THE CANDIDATE

A POLITICAL THRILLER

J. R. MCLEAY

The Candidate is a work of fiction. All depictions of characters and events are the products of the author's imagination. Any resemblance to actual persons or events is unintended and coincidental.

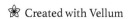

OTHER BOOKS BY J. R. MCLEAY:

Crime Thriller:

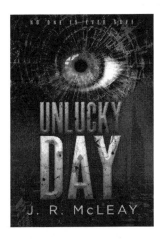

Everyone has to come out in the open eventually.

Medical Thriller:

Remember when you said you never wanted to grow up?

PART I

RISING STAR

1

Garfield Heights, Washington DC

July 15, 10:30 p.m.

B reanna Marshall's eyes narrowed as she surveyed the smoky room. She'd been invited to a house party on the wrong side of town, and her heart was racing a mile a minute. Her boyfriend told her it would be the biggest party of the semester and that all the heavy hitters would be there. Against her better instincts, she'd reluctantly agreed to go. But as she scanned the crowd, she felt uneasy.

It was a decidedly different demographic than she was used to. As the teenage daughter of Congressman James Marshall, she was accustomed to socializing with mostly white, upper-middle-class kids from the political elite. But instead of the skinny jeans and designer tank tops favored by her friends on Capitol Hill, most of these party-goers sported baggy low-riders, cornrows, and crooked baseball caps. She hadn't been exposed to this degree of cultural diversity in her neck of the capital.

As Shaun led her by her hand through the packed crowd into the main room of the house, Breanna pulled up. In the corner of the room, a group of people huddled over a coffee table taking turns snorting lines of white powder off the glass surface.

Her boyfriend felt the tug on his arm and turned around.

"What's the matter, babe?" he said, raising his voice over the din of thumping rap music.

"*Heavy hitters*, huh?" Breanna said, leaning in to her boyfriend's ear. "Looks more like a bunch of *gang-bangers* to me. What have you gotten me into?"

Shaun shook his head and laughed.

"It's a little outside your normal world, I'll admit. But the music is cool and the place is packed with interesting people. I heard that Jay-Z dropped in to their last gig—maybe we'll get lucky and bump into Beyoncé."

Breanna's nose wrinkled at the heavy scent of marijuana smoke permeating the room.

"Something tells me this is not the kind of party Beyoncé goes to. I don't think my parents would approve of my being in a place like this. I'm not feeling comfortable—let's go."

Shaun placed his arm around Breanna's waist and pulled her toward him.

"Come on, Bree—live a little. Just because most of these partiers have a darker shade of skin doesn't mean you've got anything to be afraid of. You need to stretch your wings and move outside your sheltered existence on Capitol Hill."

Breanna furrowed her brow.

"Shaun, you know I'm not racist. My Dad's been a supporter of minorities and the underclass for as long as I can remember. I've got no problem mingling with people of color."

Her eyes widened as a tall black man wearing a do-rag and a thick gold cross approached them.

"It's just that some of these characters scare me."

The man sauntered up to Shaun and swung his arm over his shoulder.

"Shaun, *my man*. Glad ya could make it." He looked Breanna up and down and smiled. "Who's da lovely lady?"

"Ty, this is my girl, Breanna Marshall. Breanna, this is Tyson Booker. This is his crib."

Tyson cocked his head and squinted at Breanna.

"Name sounds familia'. Yo' wouldn't be related to Jimmy Marshall, the fly congressman, would ya?"

Breanna hesitated. She never liked to raise her standing on the coattails of her father. Plus, she wasn't sure being recognized as a member of the DC political establishment would improve her status in this situation.

"Yes..." she said tentatively, "he's my father."

"No *shit*," Tyson said, raising his eyebrows. "I'm an admira'. He's one of da few politicians fightin' for da rights of African-Americans. Come," he said, pointing to the bar, "make yo'self comf'table. I got Hennessy, Ciroc, Crystal—whateva yo' pleasha." Tyson reached out and clasped Breanna's hand firmly. "I look fo'ward to jawin' wit' ya lata tonight."

Tyson melted back into the crowd and Shaun turned toward Breanna.

"See babe, I told you this party had it going down."

The party DJ flipped on a new track, and the sound of Nelly's song Hot in Herre filled the room.

"Come on, let's get our groove on."

Breanna hesitated for a moment, then she smiled as her hips began swaying to the seductive beat. She followed Shaun to an outdoor patio where a thick crowd was gyrating to the hip-hop music.

"*Crib? Jawing?*" she said. "Where exactly do you know this Tyson guy from?"

Unlike many of her politically connected friends who went to private schools, Breanna's father insisted she attend public schools to stay grounded. But Garfield Heights was a long way, geographically and culturally, from their upper-class neighborhood on the other side of town.

"We've been collaborating on a couple of personal projects," Shaun said.

"*Personal* projects, hmm?"

Breanna decided she'd ask Shaun about the nature of their business together another time. For now, she just wanted to enjoy the music.

As she stepped onto the patio, she glanced to the west where she could see airplanes taking off from Ronald Reagan airport across the Potomac River. It was a clear summer night, and Breanna felt her tension level begin to subside as she looked at the sparkling lights in the night sky. Just below her line of sight, a rumbling SUV rolled by on the street at the front of the house. She didn't see the windows slide down and three machine guns point toward the house.

Suddenly, the music was drowned out by the deafening roar of automatic rifles shredding the face of the house. All Breanna could hear for the next few seconds was the sound of breaking glass and terrified screams as party patrons ran for cover. Shaun yanked her behind the cover of a hedge, and they fell to the ground as green foliage rained down on their heads.

It was over almost as quickly as it had begun. The sound of gunfire stopped, and people could be heard yelling and pointing toward the street. Breanna thought she heard someone say something about The Crips, as a group of young men suddenly appeared running toward the road holding Uzis.

Shaun rose up to look at his girlfriend.

"Bree—are you okay?"

To his horror, he saw that Breanna's white blouse was stained dark red with two holes oozing thick liquid onto his hands.

"Breanna!" he yelled. "You've been shot! Someone call 9-1-1!" he screamed, looking around frantically.

But everyone was attending to other wounded bodies surrounding them on the patio. Shaun fished his cell phone out of his pocket and fumbled to tap the screen with his sticky fingers. He glanced at Breanna. She was breathing in spasms and staring at him with wide eyes.

"It's okay, babe," he said. "Someone will be here soon. Hang in there."

Suddenly Breanna coughed and blood spurted from her mouth. Her body heaved, trying to draw in air, but it was no use. After two more spasms, her body fell limp, and the life drained from her eyes. As the sound of sirens filled the neighborhood, Shaun held his girl-friend in his arms, shaking in disbelief.

2

DC Metropolitan Police Station, Seventh Precinct

July 15, Midnight

Detective Lewis Ferguson shifted uncomfortably in the interview room of the Metropolitan Police seventh precinct. For the past twenty minutes, he'd been consulting with Congressman James Marshall and his wife about their daughter's murder. It was never an easy task talking with grieving parents of violent crime, and it was particularly difficult when it involved politicians. The fact that this one appeared to be another interracial crime made the matter all the more sensitive.

He'd returned from the crime scene with few clues. From all appearances, it looked like another drive-by shooting in DC's gang-infested southeast quarter. It was the third multiple-fatality shooting this month, and the DC police had been unable to contain the escalating violence. Most of the killings involved drugs, where neighborhood gangs viciously fought to defend their turf. But this shooting was a little different, in that it involved rich white kids from the other side of town.

Congressman Marshall clenched his jaw as he listened to the detective.

"Let me get this straight," he said, summarizing what he'd heard. "You're saying you've got no leads and no motive for the execution-style murder of our daughter?"

Detective Ferguson knew to tread lightly on the raw emotions of family members in these types of situations. It was normal for parents to lash out at the first person connected with a crime, even if it was the police who were only trying to help. He looked at the congressman's wife, whose face was contorted in anguish over the loss of their daughter. Her eyes were swollen and she was visibly shaking as she held onto her husband's arm.

"I don't think anyone had a motive for killing your daughter, specifically," Ferguson said. "This appears to be a gang-related drive-by shooting. The assailants were probably trying to send a message to the known drug-dealers that frequent this address. Unfortunately, your daughter was in the wrong place at the wrong time. I'm very sorry for your loss."

Marshall shook his head trying to make sense of the random killing.

"So the house was a known haven for drug-dealers?" he said.

Detective Ferguson nodded.

"We've been shadowing the owner of the house for some time. We believe he's the head of one of the largest distribution networks in the city. We interviewed other persons attending the event who have criminal records for drug trafficking. This particular gang has been pretty aggressive about expanding their territory."

Marshall looked at his wife with a confused expression.

"It doesn't make sense. Our daughter was a straight-A student who rarely ventured outside her regular circle of friends. What was Bree doing in a place like that anyway?"

Detective Ferguson leaned toward the couple.

"We understand she went to the event accompanied by a young

man named Shaun Jackson," he said. "Do you happen to know him and what connection he might have to this gang?"

Marshall and his wife looked at each other in surprise.

"Yes," Marshall said, "Shaun and Bree had been dating for a few months. I know his family well. His father is the managing editor of the Washington Post. I don't have any reason to believe he was mixed up in any drug-related activity—"

"Did they attend the same school?" Ferguson asked.

"Yes, they were both seniors at Cesar Chavez high school."

The detective nodded slowly.

"We've been monitoring that school as a hub for cocaine distribution in the Capitol Hill region of DC for some time. I'll look into Mr. Jackson's possible connection to the drug trade at the school."

Marshall's eyes widened.

"You think Shaun might have been *dealing cocaine* out of their school?"

"It's just a theory. You said it was unusual for your daughter to be mingling in these circles. *One* of them must have had a connection to someone at the party to have traveled so far outside their usual social circle."

Marshall looked at Detective Ferguson blankly for a few moments.

"I had no idea the drug problem had invaded our neighborhoods at this level. I thought teens were experimenting mostly with marijuana and methamphetamines these days."

Ferguson leaned back in his chair and shook his head.

"We're finding the most popular drugs for young people today are harder substances such as cocaine and ecstasy. Even the escalating heroin epidemic has been finding its way into high schools and middle schools."

"Isn't there anything you can do to stop it?"

"We're trying, believe me. But it's like trying to hold back a flood with your bare hands. The demand for recreational drugs is unstoppable, and the criminal element is only too eager to provide a limitless supply with the enormous profit involved."

Marshall's eyebrows pinched together as he thought about the detective's comment.

"But cocaine and heroin are produced *outside* the U.S. How are they getting into the country so easily?"

"The dollars involved run into the hundreds of billions per year. With that kind of money, there's a never-ending supply of people willing to step in at every link in the distribution chain. Whether it's farmers in Colombia and Afghanistan, couriers along the Mexican border, or local street dealers, everyone profits handsomely. We do our best to capture and put away known offenders, but someone always seems to pop up to take their place. We're fighting a losing battle in the war on drugs. All we can do is focus our limited resources on the violent consequences of the trade."

"Like our daughter?" Marshall said.

The detective looked at Marshall and his wife with a grim expression.

"Honestly, Congressman, it's people like *you* who can make the biggest difference. We need stronger laws and sentences for the criminals who are getting young people addicted to hard drugs and paying no mind to the consequences of their actions."

Ferguson rose from his chair.

"I'll do everything in my power to find the people who killed your daughter and bring them to justice. I'll let you know as soon as there's a break in the case."

Marshall put his arm around his wife's shoulder and helped her to her feet.

"Thank you, detective," he said. "I know you and the DC police are doing everything you can."

Marshall handed the detective his business card as he led his distraught wife to the door.

"Please call me as soon as you hear anything," he said.

3

Marshall Residence

July 16, 4:00 a.m.

J ulie Marshall woke up in a cold sweat and instinctively moved her hand to her husband's side of the bed. She'd had terrible nightmares and wanted the comfort of his warm body. But the sheets were cold and empty. Looking toward the window, she saw that it was still pitch-black outside. She put on her nightgown and walked downstairs. A sliver of incandescent light shone from the partially open door of the study. She tiptoed to the entrance and saw her husband hunched over his computer. He looked troubled as he scanned the screen, with his chin resting on his propped up left hand.

She opened the door, and James looked up from the screen. They didn't need to say a word. The silent look they shared indicated they were both thinking of their daughter. James's eyes were bloodshot, and his cheeks were sallow. It was obvious that he hadn't slept since getting home from the police station.

Julie walked up behind his chair and put her arms around his shoulders, resting her head on his shoulder.

"Have you been up all night?" she said.

James nodded.

"I couldn't sleep. I've been racking my brain all night. I keep thinking, if only..."

Julie swiveled James's chair around and looked him in the eyes.

"Hon, don't do this to yourself. There was nothing else we could have done to save Bree. She was a grown girl. We brought her up right, and she had her head screwed on straight. You can't stop teenagers from going to a party on a Saturday night."

"But *this* one...she should have known—"

"She likely didn't know what she'd gotten herself into until she got there. She's a smart girl. She probably was thinking about leaving before the shooting started."

James thought back to the last moment he saw his daughter.

"I asked her where she was going and who she'd be with before she left. I should have asked her to call me when she got there."

Julie knelt beside her husband and placed her hand over his.

"There's only so much a parent can do when kids get to this age. We have to give them a little room to make their way in the world. She would have been off to college in a few months—"

Julie's voice caught in her throat as the full weight of what had happened struck her. Their young daughter's life had been prematurely snuffed out. All her hopes and dreams had been suddenly extinguished. Julie collapsed into James's arms and sobbed. They held each other for several minutes as they both flashed back to precious memories of their daughter.

When Julie finally lifted her head, she glanced at James's computer screen. A website was loaded showing statistics for drug-related crimes.

"Oh, James," she said. "You're always trying to save the world.

Can't we focus on ourselves and our poor baby this once? There's nothing we can do to bring Bree back."

James gently pulled his wife up and rested her on his knee.

"I know hon, but just take a second to look at some of this."

He clicked his computer mouse and opened some tabs.

"Look at these numbers. It's insane how prevalent illegal drugs have become. This study shows that more than half of all teens have tried illegal substances, with one in five using hard drugs such as cocaine and heroin. Even five percent of *eighth-graders* have experimented with something beyond marijuana."

Julie looked up from the screen.

"You don't actually think *Bree* was abusing drugs? You know our daughter—that wasn't her style."

"I agree. But if their friends are taking them, it's easy to get pulled into the culture. And Brooklyn will be starting middle school next year."

Julie stood up and rested her hips on the edge of James's desk.

"All we can do is continue to teach our children sensible values. As best we can tell, none of our kids have even touched a cigarette. Heath's in college and hardly even has one beer when he's home watching football with friends."

James glanced back at his computer.

"Yes, but as we saw yesterday, it's not just the consumption side we have to worry about. The crime syndicates controlling the supply of drugs are making the streets unsafe even for average citizens."

He clicked his mouse and opened another tab.

"Look at this—more than fifteen percent of all homicides involve drugs and gangs. And almost *half* of the country's two-million-plus federal inmates are in prison for drug offenses."

Julie stood up and walked to the window, throwing open the shades. The morning light was starting to appear over the horizon.

"How does all this bring our baby back?" she asked. "Like the detective said—it's impossible to stop it. How can any of this help our children?"

James sighed.

"If even one child can be saved from the consequences of drug abuse, wouldn't it be worth it? Anything we can do to make the world safer for our children and grandchildren is worth the effort."

Julie smiled at her husband. She'd always admired his passion for helping others. It was his commitment to public service that had gotten him into politics in the first place. His job as a district attorney had convinced him that taking a piecemeal approach to the problem was only making a small dent. He believed that too many people were filling the courts with minor drug offenses, while the really violent criminals were getting away with their crimes. He hoped that being a congressman would give him an opportunity to pass laws that would help everyone's quality of life.

"How will tougher laws and longer sentences help?" Julie said. "You said yourself—prisons are already overcrowded with drug-related criminals."

James turned his chair around and let the rising sun warm his face.

"Actually, I was thinking of a different approach. Drug interdiction and steeper sentences are only treating the symptom. We have to address the root cause, which centers on the criminalization of drug distribution. Prohibition in the twenties only increased alcohol-related *crime*—it didn't stop people from drinking. We'll never stop people from consuming mind-altering substances if they really want to. Smoking and alcohol abuse kills many more people every year than hard drug use, and they're entirely legal. I think the only way to end violent crime related to drug use is to remove the criminal element, by decriminalizing them."

Julie's eyes widened.

"*All* of them? Not just marijuana?"

"Everything. Opening up distribution would put organized crime out of business virtually overnight. We could then tax the sale of drugs and use that money to help rehabilitate users. Think of how much the country would save by releasing a million non-violent prisoners. The cops would then be able to focus their resources on tracking down the *really* bad guys committing violent crimes instead of fruitlessly chasing down drug dealers."

"And you think all those criminals currently dealing drugs are just going to suddenly turn to operating car washes and laundromats?"

James chuckled. His wife had led her debate team at college and always seemed to have strong arguments for any weighty subject.

"At least if their limitless profit is eliminated, they won't have a reason to *kill* people to protect it any longer. They'll be running law-abiding businesses, paying taxes like the rest of us."

Julie shook her head as she walked toward the door.

"I think you'd be committing political suicide by introducing such a motion in the House. Look how difficult it was to get one state to legalize marijuana. Even if you're right about this helping to reduce crime, it's going to be virtually impossible to get your fellow congressmen to pass this legislation."

"I can always fall back on practicing law if they throw me out," James kidded.

"That is if anyone in the legal community would even *hire* you after pulling a stunt like that. I'm going to put on a pot of coffee. Why don't you stop dreaming for a while and let me get you something to eat. Brooklyn will be getting up soon, and we've still got the difficult task of breaking the news about Bree to our two other children."

James's expression suddenly changed as he looked up at his wife. He closed his laptop and rose from his chair. Julie was right. There were far more important things to attend to right now than trying to save the world.

4

Longworth Building, DC Congressional Offices

August 21, 9:30 a.m.

J ames tapped on fellow legislator Ray Bradley's open office door. As mutual first-term members of Congress, they shared a similar experience as junior legislators in the House of Representatives. Both lawyers in their early forties, they'd entered public service with visions of shaping the legislative landscape to improve American citizens' quality of life. But they soon discovered that the real power rested with a few senior members who chaired special committees. As low-ranking congressmen in the minority Democratic Party, they had little ability to influence the legislative agenda. It hadn't taken long for them to become close friends and confidants.

Ray looked up from a briefing he was reading and smiled. He always enjoyed chatting with his idealistic fellow congressman. But he knew James was still struggling to deal with the loss of his daughter, and he hoped to lighten his mood.

"Jimmy! Have you come to save me from death by boredom? I was just thinking of jumping out the window. This appropriations bill is killing me. Two thousand pages of overcooked pork in mind-numbing legalese. It's a wonder the government doesn't implode under the weight of its own hubris."

James laughed.

"You gotta admire how our fellow lawmakers always manage to cram their special interest earmarks into these omnibus bills. I guess they figure all their wasteful projects will get lost among the minutiae."

"It seems to be working," Ray sighed. "Sometimes I think the only people who read these bills are the sponsors and lawyers who write them. Maybe it's time you and I climbed on board and got a piece of the action. Our constituents will need to see some progress from us if we want to hold our seats in the next election."

James folded his arms and looked at Ray disapprovingly.

"I thought we agreed we'd stay above this practice. That we'd only promote and vote for bills that champion the greater good. Don't tell me you've joined the other side and become another beltway bootlicker?"

Ray cocked his head in disbelief.

"I'm kidding, bro. Loosen up—I'm still on your side. What's got you spouting off like Mahatma Gandhi so early this morning?"

James closed the door and took a seat in one of the armchairs opposite Ray's desk.

"Actually, there was something important I wanted to float by you. I've been doing a lot of soul-searching lately and wanted to see if an idea I have is totally off-base."

"You better not be thinking of quitting. You can't leave me here alone with all these stodgy old career politicians."

James chuckled.

"Worse. I've been contemplating becoming one of them, in a manner of speaking."

"What—are all these congressional perks going to your head? You have to admit, the cafeteria food is pretty awesome."

James shook his head. Ray could always be counted on to bring a little levity to any serious discussion.

"I hear the food at the *White House* is even better. I'm thinking of running for President."

Ray choked as he caught his breath.

"You've got to be kidding me. The guy who said he'd always stay above petty politics? Now you want to take the *ultimate* plunge. Why the sudden change of heart?"

"For the same reason we both entered politics—to improve the quality of life for average Americans. You and I both know there's very little we can do in our present roles to effect change. Even if we were to advance a meaningful bill in the House, it would just get voted down by the majority party or vetoed by the President. The only way to pass important new legislation is for our party to take back control of both houses and install a like-minded chief executive. I'm tired of watching the old guard maintain the status quo."

Ray's expression suddenly became serious.

"Jim, I know you're going through a tough time, with what happened to Bree. But you've got to think this through. A first-term congressman has never been elected President. You haven't earned the political capital to take a legitimate run at the office, let alone win our party's nomination. What's driving this—is there a particular agenda you had in mind?"

James leaned back in his chair and rested his hands behind his head.

"Yes, actually. I don't want to go half-cocked on any policy issue anymore. I want to propose some radical changes and see if we can build the popular support to truly change the way government helps the people. Starting with drug enforcement. I want to decriminalize drugs to make our streets safer."

Ray nodded, suddenly recognizing James's motivation.

"You know there's *already* a bill before the House to legalize marijuana at the federal level? Its chances of passing is virtually nil. The old guard would never risk alienating their base."

"Not just marijuana," James said. "*All* drugs."

Ray's eyes opened wide.

"Are you crazy? Cocaine, meth, heroin? You know this can never fly. You'd be committing political suicide. And not just defeating your chance to be President. You'd never hold your seat in Congress on that platform. Have you thought this through?"

James held up his palms defensively.

"Hear me through for a minute. I know it sounds absurd on the surface. But it's been done elsewhere. More than twenty countries have decriminalized drug possession in varying degrees. For twenty years, Portugal has made it legal to carry drugs for personal use— including marijuana, cocaine, heroin, ecstasy, and amphetamines. Since the law was passed, there's been little change in the level of drug use. Plus, infectious diseases are down sharply, and overdoses have dropped by a factor of five."

"Huh," Ray said, raising his eyebrows. "I had no idea it had been tried in other countries. If those are typical results, your idea might hold water. But how does this make the streets safer?"

James had done his homework and was ready for the objections he knew would be coming.

"More harm is caused by criminal prosecution than by the use of drugs themselves. You only need to look at the example of alcohol prohibition to see the effect. It did virtually nothing to deter use and only attracted organized crime, while diverting law enforcement resources. The best way to eliminate organized crime and the violence that comes with it is to remove the lucrative profit that comes with an artificially constrained supply. Plus, we can tax the money earned from the legalized drug trade and use that money to help rehabilitate homeless addicts. The bottom line is, people are going to go on doing what they want to do with their own bodies, and we're losing the war on drug interdiction."

Ray sat still for a long time, looking at his friend.

"You've got some strong arguments, as always," he said. "But you know this is a huge uphill battle. Half the country will never go for it, not to mention virtually every Republican in Congress. Even if by some miracle you became President, you'd never get enough support in the House to advance the bill."

"Well then, I guess we'll just have to capture the other half of the popular vote and make sure our side wins a majority in both houses in the next presidential election."

Ray smiled and shook his head.

"Bernie Sanders damn near won the party's nomination in the 2016 presidential election, and his platform was almost as radical as yours. And you're a damn sight younger and prettier than he is. If anybody can summon the public support to pull this off, you can. I'll support you in this cause as best I can. When were you thinking of announcing your candidacy?"

James's cell phone suddenly buzzed in his pocket. He pulled it out and tapped the screen, then held it to his ear.

"Good to hear from you, Detective Ferguson," he spoke into the phone. "That's wonderful news. When is the court hearing? I'll see you then."

James put his phone back in his pocket and looked at Ray.

"I'm thinking in one week's time. I may have just found the perfect podium for declaring my candidacy."

5

Courtroom 8, DC Superior Court

September 30, 10:00 a.m.

James sat in the back row of the court awaiting the verdict of his
daughter's alleged killers. Four men had been jointly charged
with three counts of first-degree murder in the drive-by
shooting at Garfield Heights. The prosecution had presented an
airtight case, with eyewitnesses identifying the individuals occupying
the car involved in the shooting. Their machine guns had been recovered by the police and ballistics had matched the fatal bullets with
the weapons. The jury had deliberated for less than an hour before
beginning to stream back into the courtroom.

The case had attracted the attention of the local press, and the
gallery was overflowing with observers. Every news station was eager
to report the court's finding in the gangland slaying of the congressman's daughter. In a vain effort to remain unnoticed, James had taken
a seat in the back corner, but he noticed many people stealing furtive

glances in his direction. As the jurors took their seats and a hush descended over the courtroom, he could feel his heart pounding in his chest.

Even though he'd had more than a month to prepare for this moment, his reaction surprised him. He knew that the four young men sitting at the defense table hadn't targeted his daughter directly. She'd simply been an unlucky bystander in a turf war between rival gangs. From his position in the corner of the courtroom, he could see that the defendants barely looked out of their teens. He wondered if they'd considered the consequences of their action when they took aim at the drug dealer's house or if they were merely pawns in a larger criminal enterprise. He knew that many new gang recruits were required as part of their initiation to demonstrate their loyalty by killing a random person. Many of these young men had likely grown up fatherless and without direction, knowing no other life on the hardscrabble side of DC. But the fact remained that they'd knowingly committed a horrible act that had ended three lives, including Bree's.

After the jurors had all been seated, the court clerk stood to address them.

"Will the jury please rise," he said. "Will the defendants also rise and face the jury. Mr. Foreman, has your jury agreed upon a verdict?"

A gray-haired juror cleared his throat.

"We have."

"What say you, as to the charge of first-degree murder, in the case of each defendant so charged?"

The gray-haired gentleman looked straight ahead as he spoke.

"We find each of the defendants guilty of first-degree murder on each count," he said.

The foreman handed the clerk a piece of paper, and the clerk placed it on the judge's bench. The judge glanced at the form, then turned to address the jury.

"Members of the jury, your service is complete. Thank you for your deliberation and your public service. The court officer will escort you back to the jury assembly room, where you will be discharged."

The jury members filed out of the courtroom in single file. When the last juror left the room, the judge turned to the prosecution table.

"We now turn to the matter of sentencing. I would like to hear the prosecutor's recommendation first."

A lawyer from the prosecution table stood up.

"Your Honor, in view of the premeditated and brutal nature of these crimes, we recommend life sentences on each count for each defendant, to be served consecutively. It is worth noting that these individuals operated in concert to plan and execute this shooting. Furthermore, they would have known from their choice of automatic weapons that there would be multiple casualties. We believe that a clear message should be delivered that this kind of indiscriminate killing will not be tolerated."

The judge scribbled a few notes, then looked toward the defense table.

"And what does the defense counsel recommend?"

The lead counsel at the defendants' table stood to address the judge.

"Your Honor, I would like to point out that none of these young men have prior convictions for violent offenses. Mr. Stevens has a conviction for possession of cocaine, and Mr. Clayton has two prior convictions for drug trafficking. Mr. Hamilton and Mr. Wayne have no prior convictions. Moreover, Mr. Hamilton's fingerprints were not found on any of the recovered weapons, since it has been determined he was the driver in the incident in question."

The defense lawyer turned to face the four defendants, who were looking ahead with vacant expressions.

"These men were forced at a young age to support their families, in a district where opportunities are few and far between. Unfortunately, joining a gang is one of the easiest and quickest ways to make a living in their impoverished neighborhood. My clients were victims of their circumstances and pressured into this act by the leaders of their gang. They have expressed contrition for their crime and deserve a chance to rebuild their lives while they are still young. For these reasons, we recommend fifteen-year terms for Messrs. Wayne, Clayton and Stevens, and a five-year term for Mr. Hamilton, to be served concurrently on each count."

As James listened to the arguments, his jaw tightened. He knew that with good behavior, many inmates served only one third of their sentences. If the judge accepted the defense recommendations, the killers of his daughter would be back on the streets in two to five years. On the other hand, if the judge sided with the prosecution, the young men would likely spend the rest of their lives behind bars.

The judge scribbled some more notes, then looked directly at the defendants.

"The court only has the testimony of the defendants regarding their motivation for committing this crime. I don't believe they were coerced into shooting indiscriminately into the crowd, and that they fully understood the likely consequences of their act. Furthermore, I do not accept the argument that these men had no other choice but to join a gang because of their impoverished circumstances. Many other young men living in similar conditions finish high school and go on to secure legitimate jobs or attend college."

The judge paused as the gallery watched in silence.

"The point that none of the defendants have prior convictions for violent offenses is one aspect in their favor. However, the fact of the matter is that three people lost their lives as a consequence of their actions, with the victims' families irreparably torn apart. As for the driver receiving leniency because he did not carry a gun, this is a spurious argument. I believe all four of these men planned this act together and they must be held equally to account. Accordingly, I hereby sentence each defendant to life sentences on each count, to be served concurrently."

The judge raised his gavel and slammed it on his desk.

"This court is adjourned."

A loud buzz immediately filled the courtroom as members of the gallery exchanged opinions about the sentence. Family members sitting behind the defense table sobbed as the four defendants were handcuffed and led out of the courtroom.

Suddenly, a loud cry pierced the sober mood of the courtroom.

"I hope you *rot in jail*, scumbags!" an enraged man yelled, as the distraught mother of one of the victims trembled on his arm.

Many reporters in the gallery turned to James to register his reaction. He didn't want to distract attention from the other grieving families and quickly rose to work his way out of the courtroom. But as soon as he stepped into the hall, he was surrounded by a mob of reporters.

"Congressman Marshall!" one of the reporters said. "What is your reaction to the verdicts? How are you feeling at this moment?"

James continued toward the courthouse main entrance, surrounded by the mob.

"I'm saddened for the families of the victims," he said, as he walked. "I know what it's like to lose a daughter, and my thoughts and prayers are with those whose lives have been taken and for their loved ones."

The crowd edged closer to the congressman, jostling for position.

"Do you feel the verdicts were *fair*?" another reporter yelled.

James picked up his pace as he approached the courthouse exit.

"I agree with the judge's assessment and decision in the matter. There's no restitution that can bring my daughter and the other victims back. I only hope that these young men understand the gravity of their actions and have learned from their mistake. Our jails are filled with misguided individuals who've made horrible mistakes, who'll spend most of their adult lives behind bars. There are no winners in this situation."

As James stepped through the front door onto the courthouse steps, he was greeted by a phalanx of television news trucks and flashing camera bulbs.

"Are you saying you feel *sorry* for the men who murdered your daughter?" one of the reporters asked.

James stopped at the top of the steps, as television news camera operators zoomed in on his face.

"I don't believe there are bad *people*—only people who do bad *things*. Everyone should have a chance to amend their ways and find a constructive path in life. These men did a very bad thing and need to pay for their crimes. Unfortunately, their sentences will do nothing to deter the underlying impetus for this crime, which is the organized gangs that feed off the drug trade in this and other cities across America."

The reporters moved closer, sensing a new story for their evening newscast. A reporter stepped forward and thrust a microphone under his chin.

"As a congressman, what do you believe can be done to stop the violence?"

James paused for a moment and looked directly at the reporter who asked the question.

"The United States has tried for too long to contain drug violence through tougher law enforcement. This trial and thousands of similar others demonstrate that it isn't working. We'll never stop people from using psychoactive substances, as alcohol and cigarette containment efforts have clearly demonstrated. It's time for our government to take a more progressive approach to the escalating violence attending the drug trade. I believe it's time to consider legalizing drugs in order to remove the criminal element from the equation. Then we can use the taxes collected on the legitimate trade of these substances to rehabilitate users in need."

For a brief moment, the crowd of reporters fell silent. For a sitting member of Congress to propose such a radical plan was unprecedented. Whether they were in shock or simply had to replay the congressman's words to be sure they heard them correctly, all eyes were centered on the junior congressman from Maryland.

The mob of reporters suddenly erupted with a flurry of questions.

"Are you proposing to legalize *all* drugs?" someone asked.

"Won't legalization just lead to increased drug abuse?" another asked.

"How do you propose to enlist the support of a divided Congress on such a polarizing issue, as a first-term congressman?"

James peered directly toward the line of video cameras pointed at him from the street.

"To answer your questions—yes, no, and I don't propose to enlist support for this initiative as a member of Congress. I propose to lead the charge as executive-in-chief and sign the bill as President of the United States. As of today, I'm formally declaring my candidacy as a presidential candidate for the Democratic Party."

The tumult of reporter questions ratcheted up so much that no one could make out what anyone was saying.

James held up his hand and began to speak.

"I will answer all of your questions in due course. I'll be releasing a policy statement summarizing my position on this matter, along with the costs and benefits of implementing the program. I look forward to continuing our dialogue over the course of the primary season, where we'll have many forums to debate the merits of the plan. God bless America."

James pushed his way through the crowd and descended the courthouse steps, where he flagged a waiting cab. As he closed the taxi door and the car sped away, he saw the reporters disband and pull their cell phones from their pockets.

They'd all found the evening's top news story.

6

Charambira, Colombia

September 30, 5:30 p.m.

Carlos Rojas sat in his seaside villa watching the CNN evening news with his three lieutenants. As the leader of the Norte del Valle cartel, he controlled over half the cocaine distribution in Colombia. The Norte del Valle cartel had formed from the remnants of the Cali cartel after its leaders were arrested and extradited to the United States. With over one billion dollars' worth of cocaine leaving Colombia every year, Rojas had become extremely wealthy in a few short years. Enlisting the aid of the AUC right-wing paramilitary group to protect its laboratories and drug routes, he had quickly consolidated his control over the cocaine trade in South America.

He liked to watch the U.S. news to stay abreast of developments in his biggest market. With the majority of his profits originating from the U.S., it was critical that he recognize demographic and political shifts that could affect his business. As he peered through his floor-to-ceiling living room windows at the setting sun over the Pacific Ocean, he smiled. Life as a cocaine drug lord was good.

"Another beautiful day in paradise, boss?" one of his lieutenants said, noticing his master taking in the view.

"Si, Diego. The gods are shining on us for another day. We must savor these peaceful moments when they are presented to us. There is too much violence and suffering in this world. We are truly blessed."

Diego was Rojas's main enforcer and bodyguard. A vicious *sicario*, he had personally been responsible for killing and torturing hundreds of men and women who were thought to be disloyal or working against the cartel's interests.

The nightly newscast began with Wolf Blitzer standing in front of the network's *Situation Room* logo.

"Good evening," he said. "These are today's top news stories."

The camera cut to an image of Congressman Marshall standing atop the DC courthouse steps.

"In an unexpected turn of events, first-term congressman James Marshall announced his candidacy for President of the United States. As many of our viewers may remember, his teenage daughter was gunned down in a gangland shooting just over a month ago. Listen to his comments after he left the courthouse where his daughter's killers were sentenced earlier today."

The telecast replayed Marshall's comments about the failed judicial system and his plan to legalize drugs to reduce violent crime.

Blitzer shook his head as the camera cut back to him.

"This is a truly unprecedented event in the history of U.S. politics. It was only recently that marijuana was legalized in Colorado and seven other states, after years of grassroots efforts to decriminalize the soft drug. Congressman Marshall is advocating the legalization of *all* drugs at the federal level and intends to lead the charge as a presidential candidate. Let's weigh in with our senior political analyst, David Gergen, to assess the candidate's motivation on this initiative. David, do you think this is simply a gut reaction by the congressman to the drug-related slaying of his daughter?"

The camera cut to Mr. Gergen, who shook his head.

"I don't think so, Wolf. It appears that Congressman Marshall has carefully thought through the ramifications of his proposal since the murder of his daughter more than a month ago. He's prepared a detailed policy paper outlining the costs and benefits of the program, which he'll make public in the coming days. I think he was simply using the courtroom setting of his daughter's killers as a convenient platform from which to announce his candidacy."

Blitzer looked at Gergen with a puzzled expression.

"But isn't this an extreme departure from U.S. policy on this issue? For decades, the U.S. has been resolute in its opposition to illegal drug use, using heavy prison sentences and drug interdiction as its main weapons in the war on drugs. How can the junior congressman possibly hope to gain traction on this radical plan and win the hearts of the voting public? Not to mention the many conservative members of Congress?"

Gergen nodded.

"I think he recognizes that his chances of introducing, let alone advancing, such a bill in either of the legislative houses is extremely remote. That's why he's looking to bypass the legislative branch entirely and take the issue directly to the people. He seems to think he can win the minds of the voters on the premise that his program will eradicate the organized crime that is tied to the illicit drug trade. He believes this program will actually help reduce drug use in America."

"What is your assessment of his chances to capture his party's nomination and go on to win the Presidency?"

"To be honest, Wolf, his chances on both fronts are practically nil. Even within the Democratic Party, most of the delegates lean to the right on this issue. They are unlikely to stomach the idea of letting loose a flood of legal heavy drugs onto the streets of America. His chances with the other half of the conservative voting public is even more remote. On the surface, this looks like a wild fantasy."

"Thank you for your considered analysis, David," Blitzer said as he looked back into the camera. "We'll follow this unfolding story as it develops. After the break, we'll cover another outbreak of violence in London, where terrorists have bombed the underground transportation system."

As the telecast cut to commercial, another one of Rojas's lieutenants looked to Carlos for his reaction.

"What do you make of this gringo politician, boss? Is he loco?"

Rojas's eyes narrowed as he stared out the window.

"So it may seem, Miguel. But I think we should be careful not to judge this politician too quickly. We've seen other radical U.S. candidates rise to power recently, who were written off at the beginning. This candidate is young, articulate and handsome. I think we should keep a close eye on this congressman. His chances may be low, but we cannot afford to have him sway the opinion of the American public on this matter. Our entire enterprise rests on the United States maintaining their present course."

Miguel looked at his boss confused.

"Wouldn't making cocaine legal make our business *easier*? We wouldn't have to smuggle our product across the border any longer and pay the AUC to protect our operations."

Rojas nodded.

"It might make our business easier, Tomas, but I'm afraid it would steal our business away from us. It's the superhuman effort by the United States to *block* the trade that keeps us in business. If they make it legal to grow and distribute cocaine, people will no longer have any reason to hesitate supplying the product. We would have infinite competition and no way of controlling the flow of drugs."

"But, don Carlos, no one else has our resources," Tomas said. "Couldn't we use our private army to enforce submission and the continued loyalty to our organization?"

Rojas shook his head.

"If cocaine is legalized, the U.S. government would stop pressuring our local government to block the production and distribution in Colombia. Every coca farmer and trafficker in South America would be free to produce and distribute as much cocaine as American consumers crave. We couldn't control the flood of suppliers any more than the U.S. government has been able to stop the millions of cocaine users in the United States."

Rojas's expression turned serious as he looked at the darkening horizon.

"Let's hope this congressman fails in his ambitious plan. Otherwise, we will have to find a way to stop him ourselves."

7

Longworth Building, Congressman Marshall's Office

October 1, 9:30 a.m.

On the morning after James's presidential candidacy announcement, House Minority Leader Thomas Akerman stormed into the congressman's office. As the leader of the Democratic Party in the House of Representatives, his role as the party's chief spokesman was to establish and represent its legislative agenda in Congress. He wielded tremendous power within the party, and almost every member deferred to his leadership. He hadn't been consulted on James's drug legalization agenda nor his plan to run for President, and he was outraged.

"What the hell was that stunt you pulled yesterday?" Akerman said as he slammed James's door behind him.

James looked up alarmed and put aside a policy paper he'd begun working on. He'd had a testy relationship with the mercurial minority leader during his short stint in the House, refusing to support him on various contentious issues. He'd made it clear that he would vote with his conscience in the best interests of the country, rather than following most other members of Congress, who almost always voted along party lines.

"You mean the announcement of my candidacy for President?" James said.

"That, and this insane idea you have about legalizing hard drugs." James sat back in his chair.

"It's not such a crazy idea, Tom. I'll have this policy paper ready for your review later today, summarizing the cost and bene—"

"I'm the ranking minority member of the House Judiciary Committee!" Akerman interrupted, his eyes flaring in anger. "You know it's protocol to forward new legislative ideas to me first. Where do you get off bypassing the party chain of command with this grandstanding act?"

James had anticipated this reaction from Akerman and had prepared his response. Although he was no fan of the minority leader, he knew his support would be helpful, if not essential, to advance his agenda.

James got up from behind his desk and approached Akerman. At six feet two with two hundred pounds of trim muscle, he towered over the much shorter congressman. His body language made it clear he would not be bullied by the minority leader, and Akerman subconsciously took a step back.

James motioned to two armchairs sitting next to a coffee table in the center of his office.

"Please have a seat, Tom. Give me a few minutes to explain my reasoning."

Akerman paused for a moment considering his options, then slowly sank into one of the chairs. James sat in the opposite armchair, projecting a position of equals.

"I'd hardly call this an act of reason," Akerman declared. "It feels more like an *emotional* impulse from this side of the table." He crossed his legs and sat back in his chair. "What were you thinking? You know there's zero chance of this proposal moving forward in the

House, whether you're President or not. Which, by the way, is another pipe dream. You've got a lot of nerve announcing your candidacy alongside more senior members of our party."

Akerman himself had thrown his hat in the ring for President two election cycles ago and failed in the final primary run-off against a younger candidate. James wondered how much of the minority leader's reaction was informed by social conscience as opposed to his previous bitter experience.

James crossed his legs to mirror the leader's posture.

"I know it must look like this is a reaction to the killing of my daughter by drug dealers. But I've had a lot of time to think about this, Tom. My daughter's murder simply concentrated my thinking on the issue. It's actually a pretty common-sense proposal. You know as well as anyone how poorly the government has fared in its strategy to curtail illicit drug use by stepping up law enforcement. It's proven that interdiction and longer sentences don't stop the flow of illegal substances to people who insist on taking them."

James took a sip of coffee from his mug and asked Akerman if he'd like one as well. The minority leader shook his head and tapped his foot impatiently.

"Prohibition of alcohol," James continued, "demonstrated that this strategy only increases the degree of criminal involvement with its attendant violence. When you read my paper, you'll see the large savings in drug enforcement and incarceration costs that will follow wide-scale legalization. The experience of many other countries actually shows that decriminalization *reduces* drug abuse. Plus, we'll be able to fill our coffers with new tax money from the sale of legalized drugs that can be used to support other programs important to our party."

Akerman looked at James blankly for a long moment before he replied.

"Regardless of the logical merits of your program, you know this plan will never fly in this country. The conservative right and the majority of Congress don't support the legalization of illicit drugs, by any measure. This rash act is just distancing you from your party and alienating you from your constituents. What makes you think you've got a shot in hell of winning the *Presidency*?"

James nodded calmly as he looked the minority leader square in his eyes.

"You're right, Tom, about our fellow members of Congress. That's why I chose to bypass this route in the first place. No other sitting congressman would have the guts to introduce this kind of bill, let alone publicly vote for it. It would be political suicide, even if it *is* in the best interests of the country. The only way to pull this off is to build grassroots support for the plan at the voter level and capture the White House on the strength of this platform. Then Congress would have no other choice but to support it."

Akerman threw up his hands in disbelief.

"You're dreaming, James. The average citizen opposes illicit drug use and will never support its legalization at the federal level. I'm afraid you've signed your own death sentence. Nobody's going to support you, in this House or elsewhere, with this wild scheme of yours."

Akerman stood up to face James, placing his hands on his hips.

"And as for your bid for the Presidency, as Bernie Sanders learned with his similarly delirious run in '16, you *also* have to gain the support of the four hundred and thirty-seven superdelegates in our party to have any chance at earning the Democratic nomination. And I've got most of them in my pocket. Good luck with your campaign, James."

Akerman scurried past James, flung the door open and stormed down the hall. James stood motionless as he listened to the clicking of the democratic leader's heels on the cold granite floor of the congressional building fade into the distance.

8

Congressman Marshall's Office

October 1, 10:15 a.m.

Nick Garcia hesitated as he paused outside James's open door. He'd heard the raised voices from his adjoining office and seen minority leader Akerman storm down the hall. As James's only official aide, Nick was responsible for assisting the congressman with constituent and legislative matters. While most members of Congress hired many staff assistants, James found this practice wasteful and often joked with his lone assistant about his chief of staff title. But the fact of the matter was that he was James's top advisor, and the congressman counted on him to provide guidance on important policy and political matters.

Nick tapped twice on the door jamb.

James looked up and smiled at his aide.

"Did we wake up the whole wing?" he joked. "How much of that did you catch?"

"Not much. Some bits about him being the ranking member of the Judiciary Committee and having the superdelegates in his pocket. And the slammed door. That was pretty hard to miss."

James laughed.

"Our minority leader's got a pretty short fuse. Sorry to disturb you from your duties."

"No worries, I needed a break anyway. I was just reading up on the latest iteration of the House appropriations bill."

The congressman shook his head and sighed.

"That would put anyone to sleep. Come in—we've got more important matters to discuss."

James took a seat in one of the armchairs and Nick followed suit.

"I take it Akerman wasn't too pleased with your announcement?" Nick offered.

"Just as we anticipated," James nodded. "I can't blame him, though. From his perch on the Hill, it must look like we're lobbing broadsides at him. He's feeling a little blindsided."

"We didn't have much choice," Nick said. "He would have shot down your drug legalization motion in a flash. What did he say about your run for the Presidency?"

"He says I have no virtually chance at winning the party's nomination and he intends to block me at every turn."

"I suppose that's expected. He's got his *own* favorites in mind for the nomination. You're complicating his plans."

James nodded.

"It's going to be an uphill battle, to say the least. Are you sure you're fully on board with this? We're going to make a lot of enemies along the way. This might not be the ideal way for you to advance your career. If I fail, you might have a hard time finding *any* job on Capitol Hill."

Nick laughed.

"I wouldn't be here if I didn't agree with what you're trying to do. No one else would have the courage to introduce this kind of initiative. You're changing the political landscape and actually trying to improve citizens' lives. That's what I signed up for."

James leaned forward and placed his arms on the chair side rests.

"Let's get to work then. Our first order of business is getting the message out to the people. I was thinking an appearance on *Meet The Press* might be a good initial forum for explaining the merits of the legalization program. How soon do you think you can slot me in?"

Nick paused as he considered the options.

"Normally, they're booked up at least six weeks in advance. But your courthouse announcement has gotten the press pretty worked up. We've got a shot at moving you to the front of the line for this Sunday's telecast."

"Make the call," James nodded. "But we'll have to scramble to have our all our ducks in a row. The show's host likes to go pretty deep with his interviews. He's likely to ask me about my position on other policy matters. I don't want to come off as a one-trick pony."

"Agreed," Nick said. "I've prepared a policy report on the major issues for your review. It summarizes each party's position on ten critical issues. I made some suggestions for where we can stake out new ground, but you'll want to flesh some of that out of course."

James nodded approvingly.

"That's good work, Nick. Bring that to me as soon as you can. We'll also have to start anticipating the objections to our positions ahead of the debates. The first Democratic Party debate is only a few weeks away."

"Already on it," Nick said. "Do you want me to start any preliminary polling? It might be a good idea to do some initial benchmarking so we can see how the public is responding to your statements and appearances."

"Good point. Let's start with a national poll to see how much support I've got as a presidential candidate. I'd also like to gauge public sentiment on the subject of federal drug legalization—both for soft drugs and harder ones. I have a feeling that the recent legalization of marijuana at the state level has softened public opinion. We can use that as a jumping off point."

"Sounds good to me."

Nick stood up to leave.

"It's going to be an *adventure* at the very least," he said, turning toward the door.

James held up his finger to stop his aide.

"Nick—one last thing. I want you to hold all of this as close to the vest as possible. There's a lot of people who stand to lose if we're successful. Watch your back."

Nick stopped and looked at James quizzically.

"You mean the other Democratic candidates and the Republicans?"

"Those, to be sure. But there are many people in the private sector to be concerned about, too. If we're able to pull off wide-scale drug legalization, a lot of people will be put out of business in short order. From the private prison operators who'll lose half their inmate population, to the organized crime operators who'll be quickly pushed out as suppliers, there are plenty of people who'll be pissed off. We don't need any more enemies than we've already got."

Nick looked at James for a moment, then nodded.

"Unfortunately, *you'll* be the one taking most of the heat, boss. But I'll keep our strategy and talking points between us until you're ready to go public. This should be an interesting ride."

9

NBC Television Studios, 400 North Capitol Street NW

October 5, 9:00 a.m.

Television host Chuck Todd reviewed his notes for the Sunday morning telecast of *Meet The Press* while a makeup technician applied final touch-up. Congressman Marshall sat beside him on the stage while Todd explained the interview protocol and the subjects to be discussed. The show format started with a half-hour interview of the candidate, followed by a panel discussion. James felt a twinge of nervousness, but he was excited about having the opportunity to present his platform to a national audience.

"Ready in ten," the show's director announced behind the camera.

As the production assistant counted down the final seconds, Todd looked at James and nodded to signal he was ready.

"Good morning," the host said, looking into the camera. "Welcome to *Meet The Press*. This week's top story is the unexpected announcement by Congressman James Marshall that he's joining the presidential race. Equally surprising is the controversial platform he's running on: full legalization of all recreational drugs."

The telecast cut to a video of the congressman announcing his candidacy atop the courthouse steps.

As the camera cut back to the host, Todd turned to James with a wry smile.

"You certainly know how to make an entrance, Congressman. Talk about drama—that was quite a bombshell."

James smiled.

"I suppose it was, for some of your viewers. But if you've followed my congressional record, I supported the recent marijuana decriminalization bill introduced in the House. And I've been speaking out on the failed policies of the administration regarding drug enforcement for years."

Todd raised his eyebrows.

"*Marijuana* is one thing. But you're calling for the blanket legalization of all illicit substances, including hard drugs like cocaine and heroin. Aren't you concerned about increased use from making these drugs easily available?"

"They're *already* easily available, Chuck. Even elementary schoolkids have access to them."

James paused to let his point sink in before he continued.

"The decriminalization of marijuana in eight states has shown it doesn't lead to increased use. Teen use has actually *dropped* since Colorado legalized pot. As for the effect on hard drugs, Portugal legalized the personal use of all drugs over twenty years ago, and there's been little change in the overall level of drug use. More importantly, infectious diseases and overdoses are down sharply."

Todd squinted his eyes and nodded, impressed with James's depth of research on the issue.

"You mentioned the experience in Colorado. Haven't they also seen a large increase in the homeless population attributed to the legalization of marijuana?"

James nodded.

"Actually, there's been a small increase, on the order of eight percent. But there's some evidence this has been caused by a swing in net migration from other states. There are a lot of people who use marijuana to control pain for medical conditions that keep them from gainful employment. These unfortunate souls are willing to travel anywhere to find relief. The good news is that the hundreds of millions of dollars in new tax revenue from legalized pot can be used to rehabilitate users and help find shelter for homeless people."

Todd paused for a moment. He was surprised by how fluidly the congressman was answering his tough questions. He looked down at his notes, then peered up.

"Your announcement on the courthouse steps painted this initiative mostly as a drive to reduce violence from organized crime. What makes you so sure that the criminal element which controls the current drug trade will just walk away and lay down their weapons if drugs are legalized?"

James smiled. His chief of staff had done his homework well, anticipating many of the questions from the host.

"I don't expect them to walk away. They'll undoubtedly try to protect their share of the market. But thousands of new suppliers will be free to grow and distribute the product without fear of prosecution. One thing this great country of ours has demonstrated since its inception is that the free hand of the market is the great equalizer. When the laws of supply and demand are allowed to operate in an unfettered manner, everyone wins. The unrestricted supply from an open supply base will dramatically lower the price of these substances. Frankly, organized crime will no longer have the motive to fight for control, once the lucrative profit is removed."

"What about the thousands of inmates who are currently incarcerated for drug-related crimes? What happens to them?"

James was beginning to enjoy the back-and-forth banter with the show host. Todd had turned out to be the perfect foil for exposing the hypocrisy of the current system and the logic for a new approach.

"It costs upwards of forty thousand dollars per year to keep each federal inmate in prison. The United States has the highest incarceration rate in the world, with over two million inmates behind bars. Time Magazine has estimated that thirty-nine percent of the prison population is locked up with little public safety rationale. The majority of these prisoners are serving time for drug-related crimes. That equates to twenty billion dollars of taxpayer money per year— enough to employ three hundred thousand school teachers."

Todd looked at James skeptically.

"Are you proposing to free *all* these prisoners?"

"The non-violent offenders who pose no public safety threat, yes. If the laws under which they were convicted are eliminated, they will no longer be criminals."

Todd put aside his notes and folded his hands on his desk.

"Well, Congressman, no one can accuse you of being faint of heart. You've certainly lit a spark in the political landscape with this daring plan of yours. We'll see if it catches fire and can attract the support of the general public. Good luck with your campaign. Thank you for coming to visit us today."

"Thanks for having me, Chuck."

Todd turned back to the camera.

"There you have it, folks. A bold new candidate has entered the presidential race, who's shaking up the political establishment. Let's turn now to our guest panel for analysis and insight on this issue."

The camera cut to a table where two members of Congress from either side of the political aisle were sitting with an NBC political analyst.

As James removed his microphone from his suit lapel, he glanced over at the large display screen behind the panel. It showed the latest poll numbers for support of marijuana legalization. The large graphic displayed *sixty-one percent*, with a green arrow indicating a five-point increase since the last poll.

Regardless of what the pundits had to say about his plan, the American people had already weighed in, James thought. His base was mobilizing, and the momentum was on his side.

10

Wolf Trap Performing Arts Center, Vienna, Virginia

October 15, 9:00 p.m.

The Filene Center at Wolf Trap National Park buzzed with excitement as the Democratic presidential candidates began to take the stage. Entering from both sides, they waved to the audience as they strolled toward their pre-positioned lecterns. Some candidates stopped by the front of the stage to talk with audience members, laughing and trying to look relaxed. A few others stooped down and shook hands with fans clamoring for their attention.

This was the first Democratic debate of the presidential election cycle, and the stakes were high. For many candidates, it was their first exposure to a national audience. The debate was a high-profile opportunity to make an all-important first impression with voters. Everybody had thoroughly prepared for the contest and tensions were high. No one was certain what questions would be asked or the subjects that would be addressed. Even more nerve-racking was the rebuttal phase of the debate. There was no way of knowing how competing candidates would respond to another candidate's comments. In previous debates, more than one presidential candidate's chances had been dashed by a cutting counterattack.

As James took the stage, he quickly scanned the audience to gauge its composition. Most of the people near the front of the stage were middle-aged or senior couples. He suspected they'd already made up their mind about their favorite candidate. They were the least likely to be swayed by the outcome of the debate. He recognized a few fellow congressmen sprinkled among the crowd, including House leader Akerman sitting in the second row. James nodded to acknowledge his presence, but Akerman quickly looked away. Towards the center of the assembly, he saw his wife and two children waving excitedly. He blew them a kiss with a big toothy grin.

The Wolf Trap concert venue was an outdoor amphitheater designed to be in harmony with its park setting. Half of its seven thousand seats were covered by a wood canopy with open sides that looked out onto tall trees and rolling hills. Beyond these, a large sloping lawn provided first-come, first-served seating for lower-priced ticket holders. James placed an open hand over his eyes and raised his head to acknowledge the large crowd that sat sprawled out on picnic blankets. They looked to be considerably younger, and a large cheer rose from outside the covered pavilion as they welcomed his attention.

"Candidates, please take your positions," a production assistant called out over the public address system. "Audience members, please take your seats."

The lighting over the audience dimmed as bright spotlights suddenly illuminated the stage. On a raised dais directly in front of the stage, debate moderator Anderson Cooper reviewed his notes. A hush fell over the auditorium as he announced the commencement of the event.

"Welcome, Democratic candidates," he said. "And welcome to our audience and television viewers, to this first presidential debate of the primary season. We will have ninety minutes to debate the critical issues among the candidates, after which there will be a panel discussion of the findings."

Seven candidates stood ramrod straight behind their lecterns as Cooper went on to outline the debate rules. Some had their heads bowed reviewing their speaking points, but most simply smiled and nodded as they listened to the moderator.

"I'd like to ask the audience to hold their applause until the end of the debate," Cooper continued, "when each candidate will make their closing comments. We have a limited amount of time to cover a large number of issues, and this will help move the agenda and maintain order. The order of candidate speaking for each subject has been determined by random sampling. Then other candidates will have a chance for rebuttal. Candidates, please remember to keep your comments to ninety seconds or less. You will hear this single tone when you have twenty seconds remaining in your segment and this double-tone when you have ten seconds left." The PA system played the soft chimes to prepare the candidates. "I will cut off any candidate who exceeds their allotted time.

"Let's get started with the first subject. The economy is always front and center in the voters' minds at this time of year. There are still millions of citizens who are without jobs after the last economic downturn. Senator Channing, how do you propose to put America back to work again and raise the standard of living for many people still living on the margin?"

As a three-term senator, Channing was one of the more experienced and well-known candidates. With a commanding lead in the polls, he was the top Democratic contender. He looked up from his notes and smiled.

"Thank you, Anderson, for addressing this important subject. There are too many people who've been left out of the recovery, who are being ignored by the current administration. The government's response has been to lower taxes and raise interest rates. They seem more concerned about controlling inflation and padding the pockets of the wealthy than adding jobs. The Republican administration regards a four percent unemployment rate as full employment, yet over seven million Americans remain out of work. Another twenty million are underemployed, working part-time jobs paying a minimum wage that is far from enough to maintain a comfortable standard of living."

It was standard protocol for presidential candidates to criticize the sitting administration's policies on key issues. Whether it was because of the wide gulf in ideological policies, or the fact that there was no one on the stage from the other party to argue with them, this was always the common theme they could unite behind. Sometimes it seemed as if they were already debating their main opponent in the final run-off, forgetting they still had many competing candidates within their own party to eliminate first.

"What is your plan to *improve* the jobs situation, Senator?" Cooper interrupted, impatient at the candidate's failure to answer the original question.

"I was just getting to that, Anderson. First, I plan to increase infrastructure spending to restore our crumbling bridges and roads. This has been neglected for far too long. Over fifty thousand bridges across our country are structurally deficient and in danger of collaps—"

Senator Channing paused, looking surprised, as the first tone sounded, signaling he was nearing the end of his allotted time. He looked down quickly at his notes to regain his focus.

"The current administration's tax cuts," he continued, "have primarily benefitted the top ten percent of wage earners. I propose to *raise* taxes on the top ten percent of earners and lower taxes for lower- and middle-class Americans who really need it—"

The senator was interrupted by the second double-chime.

"Tax cuts for high earners just pad their already comfortable savings," he spoke, more hurriedly. "Whereas tax cuts for those who really need the money will be directly injected into the economy and help people pay their bills. Furthermore—"

"Thank you, Senator," Cooper interrupted. "Your time is up. Governor *Harper*, what would you do differently to help support the jobless population?"

Each candidate responded in turn to the economy issue, criticizing their leading opponents' plans while trying to differentiate their own strategies. Congressman Marshall was the second-to-last candidate asked to weigh in.

"Thank you, Anderson," James said, after the moderator invited his response. "I agree with my fellow candidates that the current administration has failed to elevate the lives of average Americans. But I think my opponents' plans will have a negligible effect on raising the quality of life for those living near the poverty line."

James paused to underscore his next point.

"One of the first things I would do as President is correct the outrageous disparity between the highest-paid and lowest-paid workers in America. The average pay ratio of CEOs to median workers in the United States is more than two hundred to one. It's hard to imagine any chief executive's job that is two hundred times as valuable as a front-line worker's. I would start by progressively taxing those companies with the highest differential in worker pay. This way, shareholders will put pressure on overpaid executives to reduce their pay and distribute the savings to those who are putting in an honest days' work. If we elevate the take-home pay of average workers even ten percent, this will put thousands of dollars in their pockets to help support their families."

A murmur arose from the crowd as audience members looked at one another, discussing the merits of James's plan. Soft applause emanated from the rear of the theater.

"Another way we can put our tax dollars to work," James continued, "is by focusing tax cuts in those areas where they will help the most. Most new jobs are created by small and new businesses. One of the distinguishing features of this great country is its entrepreneurial spirit. Our young people are the real drivers of economic growth. The United States is the worldwide leader in internet applications that have created millions of well-paying, intellectually-stimulating jobs."

James paused as he heard the first chime sound.

"I would target business tax cuts to those companies proportionally producing the greatest number of new jobs and those offering permanent high-paying positions. Let's harness our entrepreneurial power and leverage our leadership in the technology sector to create meaningful new jobs, not just more burger-flippers."

A loud cheer rose from the back of the assembly as the double-chime sounded.

"Audience members—" Cooper chided, "I remind you to hold your applause until the end of the debate. We still have a lot of material to cover, and we want to give everyone an equal chance to be heard."

The last candidate spoke next, roundly criticizing James's platform as shallow and insufficient. But his own plan was dull and derivative, and the audience remained conspicuously silent throughout his monologue.

Round one had gone to the junior congressman from Maryland.

Cooper then moved through the issues of healthcare, foreign policy, and gun control. On each subject, the candidates trotted out familiar strategies, primarily focused on criticizing the current administration. Only James seemed prepared with a unique, detailed strategy for differentiating himself from the field. At each turn, the level of applause and cheering increased from the crowd, especially from the young people sitting on the back lawn.

Cooper saved the most contentious issue for last. The issue of wide-scale drug legalization was a hot button that had dominated the news over the last week. He knew it would be the most difficult discussion to moderate and that it would elicit the biggest audience reaction.

He started the discussion with a provocative question addressed at James.

"Congressman Marshall, you've recently proposed a radical new plan for curtailing the gang violence spreading across this country. Can you summarize the costs and benefits of your program in ninety seconds?"

James looked at Cooper and smiled.

"I'll give it my best shot, Anderson. The central argument of my plan is two-fold. First, there has been zero evidence over the last century that drug-repression efforts have reduced drug use. Second, criminalization of drug use only attracts organized crime that stops at no length to control the trade. While our streets are being overrun by drug-driven gangs, our jails are being filled by people who are consuming products with minimal public safety threat. Drug legalization efforts by other countries have resulted in lower overdoses, fewer infections, less organized crime, better drug quality control, higher taxes, and more funds for rehabilitation programs."

A loud cheer rose once again from the back of the pavilion as a soft murmur of applause slowly worked its way toward the front row. Cooper paused to wait for the clamor to subside before he responded.

"Are you saying there are *no* negative consequences associated with your plan?" he asked.

"The experience of twenty other countries that have decriminalized drugs in one measure or another have demonstrated virtually no negative effects." James paused as he heard the double-chime, signaling he had ten seconds left. "Perhaps my opponents can find some."

"Senator Channing," Cooper said, inviting the first rebuttal. "Is the drug problem as simple a solution as the congressman suggests?"

"Of course not, Anderson. This is an outrageous plan that Congressman Marshall is proposing," the senator said, striking his fist on his lectern. "To invite the general public to freely abuse their bodies in this manner is irresponsible. Regardless of the experience of other countries, the United States shouldn't encourage its citizens to consume substances with dangerous side effects. There's already enough alcoholics and nicotine addicts in this country without adding God-knows-how-many new hard drug addicts."

"Congressman," Cooper said. "Counter?"

"We'll never stop people from doing what they want to do with their own bodies," James replied calmly. "There are still laws on the books that outlaw certain sexual practices between consenting adults. Criminalization doesn't stop people from taking drugs, availing themselves of prostitutes, gambling, or doing whatever strikes their fancy in their own bedrooms."

James's voice slowly rose in volume and stridency as he continued speaking.

"The government has no place in these affairs and is only stuffing our jails with non-violent citizens who are minding their own business. It's time we let the free market and the free will of the people determine how they seek their pleasure."

James extended his arm toward the audience for emphasis.

"Let's free up your limited taxpayer resources to go after the really dangerous criminals."

The pavilion erupted in raucous cheers from the back lawn. Many audience members from the front rows stood to applaud the congressman. The other candidates looked at James dumbfounded, crossing their pens through their prepared counterarguments.

Nobody wanted to be on the wrong side of the shifting pendulum of public opinion.

11

CNN Television Studios, 820 1st Street N.E., Washington DC

October 15, 10:30 p.m.

After the debate ended with each candidate's closing remarks, the camera cut to the CNN newsroom. Wolf Blitzer stood in front of a live video feed showing the candidates mingling among the debate audience. Twenty feet to his side, a group of six political analysts sat around a glass table. As was standard practice after every presidential debate, the pundits were itching to declare the winners and losers.

"We've just witnessed a dramatic first round in the Democratic presidential debates," Blitzer said, looking into the camera. "As always, our team of seasoned political analysts stands ready to provide incisive commentary. Joining CNN senior political analysts Dana Bash and David Gergen are Republican commentators Ana Navarro and Alex Castellanos, along with Democratic commentators Paul Begala and Kirsten Powers."

Blitzer looked toward his senior political correspondent.

"Dana—this debate was not without some surprises and drama. Were there any game-changing performances?"

"I think there *was*, Wolf," Bash said. "One of the clear winners, at least based on audience response, was Congressman Marshall. On each of the debate topics, he presented a strong and distinctive position that resonated with the crowd. It seemed that each time he spoke, the audience reaction grew stronger and more positive. By the end of the debate, his impassioned case for legalizing drugs brought the crowd to their feet."

"He certainly did appear to generate the most vocal reaction," Blitzer nodded. "David, what is it about this candidate that got the audience so excited?"

"I think it's three things, Wolf," Gergen said. "First, he's obviously thought through his positions on each issue after a great deal of research. Second, he presents his positions in succinct soundbites with tremendous passion. It's obvious that he strongly believes in his programs. He's not just towing the party line or pandering to majority opinion. He's also a handsome and commanding figure on the platform-considerably younger and taller than most of the other candidates. I think a lot of the reaction he engendered tonight from the audience was visceral."

Blitzer smiled as he glanced toward the Republican analysts.

"I wonder if our commentators from the other side of the aisle share your appraisal, David. Ana, what was your impression of the young congressman's performance?"

"I'll grant you that he's easy on the eyes," Navarro laughed. "But I'm not sure the *substance* was there in equal measure. His economic plan was one-dimensional, focused almost entirely on tax incentives for a small segment of the economy. I don't see how it can have a significant impact on creating jobs or raising the standard of living. And his drug-legalization plan is simply too great a leap from current sentiment. Frankly, I don't think he stands a chance at gaining support beyond very young and very liberal voters."

"Paul," Blitzer said, inviting the Democratic commentator to weigh in. "What's your view of the congressman's chances?"

"I have to respectfully disagree with my Republican friend," Begala said. "I think it's his one-dimensional positions on the issues that makes him such an interesting and compelling candidate. Unlike most of the other candidates, his plans are easy to understand. As for his chances at gaining widespread support for his policies, the latest poll shows a majority of Americans now support marijuana decriminalization. He showed that prohibition of alcohol and marijuana only increases gang violence and doesn't reduce use. It's not that much of a stretch to see how the same argument can be applied to harder drugs."

Blitzer rubbed his silver beard as he looked to the other Republican analyst.

"Alex, many political pundits are painting Congressman Marshall as a left-wing liberal with his radical proposals. But don't elements of his platform also speak to longstanding Republican values? He wants to cut taxes to stimulate the economy. And one of the central arguments of his drug legalization plan is reducing government involvement in the private affairs of Americans."

Castellanos chuckled.

"That was quite a soundbite the congressman delivered near the end of his presentation. While he may couch his drug legalization plan as an issue of free will and reduction in government interference, the effect of his plan will be quite the opposite. Under his plan, the government would be intimately involved in the everyday trade of these substances. Not only would they be tracking and taxing the sale of every transaction, they'd be setting standards for quality control. If the experience of other countries is an example, they might even go so far as to set up supervised use and injection sites."

Blitzer raised his eyebrows and nodded toward the last Democratic commentator.

"Kirsten, where do you see the congressman standing on the political spectrum? Do you think his policies have elements that appeal to both sides?"

"It's a good question, Wolf," Powers said. "Actually, Congressman Marshall appears to be a bit of a conundrum. On the one hand, he wants to reduce income inequality with an aggressive tax strategy. At the same time, he sounds much like a Republican with his strong advocacy of American enterprise and tax cuts for small business. On the drug issue, he wants to cut drug enforcement of illicit drugs, which has been a bedrock Republican policy for decades. But he also frames it as a matter of reducing government involvement in people's private affairs. So he leans hard to the right on fiscal issues and hard to the left on social issues. If anything, he's more of a Libertarian than a Republican or Democrat."

"Interesting summary," Blitzer said. "No Libertarian candidate has ever captured more than five percent of the public vote in any presidential election. Are you suggesting he doesn't stand much of a chance with his divergent policies?"

Powers shook her head.

"On the contrary, Wolf. His positions may find a strong constituency on each side of the political aisle. His policies are quite populist, appealing to many Americans' basic beliefs. I think he has a good chance at picking up a fair number of votes from all three sides of the political spectrum. A record forty-three percent of Americans identify as political independents. His free-thinking policies may resonate with quite a few voters."

Blitzer nodded, impressed with the breadth of the analysis. He looked to CNN's senior political analyst, David Gergen, to sum up the discussion.

"Marshall still has a long way to go to catch the front-runners. Both within his own party, and if he faces off against the incumbent President. His opponents hold commanding leads in the polls over the young congressman. A first-term representative with no executive experience at the state or federal level has never captured the White House. David, what do you think his chances are for catching up with these more seasoned leaders?"

Gergen paused for a long moment.

"We'll have a better understanding in a few days, when the first post-debate poll numbers are revealed. But based on the informal body-language poll of this first test audience in Virginia, something tells me we're going to see this young candidate's star rise quite a bit higher over the coming months."

12

Marshall Residence

October 18, 7:00 p.m.

On the first Sunday after the debate, the Marshall family assembled for dinner in their Georgetown home. The congressman's son had come home from university to spend the weekend. As had become standard practice since their elder daughter's passing, there was an empty place setting at the table. It was James and Julie's way of showing that Bree was always in their thoughts and prayers. After the last of the servings were placed on the table and everyone was seated, James spread his arms and opened his palms beside him. The other family members locked hands and closed their eyes.

"Dear Lord," James said, beginning grace, "we wish to give thanks for the abundance of love and sustenance around our table. Thank you for watching over our loved ones and keeping them safe. Please let our precious Bree know…"

James paused as he choked up thinking about his departed daughter. Julie squeezed his hand and sniffed.

"...that we're always thinking of her and that we love her very much. God be with you, sweetheart. Amen."

"Amen," the other three family members said quietly.

James looked up and wiped a tear from his eye as he passed the first serving to his daughter Brooklyn.

"Roast pork—" he said, glancing toward his son. "Heath's favorite. I bet they don't feed you like this at the university cafeteria."

"Not without all the fixings," Heath said. "Nor with Mom's love. Food always tastes better at home."

Julie smiled at Heath as an awkward silence filled the room. James looked toward the empty place setting and blinked away his tears.

"So Dad—" Heath said, trying to lighten the mood. "The latest poll shows you've jumped seven points in the Democratic race. That was quite a show you put on in this week's debate. Apparently not *everybody* thinks you're crazy."

James laughed.

"Just the left-wing liberals. I'll need to capture more than fifteen percent of the voters if I hope to implement my plans."

"You've risen from last place to third place among the Democratic candidates," Heath said. "The talking heads on the news are saying you've got a real shot at capturing the party's nomination if you maintain this momentum. You're all the buzz on campus."

"There's still a long battle ahead of us. Senator Channing and Governor Harper are formidable opponents. They've got a lot more legislative and executive experience. I'm still the dark horse."

"But a much *prettier* one," Julie said, reaching out to clasp James's hand. "They're just old curmudgeons. You're the only one with original ideas that will actually change people's lives."

James looked at his children.

"What do you guys think? Do you share your Mom's opinion that your old man can make a difference?"

"I think you'll be the best President ever, Daddy!" Brooklyn said excitedly.

James smiled at his daughter. At the age of seven, she barely understood what being President meant, let alone what the congressman's policies represented.

"Thanks, pumpkin. What about you, Heath? You said your classmates have been talking. Where do *you* stand on the issues?"

"I'm with you all the way, Dad. There are too many legacy programs in place that aren't working. You're the only one who's got the courage to shake up the system and bring some clear thinking into the twenty-first century. Most of my classmates agree—they're really excited about the fresh ideas you're bringing to the table."

"Even the drug legalization plan? I know young people are more progressive than most, but there's still a lot of conservatives in this country who think all drugs should be abolished."

"Like you said—they're already freely available on campus and elsewhere. It's not like you're changing the supply and demand dynamics. You're just making our streets safer by removing the criminal element from the equation."

James's expression suddenly turned serious.

"I don't want you guys to get the wrong idea. This plan doesn't mean I'm advocating the use of drugs. I still believe they're dangerously addictive and unhealthy. There are more natural ways to get your kicks."

"We know, Dad," Heath said, rolling his eyes. "You and Mom have always told us to stay away from cigarettes and alcohol."

"Well, I'm not so naive to believe that you'll never experiment with these things," James said. "But that argument goes for any man-made substance." He picked up the bowl of broccoli and passed it around the table. "If it's not naturally grown and unprocessed, it's not good for you."

Brooklyn suddenly looked up at her father with a worried expression.

"Will we have to *move* if you become President, Daddy? I don't want to leave my friends."

James smiled at this daughter.

"Yes, but only just down the street a few blocks. You can keep all your friends and still go to your same school. Besides, I think you might like the White House. Did you know it has a swimming pool and an indoor bowling alley?"

"Cool!" Brooklyn said. "Can I invite my friends?"

James looked at his wife and winked.

"Yes, sweetie. In fact, I'll do you one better. If I become President, you can have a great big sleepover during our first week at the new place."

13

Washington, Virginia

October 23, 7:00 p.m.

James peered out over the rolling hills of West Virginia from the back terrace of The Inn at Little Washington. It had been another busy week of press appearances, and he was thankful to have a break from the campaign schedule. He and Julie hadn't been on a date for many weeks, and to mark the occasion he'd chosen the most romantic restaurant in the Mid-Atlantic region.

He'd asked for a secluded table at the country inn to afford a measure of privacy from the ever-present gaze of curious onlookers. It was a warm Indian Summer evening, and the maître d' had prepared a private table for them overlooking the courtyard. A broad lawn stretched out from the back of the plantation-style hotel, framed by heavily wooded forest. In the far distance, the final glimmer of the setting sun cast the mountains in a resplendent shade of pink.

"Gorgeous, isn't it?" Julie said, happy to see her husband looking relaxed.

James turned to his wife and smiled.

"Not as pretty as my lovely bride. You look absolutely radiant this evening."

Julie pressed her hands across the linen-covered dining table, and James held them warmly.

"Thanks for this, honey," she said, looking into James's eyes. "It's been so crazy these past two months. First Bree, then this whirlwind campaign. It seems like we've hardly had any time for ourselves."

"I know, babe. There's nothing like a presidential campaign to remove any semblance of a private life. But I promise, we'll make room to steal away whenever we can."

"I hope so," Julie said. "Because if you continue to do this well, it's only going to get worse. If you make it all the way to the White House, we'll really be living in a fishbowl. We'll be cooped up in that gated fortress with the whole world watching us."

James looked at Julie with a wry smile.

"At least we'll have our own personal staff of maids, butlers, and chefs. Just think of all the free time that'll give us."

"Ha! Maybe for me, but you'll be busier than ever. It's a pretty big job you know, running the free world. You'll barely find time to breathe."

"Well, we'd better make the best of it while we can. I've got a nice quiet hotel room waiting for us upstairs. Maybe we can find a way to exercise our lungs in the big four-poster bed."

Julie's eyes widened.

What about Brooke—"

"Taken care of. I've arranged for my mother to spend the night and look after her." James lifted his napkin from his lap and placed it on the table. "Why don't you scan the dessert menu while I take a short break. I'll be back in a flash."

James squeezed his wife's hand and excused himself to make his way to the men's room. As he wound his way through the dining room, many patrons recognized the congressman and murmured excitedly to their seat mates. He didn't notice three burly men rise from a table in the corner and follow him to the lavatory.

After James finished his business and moved to the sink to wash his hands, he saw the three men enter the men's room. One of them lingered by the door, while the other two flanked James at the sink. He knew from their body language that they had other matters on their minds. James tensed his muscles as he felt a flood of adrenaline flood his system. He'd been a linebacker in college and knew how to take care of himself in a scrum. But this was an entirely different kind of confrontation. He didn't want to make a scene in the quiet upscale restaurant or ruffle his suit if he could help it. As he shook the water from his hands into the sink and moved toward the paper towel dispenser, the two men stepped in front of him.

James stood ram straight and remained calm.

"May I help you, gentlemen?"

"We have a message for you," one of the men said, pressing his chest against James.

"No need to be so formal about it," James said. "You could have just dropped a note at the front desk."

"Always so clever, aren't you?" the man said, sneering at James. "But you've become too clever for your own good." The man reached up and grabbed James firmly by his suit lapels. "I'm afraid we can't let you go through with your plans. You're going to have to drop out of the presidential race, or some very bad things are going to happen to you and your family."

James paused for a moment to appraise the situation. One man stood immediately behind him, and another minded the door ten feet away. He was never one to shrink from a fight, and the threat against his family was the last straw. He looked in his peripheral vision to gauge the distance of the man behind him, then he struck. He pulled his left foot up sharply and hit the man behind him in the testicles. Then he planted his foot and pushed the man in front of him with all his strength. The man stumbled backward into the wall while the one behind doubled over in pain. James swung around and ducked just as the third man came at him, flinging his fist over his head. As James stood up, he swung his right arm in a powerful uppercut and heard the door man's nose break with a crunch.

Thinking he had immobilized the thugs, he moved toward the door. Suddenly, he felt a searing pain in his lower back. The first man had bounced back from the wall and struck him hard in the kidney. James fell down on one knee, and the second man grabbed him by the hair and flung his head forward onto the granite edge of the vanity counter. James's forehead struck the hard surface and bounced backward. He struggled to maintain consciousness as flashing stars filled his eyes. The first man threaded his arms between James's and pulled them back as the third man punched James as hard as he could in the stomach. James doubled over and coughed from the sudden loss of wind.

The second man moved his head forward and pressed his nose against James's. "This is just a warning," he sneered, pulling James's head back. "We won't be as kind the next time around. Do the smart thing. Stick around to enjoy your cute family. Quit—or die. Next time you won't see it coming."

The men suddenly let go of James, and he dropped to the floor. The last thing he remembered was the shocked look on an incoming patron's face as the three men hustled past him out the men's room door.

PART II

GRAVITATIONAL FORCES

14

Longworth Building, Congressman Marshall's Office

October 25, 9:00 a.m.

Ray Bradley tapped on James's open door and walked into his office. James had his head down reviewing some documents and looked up. His friend looked surprised when he saw the large purple bump on James's forehead.

"Jesus, man, what the hell happened to you?"

James rubbed the bump softly and chuckled.

"I had a nasty encounter with a counter."

"What? Did you slip and fall in the bathroom?"

"Fell, yes. Slip, no. More like I was pushed."

Ray's eyes widened.

"Were you and Jules getting a little frisky and you lost control?"

"I wish. In fact, the guys that did this put a little damper on our plans for later that evening."

"Really?" Ray said, pulling up a chair. "Give me all the dirt. How many were there? Do they look as bad as you? What was the reason?"

"There were three of them. Cornered me in the restroom at a fancy restaurant. They told me to drop out of the presidential race or else. When they threatened my family, I kind of lost it."

"Holy shit." Ray leaned forward in his chair. "Did they get away? What did the cops say?"

"Unfortunately, yes. I gave as good as I got, but the fall on the counter top knocked me out. I haven't contacted the police."

Ray furrowed his brow, looking puzzled.

"Jim, I know you think you can take care of yourself. But this is serious. You can't take these threats lightly, especially now that you're running for President. There's a lot of whack jobs out there who wouldn't think twice about taking out a high profile figure like you."

James slumped back in his chair and sighed.

"Ray, if we had a nickel for every time we got a threatening letter from a disgruntled constituent, we could have retired by now. It goes with the territory. If they were really serious, they could have shot or knifed me. It was just a warning."

"Which is exactly why you shouldn't take it lightly. Especially since they threatened your family. I think you should look into Secret Service protection. Did you know it's available for presidential candidates—not just the President?"

"The last thing I need," James said, shaking his head, "is a bunch of goons in suits surrounding me on the campaign trail. Doesn't exactly scream accessibility. I'm supposed to be the *populist* candidate, remember?"

"Maybe so, but you can ask them to keep a low profile. At least to watch your family. You've already lost one person close to you..."

James rested his head in his hands and paused as he rubbed his temple.

"Okay, I'll talk to them. It's really just Julie and Brooklyn I'm worried about. No one's targeted a candidate before."

"What did your assailants say? Who do you think they were?"

"I believe their exact words were 'we can't let you go through with your plans.' I have no idea who they were."

Ray sat back in his chair, pondering who would take such extreme action.

"It sounds like someone with a lot to lose from your becoming President."

"Or some *organization*."

Ray nodded.

"There's a *lot* of organizations that stand to lose if you enact the legislation you're proposing. Starting with big corporations, who you've threatened with heavy tax hikes. Plus, a million doctors' incomes would fall dramatically under your healthcare plan. And private prison operators will lose half their profits if you pardon every non-violent drug offender currently in jail. The list goes on. You're making a lot of enemies with your proposals."

James looked out his window at the lobbyists milling about the congressional office steps.

"I dunno, Ray. These don't seem like the kind of groups that would resort to threats and violence. Those thugs were pretty rough around the edges. I get the feeling they're from the other side of the tracks."

"Organized crime, you mean?" Ray said. "Yeah—they stand to lose a lot, too. Those guys don't mess around. You might not be so lucky next time around. Even an All-American like you can't stop a bullet. Maybe it's time to rethink this whole idea of yours."

James pinched his eyebrows.

"Running for President—or my legislative agenda?"

"Both. Is it really worth losing your life or those of your loved ones over this?"

James leaned forward and rested his forearms on his desk.

"We can't cave in to terrorists like this, Ray. It's not the American way. What kind of signal would I be sending to the people I'm trying to help, let alone my own kids? That I'm a coward and I let the bad guys win? There's never been great social progress without a certain degree of risk. If not me, who'll pick up the torch?"

Ray crossed his arms and looked away uncomfortably.

"Okay, Jim," he sighed. "Just do me a favor. Don't go anywhere alone anymore, will you? And look into that Secret Service detail."

James laughed.

"There's still a few places I don't want people watching my back. I won't be inviting them into the washroom, I can tell you that. I think I can take care of *that* much myself."

15

Secret Service Headquarters, 245 Murray Lane SW, DC

October 26, 9:00 a.m.

James sat in the lobby of the Secret Service building awaiting his meeting with the Director. He'd reluctantly called the agency upon Ray's insistence, but he felt uncomfortable taking on such high profile protection. He'd always prided himself on minimizing the trappings of political office, and this seemed like the ultimate extravagance. The black-suited agents shadowing the President with their conspicuous earpieces gave him the creeps. Their omnipresent appearance almost seemed to make their charge look like even more of a target. But the recent threat to James's family was something he could no longer ignore. As he scanned the photos of former Secret Service Directors lining the wall, a familiar figure approached from the direction of the elevator bank.

"Congressman Marshall," the man said, stopping in front of

James. "Doug Richardson. Sorry to keep you waiting. Shall we find somewhere more private to talk?"

James nodded as the two men shook hands, then the director escorted James through the security entrance to his top-floor office.

"How can I help you, congressman?" the director said, closing his door.

"Well, I..." James stumbled to find the right words. He felt emasculated asking for help. "I recently experienced an...incident."

"I heard," the Director said.

James's eyes widened.

"But how—"

"It's a small town, congressman. This sort of thing gets around quickly. Have you contacted the DC police?"

"I didn't want to draw attention. I mean, I thought I could take care of it..."

"I'm afraid you've made yourself a target, congressman. Running for the top office in the land draws out the snakes. This isn't the sort of thing you should try to manage yourself."

James paused for a moment.

"I understand the Secret Service provides protection for presidential candidates—"

"At our discretion," the Director nodded, "on a case-by-case basis. But I think your case merits consideration. Tell me more about the recent incident and what kind of protection you were thinking about."

"It was just three thugs trying to rough me up in a public restroom. But I'm concerned about my family. They threatened to harm them if I didn't step out of the race."

The Director's eyelids thinned as he listened to James.

"We take every threat seriously. Do you have any idea who these men were?"

James shook his head.

"I can only guess."

"Could you sit down with our sketch artist? Maybe we can match one or more of them with our database."

"I suppose so. What kind of protection can you provide for my family?"

The director sat back in his chair and interlocked his fingers on his desk.

"We have limited resources. The agency's policy is to provide protection to leading candidates and their spouses only."

James looked at the director confused.

"What qualifies as *leading*?"

"The guidelines require the candidate to have earned ten percent of more of the vote in two consecutive primaries and raised at least two million dollars in campaign contributions."

"I meet the second criterion," James said, "but the primaries don't start for another three months. Do you make any exceptions?"

"The final decision to grant Secret Service protection rests with a five-member panel of congressional majority and minority leaders. I could bring your case to their attention if you wish."

James looked at the director for a long moment.

"You don't provide protection for candidates' children?"

"Technically, we provide protection for the candidate and their spouses only. But this includes close oversight of your home, so to the extent your children remain in the house, they'd be protected there as well."

James paused to consider his options. He wasn't thrilled with the idea of going hat in hand to the House minority leader to help support his campaign. After a few seconds, he stood to shake the director's hand.

"Thank you, Director. I've got a few things to think about. Let me get back to you. Thank you for your time."

The Director took a step toward James to slow his exit.

"In the meantime, I recommend you at least see the local police about putting together a sketch of the suspects. They can run it through our database. If these guys are part of any known extremist groups, we might be able to help apprehend them."

James cocked his head skeptically toward the Director. His experience as a district attorney gave him a good idea of how that would go down.

"Then what? Charge them with common assault? Threatening to kill someone other than the President? They'd be back on the streets in a matter of months. It's not these guys I'm worried about. It's who they *work* for."

16

Marshall Residence

October 26, 10:00 p.m.

James leaned back in his office chair, contemplating the last three days' events. After his encounter at the restaurant, Julie had urged him to reconsider his candidacy for President. He'd been open about the risks, and she was worried for him and their children. She'd agreed to allow him to investigate Secret Service protection but still felt uneasy about the black cloud looming over their heads. It was time for James to make a decision, and he was enormously conflicted. As he closed his eyes to think, he heard footsteps at his door.

"Penny for your thoughts?" Julie said.

James tilted his chair forward and sighed.

"How many do you have? Because I've got a million things running through my head right now."

Julie closed the office door behind her and took a seat on the office sofa.

"Come, rest your head on my shoulder," she said, patting the cushion beside her. "Maybe I can help lighten your load."

James walked over to the sofa and lay down with his head on Julie's lap.

"How did your meeting with the Secret Service Director go?" she asked.

"Do you want to hear the good news or the bad news first?"

"Let's start with the good."

"We qualify for protection. But it won't start until after the second primary."

Julie's eyes widened as she caressed the bump over James's eye.

"Even after such a direct threat?"

"There are exceptions, but it's a big production. They have to get the approval of the majority and minority leaders, in both the House and the Senate. The Director of Homeland Security makes the final decision."

Julie looked at James carefully. She knew he had a contentious relationship with the House minority leader and that he felt uncomfortable asking for any favors.

"What did you say?"

"I said I'd think about it."

The couple lay in silence for a minute as Julie massaged James's temples.

"You know there's a much simpler solution," she said.

James opened his eyes and tried to get up. Julie placed her hand on his chest and gently pushed him down.

"You know I'm not a quitter, hon," James said. "I wasn't sure about my chances when I started, but now I see the path clearly ahead of me. We have a chance to make a meaningful difference in the lives of millions of people."

"And I don't want you to quit," Julie said. "But it's not just your constituents you have to think about. I don't want to lose anybody else. I don't think I could handle another..."

James lifted his arm and squeezed Julie's hand.

"I know babe. I'm being irresponsible. Nothing's worth breaking our family apart any further."

He turned his head and stared at the soft glow of the lamp illuminating his desk.

"I'll announce my withdrawal tomorrow."

Julie looked at her husband's contorted face, knowing how hard this was for him. She paused for a moment, then propped him up beside her.

"Maybe there's another way," she said. "Why don't we look into *private* security, at least until the primaries start in a few months. You'll just need to keep a fairly low profile until then. We can make our own date nights at home."

James peered at his wife, trying to read her feelings.

"Are you sure? It's not just these crazies we have to worry about. The press will be invading our privacy, putting us under a microscope, looking for any dirt to make headlines. It won't be easy—"

Julie raised her hand to caress her husband's cheek.

"I know how much you want this, James. I'm so proud of you. No one would have the courage to do what you're doing. You'll make a fabulous President."

James smiled as he leaned in to kiss his wife.

"And you'll be the most gorgeous First Lady ever."

Julie put her hand on James's chest and pushed him back.

"Just promise me one thing," she said. "No more going out alone in public. As strong as you are, I don't want you in any more fist fights between now and February."

"Deal," James said, pulling Julie down onto the sofa. "Besides, who wants to go out when I can have so much more fun right here in my own home?"

17

The House of Representatives, Capitol Building

November 1, 10:00 a.m.

On the scheduled day of voting for the new healthcare bill in the House of Representatives, James walked down the center aisle toward the front of the assembly room. As he passed his fellow representatives seated to the left, he noticed the members appraising him warily. The announcement of his candidacy for President had raised the eyebrows of many politicians on both sides of the aisle. His visibility in the press and in the recent debate had gained him a newfound respect—and animosity—among his peers.

The healthcare bill was a contentious issue that had been widely debated within closed committee meetings, and both parties were eager to count the vote. The bill had been introduced by the Republican party as a measure to roll back many of the provisions of the previous administration's controversial program. After many debates and amendments, a consensus measure had been put together that seemingly satisfied both sides. Now it was just a matter of polling the members to see if a majority vote could be achieved.

Following the rules of the House, any member who wished to debate the bill sat in the front row of seats on their party's side of the floor. The House Speaker recognized each member in turn, alternating between the majority and minority sides. Today, there were three members sitting on the Democratic side and two on the Republican side. As James took his seat on the Democratic side, he glanced toward Minority Leader Akerman sitting directly behind him. The minority leader had a sour look on his face and scowled at James. Although James had let his views on the bill be known to Akerman, the minority leader had refused to invite him to the internal committee debates. This was James's last chance to sway the House vote.

After all the other members had spoken, the Speaker recognized James last. He stood and proceeded to the podium in the Well to deliver his speech. He knew he had a brief allotment of time to give his remarks, after which the Speaker would cut him off.

"Mr. Speaker," James began. "I would like to address the limitations of the proposed bill. As most of you know, this measure is a watered-down version of the previous health bill passed in this House. That bill had its flaws, as we've seen with the millions of Americans that have been denied healthcare coverage. As currently drafted, this bill does nothing to lower premiums, broaden coverage, or improve support for Medicaid."

James scanned the arched rows of seats in the assembly hall. Most members remained frozen with non-committal expressions, but a few nodded in agreement. As his vision returned to the front of the room, he glanced toward Akerman. The minority leader sat with his arms crossed and his shoulders hunched, avoiding the congressman's gaze. James glanced at his watch and realized he had only a few seconds left in his allotted time.

"Instead of rushing through another half-measure bill," he continued, "I ask my fellow members to vote no on this measure and open the floor to full debate on a more progressive bill that will be inclusive for *all* Americans. The United States has the most expensive healthcare system in the world and ranks dead last among the top ten developed nations in the quality and accessibility of healthcare. Voting yes on this bill will only maintain the conspiracy of privilege shared among private insurers, wealthy doctors, and large pharmaceutical companies."

"Congressman," the Speaker interrupted. "Your time is up. Please step down."

"Our citizens' health lies in your hands today," James said. "Do the right thing and give it back to them."

James stepped down from the podium and walked back to his regular seat in the back of the room beside Ray.

"That should right duly piss Akerman off," Ray whispered in his ear. "This is gonna be a close one."

The Speaker stood up and slammed his gavel on his desk.

"The debate on this bill is finished. We will now tally the vote. Members, please proceed to the voting stations to cast your vote."

James and Ray made their way to the closest electronic voting box and waited in line as each member inserted their card into the voting machine and punched 'Yea' or 'Nay'. A large panel above the press gallery seats displayed each member's vote, along with a running count of the totals and the time remaining. As the minutes ticked down, the totals toggled back and forth between for and against. When the buzzer sounded marking the end of voting, the numbers showed two hundred and sixteen Yeas and two hundred and nineteen Nays.

A loud cheer rose from the Democratic side of the assembly, while the Republican members looked on impassively.

"*Two votes*," Ray said, shaking his head. "Thompson and Bannerman switched. Your speech may have made the difference."

He watched Akerman rise from his seat and storm out of the room, casting daggers in James's direction.

"But I think you may have made a few more enemies in the process."

18

Capitol Hill

November 1, Noon

J ames and Ray walked along the footpath leading from the Capitol building toward their congressional offices. It was a brisk fall day, and the sun was shining brightly in a cloudless sky. James tilted his face up and closed his eyes. After the stuffiness of the House assembly, it felt good to get some fresh air.

"The gods are shining on you today," Ray said, seeing his friend soak up the sun. "Enjoy it while it lasts. You're gonna need some divine intervention to get your own version of the health bill passed."

James chuckled.

"I'm sure not getting any help from my own party. Akerman's been blocking me at every turn. Every draft I've submitted has been shot down in the Health Subcommittee. And he's not even the chairman."

"But he's tight with Spurling, who is. It isn't helping that he's running against you in the presidential race. You've been killing him in the polls."

"Those guys have had it in for me long before then, from the first day I became a congressman," James said, shaking his head.

Ray looked at James as they stopped at the light to cross Independence Avenue.

"You have to admit, Jim—you haven't exactly been a team player. Your positions on most of the issues are dancing on the fringes. You know how this town works. You have to suck up to the establishment if you want to get ahead in this game."

"That's why I entered politics," James said. "To break down those walls and create a progressive agenda. If we left it up to the old guys, nothing would ever get done around here. They're only interested in padding their pockets and boosting their egos. I'm tired of playing by the rules. That's why I'm going for the top job."

As they waited for the light to turn, three youths carrying backpacks approached the congressmen. One of them pointed at James, and they rushed toward him.

"Congressman Marshall," a pretty coed said excitedly. "We're huge fans. We watched your debate and love your ideas about updating the law to reflect modern values. It's high time someone came forward with fresh ideas to help the little guys."

"I hope my plans help more than just the little guys," James laughed, as he shook each youth's hand. "Tell me about yourselves. Are you in school? What are your plans?"

"We're students at GWU. My name's Emma. Britney and I are studying communications, and Noah's studying finance. We're all members of the Young Democrats. I'm the leader of our university's debate team. I took lots of notes during your last debate."

"That's very impressive, Emma," James said. "I bet I could pick up a few tips from you as well. If you really want to help your party, I can always use some part-time help in my campaign office. Even just a few hours on weekends can make a difference."

"Really?" Emma said, her eyes opening wide. She looked at her friends, who nodded excitedly. "We'd love to. When can we start?"

James handed each of the students his business card.

"Call my office, and my assistant will give you the details. Tell them you spoke with me about volunteering for my campaign. I look forward to seeing you again soon."

The light turned green, and the two congressmen crossed the street, headed toward the Longworth Building.

Ray shook his head and laughed.

"I may have underestimated you, Jim. You're a shameless politician after all. You realize that even if you become President, you won't have a chance in hell getting these great ideas enacted if you don't win majorities in both houses. Even then, there's no guarantee you'll capture a quorum within our own party for some of your plans. You're so far out there, it's going to be difficult to get many of the members to support you."

"Maybe so, Ray," James said. "But if I can get the majority of the citizens on my side, it'll send a strong message that the country wants to see progressive change. And if I help get some of the members reelected, they'll have no choice but to support the will of the people."

"That's assuming you don't get torpedoed by certain of your followers before then. Akerman isn't the only one gunning for you. Did you talk to the Secret Service about getting protection?"

"I did. The rules don't allow it until after the primaries begin."

"That's a long way out. What are you going to do?"

"Jules and I talked about it. She wants me to stay in. We're going to look into hiring private security to watch the kids. In the meantime, I'm just going to have to watch my back. If I make it through the second primary, we'll consider official protection then."

As the congressmen walked down the corridor of the Longworth Building toward their private offices, James heard some voices coming from Minority Leader Akerman's open door. Passing by, he glanced inside and saw Senator Channing sitting in a chair opposite Akerman's desk, laughing. Akerman looked up and made brief eye contact with James, then continued talking with Senator Channing.

James stopped and looked down. It was unusual for the senator to be so far from the Senate congressional buildings on the other side of the Capitol, especially so soon after a House recess.

This might be my last chance, he thought.

"I'll catch you later," he said, turning to Ray. "I'm gonna do some of that sucking up you suggested."

Ray looked at James like he'd lost his mind.

"This might not be the ideal time—"

"I'll be fine. Grab me a ham and swiss in the cafeteria. If I'm not down there in twenty minutes, send up the cavalry."

Senator Channing noticed James outside the door and motioned to him.

"James," he said, "we were just talking about you. I hear you stopped the latest health bill moving on to the upper chamber. I'm not sure whether to thank you or scold you. The Republicans are determined to rewrite our previous legislation."

James looked at Akerman for his consent to enter. The minority leader jerked his head to the side to invite him in.

"Good to see you again, Senator," James said, shaking Channing's hand. "Sorry our last meeting was under less friendly terms."

Channing chuckled.

"That was quite a battle you put up in the debate. You comported yourself surprisingly well. Have a seat—there was something I wanted to talk with you about. And please, call me Ken."

Akerman motioned to one of the chairs as he closed his office door.

"James," Channing said. "Tom and I have been talking about how much you've emerged as a leader these past few weeks." He crossed his leg and leaned back in his chair. "I wanted to bounce a proposal past you."

James raised his eyebrows and glanced toward Akerman, who nodded silently. For the two congressional leaders to be holding out an olive branch at this point in the presidential race seemed surprising—and suspicious. Nonetheless, James decided to heed Ray's advice and seek to make allies, not more enemies.

"Any partnership with my esteemed colleagues is worthy of consideration," James said.

"I'm glad you feel that way," Channing said. "Your performance in the debate was impressive. And your management of the media has been masterful. You're obviously resonating with a certain segment of the population."

James glanced between Channing and Akerman to gauge their body language. While the senator seemed relaxed and jovial, Akerman looked tight and uncomfortable.

"Your rise in the polls has been admirable," Channing continued. "But you're still ten points behind me and even further behind Templeton in a presidential run-off. You've got to realize your chances of going all the way are next to impossible."

James didn't flinch and simply smiled at the senator.

"I'd like you to be my running mate," Channing said. "Together we'd make a formidable team. I'll capture the older centrist voters, and you'll capture the younger left-wing voters. Templeton would be isolated on the right. We can win this. Of course, it would mean you'd have to withdraw from the race and throw your support behind me."

James looked at the senator, then the minority leader. It was obvious what they were trying to do. If he were to step down and join Channing's ticket, he'd be eliminated as a threat. He'd have to support Channing's platform, which would mean he'd also have to toe the party line on legislative measures. Although James's political standing would rise overnight, along with his chances of getting to the White House, he'd be marginalized in a number two role.

James paused for a moment.

"That's a very generous offer, Ken. While I have the utmost respect for you, I'm not sure I see how this will advance my agenda. We're pretty far apart on the policy issues. How much are you willing to adopt my proposals under a unified banner?"

Channing's eyes darted across James's face as he appraised the young congressman.

"We obviously can't embrace this universal drug legalization plan of yours. But we can move in small steps with a marijuana decriminalization bill. Colorado and Washington proved it can fly. I don't see why we can't support it at the federal level. We're actually not far apart on many economic issues. I'd be willing to support some of your programs if you throw your support behind mine. We'll work together on finding middle ground."

James knew how this worked. While the Vice President enjoyed a lofty titular status on the national stage, in reality, most sitting Presidents gave the VP a minor role in the actual decision-making process. This was an easy way to put James out to pasture for the next four years.

"You've given me a lot to think about, Senator," he said. "Can you give me a few days to process this? I'll need to consult with my wife and—"

"Come on, James," Akerman interrupted. "Don't be a fool. This is a once-in-a-lifetime opportunity to hitch your ticket to a proven winner. Don't get shot down and pushed to the side any further. You know as well as anyone that the Vice President is usually the frontrunner in the next election cycle. If you really want to be President some day, this is your best chance."

"That may be true, Tom. I'm just not sure I want to wait eight more years to get there."

James stood up and shook both men's hands.

"I'll give this serious consideration, Senator. Thank you for thinking of me so highly. I'll give you my decision in the next few days."

As James walked out of Akerman's office, he could feel his heart thumping in his chest. Going from junior congressman to vice presidential nominee in the space of a couple of years would be a huge honor. Akerman was right in stating this would vastly increase his chance to become President if Channing beat Templeton in next year's election. But something deep down told him Channing and Akerman had less honorable plans.

19

Georgetown University

November 2, 2:00 p.m.

Heath Marshall strolled with his girlfriend across the Georgetown campus between classes. Since his father's debate performance three weeks ago, he'd been getting a lot of attention. Most of it was flattering, with the majority of his schoolmates leaning to the left on the political spectrum. But the university had a strong and vocal College Republican faction that viewed him as the enemy, and they didn't hesitate to taunt him whenever they could. Heath generally shied away from engaging his fellow students on political matters, knowing it inflamed passions on both sides. He just wanted to live a normal college life and blend in on campus with the rest of his friends.

As he and his girlfriend turned off Library Walk onto the footpath leading into McDonough Hall, Heath noticed a group of three boys walking toward them. They were gesturing toward Heath and laughing amongst themselves. Since the path wasn't wide enough for both groups to comfortably pass, Heath pulled his girlfriend's hand and led her across the lawn. Seeing the couple trying to avert a confrontation, the three boys veered off the path and blocked their passage. Heath held up and rolled his eyes.

"Sorry, Liv," he whispered in his girlfriend's ear. "This shouldn't take long. I just have to humor these buffoons and let them massage their egos. You go ahead to class, I'll be there in a few minutes."

Olivia squeezed Heath's hand and pulled in closer.

"Two against three is better odds," she said. "I'm not going to leave you alone to get insulted by a bunch of rednecks."

"What's the matter, *Heath-en*," the tallest boy said, taunting Heath. "Afraid to stand up to some *real* Americans? Are you and your girlfriend looking for a hiding spot to shoot some crack? Is your dad your supplier? He must keep quite a stash, with his pro-drug rant."

Heath shook his head and sighed. These confrontations had become far too common on campus, and he was nearing the limit of his patience.

"My dad hasn't even tried *weed*," he said. "He's just trying to open the market, so people who want to use recreational drugs aren't treated like criminals. I'm sure you potheads can appreciate that."

The ringleader looked at his buddies and laughed.

"Yeah, well, we're med students, so we know that some drugs are bad for you. Unlike your daddy, who thinks the whole country should be using. Doesn't he realize there's an epidemic of addicts dragging our values into the gutter?"

Heath glanced at his girlfriend and smiled.

"You mean our *puritan* values?" he laughed. "People who want to use are going to find their fix, no matter what. Legalizing the trade just makes it safer to supply it. The tax money can actually be used to educate and rehabilitate addicts. You doctors never seem able to see past the symptoms of the disease to treat the real cause. But don't worry, that's something *else* my dad plans to fix. You might want to consider another major—MDs won't be making nearly as much money from all their unnecessary tests and procedures once he's in office."

The tallest boy stepped forward and looked Heath directly in his eye.

"Your dad doesn't stand a chance in hell of becoming President," he said. "He's just another left-wing whack job with grandiose fantasies of occupying the White House. In ten years, I'll be making more money than both of you combined. Now run off to your pathetic little law school. The only reason you were accepted here is because it's your father's alma mater."

The boy pushed Heath with both hands and Heath staggered backward.

"Don't *touch* him, you ape!" Olivia said, rushing forward. "He's ten times the man you'll ever be."

The tall boy grabbed Olivia by the arm and flung her onto the grass. Heath lunged forward and landed his fist on the boy's jaw, flinging blood from his mouth. The other two boys moved in and restrained Heath, while the tall boy caught his breath and faced him.

"You bleeding heart liberals will never understand," he said. "This country was founded as a republic and will always be ruled by men who recognize the need for law and order. If you want to waste yourself on drugs and hookers, move to *Denmark*!"

The ringleader reared back and punched Heath as hard as he could in his stomach. Heath doubled over and gasped for breath as Olivia rushed to his aide.

As he watched the three boys walk away laughing amongst themselves, he realized he and his father weren't so different after all.

20

Marshall Campaign Office, Foggy Bottom

November 4, 10:00 a.m.

James walked into his newly opened campaign office on Saturday morning to loud cheers. The office was packed with many volunteers he didn't recognize, and everybody was standing and clapping. At the back of the room, Nick stood with a huge smile. Campaign contributions had been flooding in, and he'd spared no expense outfitting the office with state-of-the-art equipment. Large television monitors lined the office walls, streaming clips from his last debate and the *Meet The Press* interview. Banks of phones lined the horizontal rows of tables, with young staffers ready to take calls from James's growing legion of fans. A large banner hung from one side of the room to the other reading *Ride The Wave — Marshall for President.*

James walked up the aisle toward his office at the back of the room, stopping to exchange greetings with the new volunteers he'd met outside the Capitol building. When he reached Nick, he looked at him with a wry smile.

"You've been *busy*," he said, appraising the office setup. "Who's paying for all this?"

"Your fans," Nick said. "You won't believe the pace of contributions we've been receiving. Come into the office—let me give you a full update."

James followed Nick and turned to the staff before he entered the rear office.

"I look forward to talking with you all soon," he said. "We've got a lot of work to do. Thank you all for coming in."

He gave a wave of acknowledgment, then closed the door behind him.

"It's absolutely incredible, Jim," Nick said, grasping James by his shoulders. "We're pulling in more than a hundred thousand bucks a day—almost all of it online in increments under fifty dollars. We just passed over three million in total contributions. Your base has really responded to our outreach."

James smiled at his chief of staff.

"I couldn't have done it without you, Nick," he said. "The website is fabulous. I noticed we've passed one million followers on Facebook and Twitter. And the new text-to-donate platform you've put together is brilliant. You're making it super-easy for our followers to get involved."

Nick motioned through the office window to the staffers talking into telephone headsets in the main room.

"And don't forget about the old-fashioned technology. The phones have been ringing off the hook from the moment we opened the office. I can barely keep up with enough staff to field the calls."

"Where did all these volunteers come from, anyhow?" James said, looking at the scores of people manning the tables.

"I started getting inundated with requests about three days ago. Most of the volunteers seem to be coming from local colleges, but we're getting a fair number of stay-at-home Moms and unemployed people as well."

James appraised the diversity of his volunteer staff and nodded approvingly.

"Let's make sure they're well fed and hydrated. I'd like to bring in a fridge and have it stocked with nutritious treats. We can hire a caterer to keep it replenished. What about setting up a ping-pong or foosball table to break the monotony? It'll keep the creative juices flowing and create a sense of camaraderie."

"Great idea," Nick said. "I'll get on it before the end of the day. Have a seat—I wanted to give you an update on the latest poll numbers."

Nick clicked his computer mouse and motioned to a large monitor on the office wall.

"Harris has us at twelve percent, Gallup at thirteen, and CNN at fifteen. That's up almost ten points since before the debate, putting you in a solid third place behind Channing and Harper."

"Those are good numbers, Nick," James nodded. "But they haven't climbed appreciably in the last few days. We need to reestablish our momentum with another strong showing at the next debate in two weeks' time."

James looked out the office window at his office staff.

"I thought maybe we could use some of our enthusiastic new staffers to help us set up a mock debate. Maybe they can come up with some creative new talking points to help me think on my feet. I didn't feel completely prepared for some of the questions and rebuttals in the last debate."

Nick stood up and walked over to the large whiteboard on the wall of the office. It was divided into ten rows and three columns, summarizing the positions of the Marshall campaign versus his opponents on each of the critical issues.

"How do you want to tackle it? I don't think we can bounce this off the whole group at one time. We need to keep most of them on the phones to make sure we don't miss any calls. Maybe we can invite a few in at a time and run it by them in stages."

James nodded.

"I agree. I think four or five ought to do it. I'd like a mixed group.

Young, old, different ethnic backgrounds, etc." James pointed through the window at one of the new volunteers. "Let's include that redhead, Emma, in the first group."

Nick stepped out of the office and invited five staffers to join them. When everybody was seated, he explained what he wanted to do.

"Thanks for giving us a few minutes of your time," he said. "Congressman Marshall and I would like to get your impressions on some of the campaign's policy positions and see if you can help us craft some good talking points. Then we'd like to run a brief mock debate, where the congressman will present his positions and you'll pretend to rebut his statements from the perspective of his Democratic opponents. I'll play the role of moderator. But first, take a look at this whiteboard summary of the candidates' positions on the issues. Does anything stand out as unclear or uncomfortable? Look at the other candidates' positions and tell us if you think our plans are sufficiently compelling and differentiated."

The group studied the whiteboard for a few minutes, then Emma raised her hand.

"Yes, Emma?" Nick said.

"Um...I'm looking at the healthcare issue," Emma said. "The other candidates are pretty much toeing the line on keeping the present plan passed by the previous administration. We're proposing a one-payer system and abolishing the private insurer program altogether. While it distances us pretty clearly from the other candidates' positions, are we sure we can sell it to the general public? It's a pretty radical departure from the free-enterprise approach embraced by the U.S. since the Nixon administration."

James looked at Emma and smiled. He was impressed with her depth of knowledge on the issue and her political insight.

"That's a good point, Emma," he said. "I agree that it's a bold shift in current thinking. But the current program is reviled by the Republicans and probably won't stand much chance staying in its current form under their repeal efforts. Allow me to present my reasons for why I think it's the best solution in our mock debate, then you can rebut it and tell me if it makes sense."

Emma nodded and scribbled a few notes on her tablet.

"Right," Nick said after the group finished providing input on the critical issues. "Let's get started with our mock debate."

For the next hour and a half, they worked through each of the key issues, with Nick posing the questions, James presenting his prepared statements, and the volunteers countering with rebuttal questions. Throughout the engagement, Nick took detailed notes on his computer and encouraged the staffers to be candid with their comments.

By mid-afternoon, James was exhausted and welcomed a coffee break. He thanked the focus group participants for their input, then circulated amongst the main office staff, getting to know them. At four in the afternoon, Nick dismissed the office and handed out a schedule of future campaign events before locking the door. James and Nick chatted for a few minutes, then James headed east toward the nearest Metro station.

He didn't notice a tall man in a dark suit tracing his steps half a block behind, scanning the surrounding scene behind dark sunglasses.

21

Royce Hall, UCLA

November 15, 8:00 p.m.

The UCLA auditorium was filled to capacity with the hum of excited observers as the second Democratic presidential debate was about to begin. The tension was high, with the race tightening after the bottom two candidates dropped out and threw their support behind Senator Channing.

ABC News Political Correspondent George Stephanopoulos sat in the moderator's chair outlining the rules while the candidates reviewed their last-minute notes. James glanced to his immediate left where Channing stood and received an icy stare. After he'd turned down the senator's invitation to join his ticket, Channing told him all niceties would be dispensed going forward. As far as he was concerned, the race to win the party's nomination was *war*, and he'd treat James as the enemy he considered him to be.

James swallowed hard as Stephanopoulos prepared to deliver the first question.

"Congressman Marshall," he said, inviting James to begin the debate. "There's been a great deal of animosity between the two main parties on the issue of healthcare in America. You recently voted against the compromise measure assembled in the House. What is your plan for providing affordable and quality healthcare for Americans?"

James nodded, forcing a smile.

"Thank you, George, for raising this important question. I voted against the bill because it would have eliminated coverage for millions of Americans and raised premiums for those who can least afford it. I think it's time the United States embraced a new paradigm for serving the healthcare needs of its citizens. We spend nearly twice as much per person on healthcare as the next nearest country. Yet on almost every measure of quality, we rank near the bottom of developed nations. There are now almost thirty million Americans without healthcare insurance, who face a crippling bill in the tens of thousands of dollars for just a few days' stay in a hospital."

The first warning sound chimed amid muted audience response. James unconsciously increased his pace.

"I propose a universal one-payer system, which will reduce the number of unnecessary and expensive tests, drug treatments, and surgeries. It will encourage healthcare providers to spend more time consulting with their patients to understand and treat the underlying cause of each illness before rushing to treat the symptoms. Every man, woman, and child in America would be covered and no longer fear oppressively high one-time healthcare bills."

The audience applauded as Stephanopoulos checked his timer. He saw that James still had a few seconds left in his allotted time.

"How do you propose to *fund* this universal plan, Congressman?"

"In the same manner we're funding the current program. Those who are employed will have half their premiums paid by their employer and pay the rest in the form of payroll deductions."

The double-chime sounded, and James rushed to finish his statement.

"And those who are unemployed will be covered by Medicare and Medicaid."

"Senator Channing—" Stephanopoulos said, beginning his invitation for the senator to reply.

"In other words, George," Channing interrupted. "Congressman Marshall's plan is funded by American *taxpayers*. More people receiving government support means higher premiums for everybody, while our highly respected doctors receive lower payments and incomes. The congressman seems to think he knows better than physicians how patients should be treated. Do you have a medical degree, congressman?"

"Congressman Marshall," Stephanopoulos said, "rebuttal?"

"I'm not a medical doctor," James said, feeling beads of sweat forming on his forehead. "I'm simply presenting the facts. A recent study found that almost two-thirds of all tests and procedures ordered by physicians have questionable merit. Unfortunately, the more invasive the test or medical procedure, the more the current system pays medical providers. My plan will rebalance these payments to encourage more thorough patient consultations, which should result in more accurate diagnoses and fewer unnecessary procedures."

"So you'll have the *government* decide what treatments and procedures doctors should prescribe?" Channing said. "Get ready for socialized medicine, folks."

The audience responded to Channing's comments with a loud cheer.

The other three candidates weighed in with their opinions on James's plan, agreeing with Channing's arguments against the one-payer system. By the time the issue was fully vetted, the audience response had swung decidedly against James. He'd lost his footing against a vicious and concentrated attack. Channing's quick and biting remarks almost made it seem to James like the senator knew in advance what James would say and that he'd had his response prepared ahead of time.

By the time the debate shifted to the issue of foreign policy, James was feeling unsteady. This time, the moderator gave Senator Channing the first opportunity to speak.

"Senator Channing, the recent escalation of rhetoric and military tests between North Korea and the United States has raised the alarm of many Americans. How would you seek to check the growing nuclear threat and keep the United States safe?"

Channing took a moment to check his notes, then looked up.

"This is a critical issue facing not only the United States, George," Channing said, "but the entire world. We simply cannot allow the totalitarian regime of Kim Jong-un to continue expanding its nuclear and missile delivery capability. The Pentagon estimates they already have the ability to strike Hawaii and other U.S. Pacific territories."

The senator paused as he looked into the television camera.

"But this is a sensitive issue, with over twenty million South Korean citizens living within thirty-five miles of North Korean artillery batteries. It's not a simple matter of using American military might to go in take them out. Although we would surely prevail, the losses would be catastrophic. The only way to peacefully resolve this issue is through diplomatic channels. I would continue to work with China to exercise its considerable influence and encourage the North Korean leader to stop the development of its nuclear program. We should also encourage the United Nations to impose more stringent economic sanctions to exert pressure on the regime."

"Congressman Marshall," Stephanopoulos said. "What is your plan for containing the threat?"

James looked out into the audience and saw that it was still and quiet. He sensed they were waiting for a more forceful proposal. He turned over his prepared notes and looked straight ahead.

"I agree this is a very serious matter, George," he began. "North Korea imposes a threat over the entire southeast Asia region. We've seen that a half-century of diplomacy has had little effect in restraining the military development of this rogue nation. The UN

Security Council is the only international body that is authorized to impose sanctions against North Korea. But two of its members, China and Russia, can veto any resolution and have shown little interest in enacting any effective measures. The United States has stood by while North Korea has systematically and decisively built up their offensive military capability. Now, parts of our country lie within range of their nuclear weapons."

James paused as he heard the first warning chime.

"It's time to stop talking and hit them where it hurts. North Korea can't fund its military program without external help. Certain nations are supplying them with essential military parts and providing necessary foreign currency by purchasing its exports. I propose to halt all U.S. trade with any country that is propping up this totalitarian regime through its direct trade of goods and services. The United States is China's largest trading partner. They will soon realize the enormous loss they will experience by continuing to support this rogue leader. Any other country that is found to be supplying North Korea with nuclear or military technology will be immediately cut off. I will send a strong message that any friend of our enemy is no longer a friend of the United States."

The audience response to James's comments was immediate and enthusiastically positive.

"Senator Channing," Stephanopoulos said, after the applause died down. "Rebuttal?"

"Perhaps the junior congressman from Maryland forgets that China signed a friendship treaty with North Korea that pledged immediate military assistance in the event of any outside attack. China has the largest army in the world and would not hesitate to use it against the much smaller American and South Korean armed forces mustered on the border. Does the congressman think that China will simply lie down from such an overt provocation? Cutting off trade with China would just escalate tensions and reaffirm their resolve to stand with their ally."

"Congressman—" Stephanopoulos began.

"Perhaps the senator has forgotten about another time we tried appeasement to mollify a threatening army," James quickly responded. "Do you remember how that turned out? Hitler proceeded to steamroll over half of Europe, while democratic nations watched idly by. The United States has never shrunk from a threat to its security, and never will. Bullies submit to only one thing—an overwhelming and decisive show of superior force. It's time to remove this rogue regime's nuclear capability—or remove the regime itself. As President, I will not stand by while this bully continues to throw stones and threaten the United States and its allies."

The entire theater stood on their feet and cheered, applauding enthusiastically for over a minute.

Suddenly, round two had gone to James.

22

Longworth Building, Congressman Marshall's Office

November 16, 7:00 a.m.

On the morning after the debate, James arrived early to his congressional office. Something hadn't felt right about the way his opponents responded so easily to some of his statements, and he wanted to talk it over with his chief of staff. He'd sent Nick a text as soon as he woke up, asking him to meet at the office. When Nick arrived, James was reviewing his debate notes, scribbling notes in the margin.

"Good morning, boss," Nick said, appearing at James's door. "You're getting started early this morning. I thought you'd want to sleep in after getting home so late last night."

"Thanks for coming in early, Nick," James said, looking up. "There's something important I wanted to talk with you about. Can you close the door?"

Nick shut the door and took a seat opposite James's desk.

"What's up? Why so serious? You killed it in the debate last night."

"It might have *ended* well," James frowned, "but it started off pretty shaky. Channing really had me in his crosshairs. It's almost as if he knew his responses to my statements ahead of time. He annihilated me on the health issue. Is it possible one of our staffers could have leaked our prepared script?"

Nick hesitated as he looked at James.

"I didn't want to worry you about this before the debate, but there was a break-in at our campaign office."

James's eyebrows shot up.

"When? Was anything stolen?"

"A few days ago. They took the hard drive from the computer in the back office. There wasn't any other sign of vandalism, other than the front door lock. It looks like they used a crowbar to wedge it open."

"Did you notify the police? Did they find anything on the CCTV?"

Nick shook his head.

"The tapes showed a single tall man wearing a balaclava. He was in and out quickly. He went right to the back office and disconnected the hard drive, then there were a couple of flashes from a camera. He was out of the office in less than sixty seconds, before the cops arrived."

James's eyes narrowed as he pondered the facts.

"We had our whole debate script on that hard drive, including your notes from the practice debate. Plus, the whiteboard had every candidate's policy position, along with our key talking notes. I didn't even think about it—we should have erased it before we left the office."

"From now on," Nick nodded, "I think we should only use laptops in the office and bring them home with us at night. I've already equipped the office with a couple of easels and drawing pads. We can roll those up and take them with us instead of leaving notes on the whiteboard."

James looked at Nick with a puzzled expression.

"But the whiteboard didn't have *all* of our talking points. Those were on the computer hard drive. Isn't that password protected?"

Nick shook his head.

"It isn't hard to hack computer passwords these days with the right technology. If the intruder was working for Channing, he'd have access to plenty of resources."

James crossed his arms.

"Channing's a piece of work, but this doesn't fit his style. I could see him planting a mole or maybe paying off one of our staffers for inside information, but a blatant break-and-enter? That's how Nixon got taken down."

"You said he told you the gloves were off after you turned down his VP invitation—"

"I dunno, Nick. It just doesn't feel right."

"Who *else* would do this?" Nick asked. "Who stands to gain from stealing our personal campaign information?"

James leaned back in his chair and ran his hands through his hair as he looked up at the ceiling.

"There's a lot of people who don't want us to win, besides our Democratic opponents. Maybe they were looking for some dirt to use against us. Inappropriate emails or photos—that sort of thing."

"I assure you, James, I haven't been surfing any porn sites or sending any compromising messages," Nick said. "Is there anything *you* could have left on the computer that might be sensitive?"

"No—you know me, Nick." James paused. "Whatever they found, they've already inflicted maximum damage. We'll just have to be more careful about protecting our information moving forward. From now on, I'd like all sensitive correspondence communicated on paper, then shredded. We can't afford another intrusion like this."

"Whatever they might have picked up, you made a hell of a recovery after the healthcare blip. Those were some pretty powerful statements on the North Korea situation. Where did you come up with those?"

"After Channing seem to have my number on the healthcare issue, I threw my notes away and just spoke off the cuff."

Nick pulled his head back in surprise.

"Well it showed. You spoke with a lot more passion and convic-tion on the foreign policy issue. It felt less prepared and genuine. Maybe you should wing it more often."

"Maybe. But there's still a lot of ground to cover in these debates. It's not just *my* positions I have to worry about. I also need to be familiar with my opponents' positions, so I can provide enough distance from them. North Korea was a good test case. Let's brain-storm how we can do the same thing on the other issues. I'd at least like to have an outline to follow in the next go-round."

Nick sat back and crossed his legs.

"The good news is the latest polls are now showing you a close second behind Channing in the Democratic race. We've got him in our sights. One more strong performance and I think you'll be tough to catch."

James looked at his closed door, knowing his bodyguard wasn't far away.

"I like the idea of not getting caught."

Then he looked his chief of staff square in the eye.

"Let's just make sure we don't get caught with our *pants* down again."

23

Marshall Residence

November 20, 9:00 p.m.

A few days after the debate, James took a well-needed rest to spend Thanksgiving with his family. The presidential campaign had been ratcheting up in intensity, and he was feeling emotionally drained. It wasn't just the preparation and stress of the debates. He didn't want to admit it to Julie, but he was still worried for his family's safety. He'd hired a private security company to keep an eye on his house and shadow the individual family members, but there was still one conspicuous hole in their arrangement. After dinner, he invited Heath into his study for a private conversation.

"What's up Dad," Heath said, as James closed the study door behind them. "You seem a little distracted today. The last debate went well. You had the crowd on their feet by the time it ended."

James smiled and motioned for Heath to have a seat in one of the armchairs.

"I got a bit lucky the moderator brought up the issue of foreign policy last. The audience was getting a bit frustrated with my opponents dilly-dallying on the North Korea problem. I guess they found my position a little more affirmative."

Heath looked at his father with a serious expression.

"Do you really think we're headed to war? Won't that crazy North Korean leader stand down when he sees the United States calling his bluff?"

James shook his head.

"He hasn't shown any sign of backing down in response to the steady buildup of U.S. troops and armaments. He thinks we won't attack as long as he holds the capability to launch nuclear weapons."

Heath furrowed his brow and looked worried.

"But we've got superior technology. We can shoot them down before they reach U.S. soil, right?"

"Possibly. But it's not a hundred percent effective. Even if one bomb were to get through, it would be catastrophic. Frankly, I'm more worried about the thousands of troops who are exposed on the front line in Korea and the millions of civilians living just a few miles from the demilitarized zone."

"But I thought there was an equal number of troops facing off against each other on each side. Isn't it a Mexican standoff?"

"Not if China were to send in their troops to join the North Koreans. Our forces would be quickly overrun, and there'd be enormous casualties. There's no simple solution here."

Heath nodded.

"Isn't that why you want to force China's hand with a trade embargo? Haven't they become too wrapped up in winning the global economic race to risk being set back so suddenly?"

"That's the billion dollar bet. But the Chinese are a proud people. Cutting off all trade amounts to a slap in the face from the one country that still stands above them economically. There are not many communist countries left in the world. If we were to take out the North Korean regime and it unified with South Korea, China would be even more isolated in the world community. It could embolden their citizens to rise up in another Tiananmen Square-like revolt. The communist leaders in China have a great deal to lose in this scenario."

Heath sat back and looked at his father thoughtfully.

"I see the dilemma. We're damned if we do and damned if we don't."

"And the pressure will only keep rising. Either we find some kind of relief outlet or the situation will eventually explode. Let's hope cooler heads prevail."

James pulled his chair closer to Heath's.

"I enjoy these political chats, son. You're well informed and passionate about the issues. But there's something else I wanted to talk with you about this evening."

Heath looked out the study window at the black SUV parked on the curb outside their house.

"It's not about those spooks again, I hope."

"Actually, it is," James said. "I want you to reconsider having a security detail on campus. I've already received a credible threat, and we can't afford to take any chances. I've taken steps to have everyone else in the family protected. It's time to bring you into the fold."

Heath slumped back in his chair and sighed.

"I'm already under a microscope from my classmates, being the son of a high-profile candidate. The last thing I need is a bodyguard following my every move. They already think I'm a privileged snob."

Heath gripped the chair's armrests more tightly.

"I can take care of myself, Dad. I'm safe on campus, surrounded by my friends. Just give me a little breathing room."

James glanced down at Heath's hands and noticed the bruise on his right knuckle.

"What happened there?" he said, motioning to his son's hand.

Heath looked at his knuckle and quickly pulled it back.

"It's nothing. Just a little scrape."

"Scrape, as in *fall*, or scrape as in *fight*?"

Heath thought for a second about making up a story, but his father's unnerving gaze would have given him away.

"It was just another jerk wanting to make a statement with his friends. He's harmless."

"Judging by the bruise on your knuckle, it looks like *somebody* got hurt. This is exactly the sort of thing I'm worried about. You're a target as much as I am now."

Heath crossed his arms.

"So now you're going to have your goons fight my battles for me?" he said. "*That'll* really help boost my image on campus."

"It's not just your *school* I'm worried about," James said. "I'm sure you and your friends go off campus periodically to bars and parties. I don't want another…"

Heath looked at his father and steeled his jaw, knowing what he was thinking.

"How about a compromise?" he offered. "If I go off campus or travel anywhere alone, I'll call for back-up. As long as the guards promise to be discreet and keep a respectable distance. I don't want to be seen as one of those overprotected political brats."

James looked at his son and paused.

"Fair enough. I've made similar arrangements with my own minder. But do me a favor. Keep your eyes and ears open. If you ever feel you're in danger, take appropriate precautions. I'd never forgive myself if something happened to another member of our family."

Heath stood up and extended his hand.

"Deal. You worry about keeping the rest of the world safe, and I'll look after my little bubble. In the meantime, keep knocking those political opponents down. I'm looking forward to the *big* challenge in the final round."

24

CNN Television Studios, Washington DC

November 25, 10 a.m.

James sat next to CNN News Anchor Wolf Blitzer, preparing for his second live interview. His rapidly rising standing in the national polls had made him a hot commodity on the media circuit. Nick thought the visibility from a national news outlet would provide a good opportunity to capitalize on their momentum from the second debate. It would also give James a chance to clarify his stance on the healthcare issue in a less threatening environment. They'd gone over their talking points, and James felt prepared to handle any question Blitzer threw at him.

Blitzer turned to face the camera as the production assistant gave the go-live signal.

"Good morning," Blitzer said. "First-term congressman James Marshall has only been in politics for two years, but he's already making a credible run for his party's nomination for President. He's joined us today to discuss his unconventional campaign style and his chances for winning the White House."

Blitzer turned to face James.

"Thank you for coming on our show, Congressman."

"Thanks for having me, Wolf."

"You've had a meteoric rise in the presidential rankings since you entered the race only two months ago. As a first-term congressman, everybody wrote you off as a hopeless dreamer with your radical positions on the issues. Yet you've arguably won the first two Democratic debates and are now in a virtual tie with the front-runner, Senator Channing. How do you think you've managed to capture the hearts and minds of so many Americans in such a short time?"

James cocked his head and gave a wry smile.

"I suppose the American public doesn't think my ideas are quite as crazy as my political opponents do."

"Fair enough," Blitzer said, chuckling. "Let's talk about some of your policies and your chances for getting them implemented, should you win the White House. Besides your drug legalization plan, one of the most contentious issues is your healthcare plan. You've proposed a universal one-payer system, which many people are calling socialized medicine. What makes you think the United States is ready for such a radical shift from the private insurance model?"

James paused for a moment to collect his thoughts.

"It's not a radical shift when compared to the practice of other developed nations. The U.S. stands almost entirely alone among democratic countries in lacking universal healthcare. Almost one half of Americans support a single-payer system. But the main reason, frankly, is that the current system is failing on just about every measure. We have the highest cost, the most uninsured, and the least healthy citizens when you look at the mortality rates from treatable and preventable diseases. This is not a program we should be fighting to defend."

Blitzer nodded, as he sized James up.

"You have some strong arguments, Congressman. But one of the strongest objections centers on who's going to *pay* for this universal coverage. Your opponents say it will increase taxes for most Americans."

"Actually, Wolf," James said, rapidly gaining confidence, "it will do just the opposite. The United States currently spends two to three times as much per person on healthcare as other developed nations. My program will reduce these costs in three ways. First, as the sole payer of medical bills, the federal government will be in a far stronger position to negotiate lower fees. Second, it will eliminate the profit markup currently being charged by private insurers. Most importantly, it will reward healthcare providers for spending more time with their patients to identify the root cause of their illness, rather than just treating the symptoms with expensive drugs and surgery."

Blitzer pinched his eyebrows and looked puzzled.

"I'm confused. Won't longer patient consultations *increase* the cost of healthcare, not reduce it?"

"At first glance, it might look that way, Wolf. But let's examine the facts. Currently, HMO rates pay doctors a higher proportional amount for the first ten minutes of patient consultation than for longer visits. They also pay much higher fees for highly invasive tests and surgery. It's more profitable for doctors to order expensive procedures and treat their patients' symptoms with drugs and surgery, than to spend the necessary time to understand and treat the underlying cause of the problem. My payment plan will reverse these incentives and encourage physicians to treat their patients holistically."

"Isn't this putting the government in the place of doctors for knowing what's best for their patients?"

James shook his head.

"Healthcare providers will still make the treatment decisions. My plan will simply encourage them to find more effective and less expensive solutions than relying on tests, drugs, and surgery to fix every problem."

"But you'll still be absorbing millions of uninsured Americans into your program. How will this not increase costs that will be passed on to taxpayers?"

"Almost a hundred million Americans are already covered by Medicare and Medicaid. My program will include the thirty or so million who aren't presently covered. If a single-payer system brings our healthcare costs down to the levels of other countries, this will more than offset the additional cost of covering every citizen."

Blitzer looked down at his notes and paused.

"Alright, let's leave this contentious issue and move on to another. You've proposed to legalize all illicit drugs at the federal level. What makes you think making it easier to access these substances won't create a whole new generation of addicts?"

James nodded at the familiar argument.

"Once again, we have the rich and lengthy history of other countries to demonstrate the reality. Decriminalizing drug use has actually reduced usage among teens and drastically lowered the amount of overdoses and accidental deaths. By taxing the legitimate trade of these substances, we can create controlled use sites to help protect users from dangerous overdoses. And because the distribution of these drugs will be more closely monitored, we'll be in a better position to control the quality of the product and prevent contamination with other dangerous chemicals."

"Won't this create more government bureaucracy to control another facet of the economy?" Blitzer asked.

James looked at Blitzer and paused for a long moment.

"Abraham Lincoln once proposed a government of the people, by the people, for the people. There are some things a central authority can do better than leaving it up to private enterprise. Taking dangerous drugs out of the hands of criminals and providing a reliable set of central checks and balances is one of them. As with healthcare, my program will neither interfere in the supply of the product, nor with people's desire to use these substances. We will simply be opening the market to legitimate providers and helping rehabilitate users who need help."

Blitzer looked at James skeptically.

"The central tenet of your program began with the claim that drug legalization will reduce street violence and organized crime.

How can you be sure that the drug gangs and cartels will simply cede the market to private producers?"

"I can't. But two hundred and fifty years of American history has shown how powerful the profit motive is in a free market system. Our country has become the most powerful nation on earth by encouraging the entrepreneurial spirit of our citizens and rewarding them for their ingenuity and hard work. Many people will want to continue using psychoactive drugs, and there's a lot of money to be made by supplying them safely. We're simply putting the power in the people's hands to use and supply these substances responsibly."

Blitzer looked up from his notes and smiled.

"Well congressman, no one can accuse you being a wallflower. One way or another, your ideas and candidacy has changed the discourse of this country and is pointing America in a new direction. Whether or not you become the next President of the United States, I wish you well. Thank you again for joining us today."

"It's been my pleasure, Wolf. I look forward to continuing our dialogue as we move toward the Democratic primaries."

25

North Capitol Street

November 25, noon

After the interview, James decided to walk the short distance from the CNN building to his congressional office. It was a sunny late fall day, and he looked forward to taking in the view of the capital along his route. As he passed through the main lobby toward the exit doors, he glanced at his bodyguard sitting by the window. He nodded that he was leaving, and his escort stood up and began following a short distance behind. He'd gotten to know Mike over the last couple of weeks and often joked that he stuck to James so well, at times he truly felt like the congressman's shadow. Still, James felt confident knowing backup was a short distance away if he ever needed it.

As he stepped outside, he breathed in the crisp air and looked up from the horizon. A few blocks away rose the imposing crown of the Capitol building. The structure never failed to impress James, with its grand neoclassical architecture. City planners had long ago passed a by-law restricting other municipal buildings from rising any higher than the base of the Capitol dome. As a result, the city spread out low and flat, enabling clear visibility of its prominent monuments from just about anywhere in the downtown area.

As he passed DC's main train terminal at Union Station, he glanced down Louisiana Avenue toward the National Mall. From his perspective on the raised elevation of North Capitol Street, he could see the long green lawn extending almost two miles to the west. Proudly rising in the middle of the park stood the Washington Monument, with the Lincoln Memorial keeping watch at the end of the Reflecting Pool. At times like this, James felt proud to be a public servant and play a role in the shaping of his country's history.

As he crossed D street, he glanced behind him to make sure his bodyguard wasn't following too close. They'd reached an agreement that Mike would keep at least ten yards distance or whatever was necessary to keep James in his sights, unless he was in close quarters within a crowd. He didn't want anyone noticing that he had a security detail tracing his every move.

But as James peered behind, he couldn't see Mike anywhere. He stopped at the light and looked in every direction. There was no sign of his man. He slowed down his pace and continued walking west along D Street instead of taking the shortcut through Senate Park. If Mike was in trouble, he'd soon know. James knew that nothing short of an emergency would have stopped him from doing his duty.

As he continued along the sidewalk, he checked his rear reflection in storefront windows. An unfamiliar tall man wearing dark glasses had taken up his shadow, trailing much closer behind. The man seemed singularly focused on James, occasionally glancing to his sides as if he didn't want any interference. James picked up his pace and turned up First Street. The man also turned, keeping his close distance.

James's heart began beating faster. Could this be the same man who broke into his campaign office? Could he be another member of the goon squad that attacked him at the restaurant a few weeks ago?

If so, he didn't want to let him escape this time. His eyes darted ahead as he formulated a plan to catch his follower. It wouldn't be as simple as pulling out his phone to call for help or flagging down a passing patrol car. He didn't want to raise suspicion that he knew he was being followed and spook the man away. He'd have to draw him into a tighter space to have any chance of snaring him.

As he approached the Hyatt Hotel, he noticed a narrow service lane between two buildings. Keeping a steady pace, he turned into the lane and walked purposefully as if on his way to a meeting. Fifty feet ahead, he saw a large metal dumpster. As he passed by, he ducked behind it and glanced around the side. The man entered the lane and began looking from side to side trying to find James. Sensing a trap, he pulled out a pistol with a long barrel and stepped forward slowly.

James knew the man would approach the dumpster cautiously, suspecting James could be hiding there. As he heard the man's footsteps approach on the hard asphalt pavement, James crept backward around the canister. He looked into the container to see if he could find anything to defend himself and saw a piece of rebar sticking up. He pulled the metal bar out of the dumpster slowly so as not to create any sound, then he crouched down and glanced under the bin. There was only about four inches of ground clearance, but it was enough for James to see the man's feet stopped at the other end of the dumpster. Suddenly he saw a hand lower onto the pavement. The man had the same idea! James grasped the top of the dumpster and wedged one foot against its side, then pulled himself up off the ground. Holding his breath, he listened for any sign of movement.

After a few seconds, he heard the man shuffling as he lifted himself off the ground, then he turned around and headed back toward the entrance of the alley. James crouched at the side of the dumpster and held the metal bar just above his shoulder. As the man passed by, he swung the bar down onto the man's arm, causing the gun to scuttle toward the side of the alley.

James rushed out and threw his shoulder into the man's abdomen. They fell to the ground together and began wrestling to gain a superior position. The man tried to reach for something in his jacket pocket, and James flung his arm against the pavement. In the midst of the scuffle, James lost his hold on the metal bar, and it rattled across the alley out of his reach.

The two men flipped over many times, each grappling fiercely to gain the upper hand. Eventually, James got on top of the man from a side position and threw his knee as hard as he could into the man's ribs. The man hollered and rolled away in the other direction. James could see the man's gun just a few feet away. As the man reached for the weapon, James picked up the rebar and rushed toward the man carrying it like a lance.

Just as the man swung around with the gun in his hand, James thrust the thin bar with all his might into the man's gut. The man's eyes flew open, and he fell backward, dropping the pistol. James grabbed the bar with two hands and pushed his assailant down onto the pavement. As the man lay moaning on the pavement from the shaft impaled in his stomach, James pulled out his cell phone and dialed 9-1-1.

This time, he thought, the *bad* guys would be the ones doing the talking.

26

Longworth Building, Staff Cafeteria

November 26, noon

Ray Bradley looked at James's meatloaf as he placed his lunch tray on the cafeteria table.

"For a guy who's raking in campaign donations by the millions, you're a pretty cheap date."

"Sorry about that," James chuckled. "I'd have taken you to the Capitol Grill, but my security team's been tightening the screws lately."

"Don't tell me you got into another scuffle?" Ray said, noticing the fresh cuts on James's forehead and hands.

"If that's what you call it when the other guy points a *gun* at you."

Ray's eyes flew open.

"What? Where was your vaunted security detail? Maybe it's time you hired a new one."

"It wasn't their fault," James said, shaking his head. "I gave them strict orders to keep a distance back. The bad guy had plenty of room to take out my bodyguard when I wasn't looking."

"So there was only one assailant this time? What happened?"

"After my interview at CNN, I noticed a strange man following me back to the Capitol. When I saw that my bodyguard had disappeared around the same time, I knew something was up. So I lured him into an alley."

Ray rolled his eyes in disbelief.

"Why didn't you just call the cops or duck into a safe building?"

"I'm getting tired of looking over my shoulder. I wanted to *catch* the guy this time. If I can find out who wants me out of the picture so badly, maybe I can dispense with this security arrangement altogether."

"So you caught him? Did he spill his guts?"

"Well, I impaled him with a steel rod—so *literally*, yes. Unfortunately, not in the way you mean. Whoever this guy's working for, he's more afraid of them than the cops. He totally clammed up."

"What about your bodyguard? Is he alright?"

James nodded.

"I just came back from the hospital. He got hit over the head with a pipe. It could have been a lot worse. He suffered a concussion, but the doctors think he'll make a full recovery."

"So what now? How can these guys protect you? This is getting serious, Jim. This new thug planned to *shoot* you. Are you sure you want to continue putting yourself at risk?"

James paused as he looked out the window.

"My whole candidacy was based on making the streets safer by reducing organized crime. If I pull out now, I'll just be giving them what they want. *Someone's* gotta stand up to these guys."

Ray shook his head skeptically.

"Your candidacy is standing up against a *lot* of powerful players. Are you sure the drug gangs are behind this? It could just as easily be private prison operators, big pharma, or the HMOs. There's a lot of people that you'll be putting out of business if you win. Hell, even the North Koreans have a reason to knock you off."

James chuckled as he finished the last bite of his meatloaf.

"I spoke with my security team about it. They're going to put two guys on me now, and I've agreed to let them follow me closer. They've assured me they won't get blindsided twice."

Ray looked three tables behind James and saw two unfamiliar men sitting quietly, wearing earpieces.

"I'll give you this much, Jim. You sure like living dangerously. I hope it's all worth it in the end."

Thirty minutes later, James met with his chief of staff in his congressional office.

"Come in," James said, when he heard the knock on his door.

"What happened to your open door policy?" Nick said as he entered James's office.

"I'm afraid circumstances have changed our rules of engagement."

"I suppose that's why there are two serious-looking guys standing watch at either end of the hall." Nick noticed the scratches on James's face. "Did you have another unexpected encounter?"

James nodded and motioned for Nick to have a seat.

"We seem to be making a lot of enemies these days. But I think we're good now. We'll just have to put up with a tighter security presence."

"That might not actually be so bad, campaign-wise. Having a visible security detail makes you look more presidential. It also sends a message that you're not afraid to stand up to the big guys to make a change."

"Possibly," James said, sitting back in his chair. "But that's not what I wanted to talk with you about today. Let's talk strategy. We've only got one more debate before the Iowa caucus. What can we do to maintain our momentum and assure a good showing?"

Nick leaned forward as he rolled up his sleeves.

"You've picked up a lot of polling points since the Arizona debate.

It's a two-horse race now. One more strong debate and we can win Iowa. But I think it's time we put some of our rapidly accumulating campaign money to work. I'd like to start work on pulling together some television ads. I think we can put some more distance between you and Channing by highlighting his weaknesses."

James shook his head.

"I don't want to run any negative ads. That's not my style. If we can't win on our own merits, then we don't deserve to be in this race."

Nick frowned as he looked at James.

"I'm pretty sure Channing won't be pulling any punches when he goes to air with his ads. He won't hesitate to portray you as the high tax, drug-loving, socialist candidate. Are you sure this is the right way to go? I understand your reticence about negative ads—but they work."

"We can counter his objections just as effectively by taking the high road. Let's focus on the benefits that citizens will experience from my policies. We can answer the opponents' arguments at the debates and in press interviews. Our millions of contributions show we're resonating with the public. What else can we do to bring our message to the people?"

Nick had been thinking about how to take the campaign to the next level.

"I think it's time we started organizing live rallies. If we can get a big turnout and generate enough excitement, this will send a strong message to the delegates that you're our best chance at beating President Templeton in November."

James sat up, excitedly.

"Great idea, Nick. If we schedule our first rally after the next debate, we should be able to peak just before the Iowa caucus in early February. Can you set up another practice session with some of our staffers to prepare for the next debate?"

Nick looked at James with a puzzled expression.

"Are you sure that's a good idea, James? What about the leak before the last debate? We can't afford to have your opponents fore-armed ahead of time again."

"We don't know for sure where that intel came from. It might just as easily have come from the break-in. Just to be sure, I'd like to plant some bait. Let's invite two of the same three staffers into our next meeting. We'll protect the rest of our data as we previously agreed."

James sat back and crossed his arms.

"If our opponents use any of the material against us in the next debate, we'll at least have our mole narrowed down to two."

27

Drake University, Des Moines, Iowa

December 15, 8:00 p.m.

The Sheslow Auditorium at Drake University was humming with excitement as the audience awaited the start of the third Democratic presidential debate. The field of contestants had narrowed to three, with only Senator Channing, Governor Harper, and James remaining in the race. The stakes were higher than ever, with just over a month remaining until the first Democratic caucus in the state of Iowa. Although the Midwest state held only one percent of the U.S. population, it carried an outsize influence in the outcome of the election. Whoever won Iowa was seen as the front-runner and carried the momentum into the subsequent primaries.

James had prepared thoroughly and felt ready to address any subject, including his opponents' rebuttals. He'd asked Nick to invite two of the three same staffers into another mock practice debate session, but to exclude Emma. There was something about her over-eagerness to join his campaign team that raised red flags. He'd planted a juicy policy statement that he knew his opponents would be unable to ignore. If either Channing or Harper played their hand too early, he'd know it was one of the other two staffers who was supplying the leak.

As CBS *Face The Nation* host John Dickerson began his debate preamble, James looked out into the audience. It was an eclectic mix of mostly white, middle-class moderates, leaning toward an older demographic. This wasn't James's strongest base, but peering further back, he saw a large contingent of young college students talking excitedly in the back rows. As he returned to the front of the stage, he caught House Leader Akerman's eye. This time, Akerman held his gaze, giving him an unflinching stare.

Dickerson turned to address the three candidates on the stage.

"As always, our first and last speakers are chosen by random," he said. "Senator Channing, you have the first question. There's been a widely divisive argument in the United States about whether recent dramatic changes in our climate are caused by human activity. Do you believe it is, and if so, what would you do to protect our ecosystem from further damage?"

Senator Channing looked down at his notes, then smiled at the moderator.

"Thank you, John, for addressing this important issue. I'd first like to thank Drake University for inviting us to this great state. The people of Iowa have been chosen to cast the first ballots in the Democratic nomination for President, and I look forward to earning your trust."

Channing paused as he flipped over a page.

"To answer your question, John, I believe that climate change is a serious threat to our planet and that it is largely driven by human behavior. We need to reduce our reliance on fossil fuels in order to preserve our ecosystem. To this end, I would join the one hundred and ninety-five countries currently supporting the Paris Accord, which set firm targets for reductions in global greenhouse gas emissions."

"The Paris Accord relies on each country to develop its *own* plan for reducing emissions," Dickerson said. "What specific policies would you enact in the United States to scale back these emissions?"

Channing paused as he looked at the moderator, seeming unsure how to answer. He shuffled through his papers then looked back up.

"The United States needs to reduce its reliance on fossil fuels," he repeated. "I would start with higher rebates for the purchase of electric cars and higher subsidies to organizations using renewable energy."

"What *kind* of subsidies?" Dickerson pressed. "And how will you measure their renewable energy use?"

"The subsidies..." Channing hesitated, "would be in the form of tax credits—"

The first chime sounded, indicating that Channing had thirty seconds left in his statement.

"We would initially rely upon self-reporting, with periodic audits. There's no need to create a whole new bureaucracy to manage this process. I believe most Americans are aware of the threat to our planet and want to do the right thing."

The double-chime sounded, warning Channing he had ten seconds left.

"Anyone who underreports their fossil fuel usage would be subject to high penalties and—"

"Thank you, Senator Channing," Dickerson interrupted. "Your time is up."

The moderator turned to James to address the same subject.

"Congressman Marshall, what is your position on this issue, and what are your specific plans for controlling climate change?"

James nodded as he looked straight into the camera.

"I agree that climate change poses a serious threat to our planet and that it is driven by human behavior. You only need look at satellite photos of Earth over the last few years to see the dramatic effect of global warming. Glaciers around the world have been retreating at unprecedented rates, and many are projected to vanish at current rates within a matter of decades. Ocean warming has accelerated alarmingly, causing an increase in the number and severity of catastrophic storms striking the United States. If we don't change our habits, within this century millions of people living in tropical zones will begin dying from heat prostration. We're living in a microwave oven that will eventually extinguish life on Earth if we don't change our habits soon."

James paused as he heard the first warning chime.

"Unfortunately, international climate agreements have failed to halt the rise in greenhouse gas emissions. We must take binding *local* action to effect change. I'm tired of watching black smoke billow into my clean air from poorly maintained vehicles and irresponsible factories. I will implement an across-the-board carbon tax for all individuals and corporations that will encourage a rapid reduction in fossil fuel emissions."

The double-chime sounded.

"If you're a reckless polluter, we will find you and hold you to account. It's time we took back our planet and delivered clean, breathable air to our grandchildren."

A cheer rose from the back of the room, as a wave of applause spread over the crowd.

Dickerson waited for the applause to subside before turning to the third candidate.

"Governor Harper, we've heard two very different approaches to managing this issue. What is your position and plan on climate change?"

Harper had been taking notes as he listened to his opponents' statements and was eager to respond.

"I agree with my colleagues that this is a serious issue that needs resolute action. However, I don't believe raising taxes for average citizens is the answer. I also believe that we should support international emissions treaties since this is a global problem, not just a local one."

As James listened to the governor speak, it was obvious he was lending his support behind Senator Channing. As the third-place candidate trailing far behind in the polls, he had little chance of catching and surpassing the front-runners. Whether he was simply towing the party line or building his case for a prominent position in Channing's administration, James couldn't be sure.

"China now produces more carbon dioxide emissions," Harper continued, "than the United States. The only way to solve this global problem is by bringing all the countries of the world together with a common plan. Within the United States, I would set quotas for how much greenhouse gas an organization can produce, while allowing them to purchase additional capacity from other entities that have underused their allowance."

As the warning chime sounded, Dickerson turned to Senator Channing.

"Senator, you have first rebuttal."

"Governor Harper's cap and trade approach has some merit," Channing said, "but it merely puts an upper limit on the emissions of greenhouse gases. And Congressman Marshall's tax plan forces producers and consumers to cut back on carbon emissions but does nothing to encourage them to find renewable substitutes. Only *my* plan provides direct incentives to switch to clean energy sources."

"Congressman Marshall?" Dickerson said. "How do you respond?"

James smiled as he looked at the moderator.

"Senator Channing is forgetting the other leg of my platform. My plan also includes rebates to consumers and producers who generate their own renewable power."

James turned to face the television camera.

"Buying electric cars simply switches the source of carbon emissions from people's tailpipes to power generation smokestacks. The energy sector produces twice as much pollution as automobiles, by burning fossil fuels to power the electricity grid. My plan empowers electricity users to generate their *own* power at home using solar, wind, and geothermal sources. This will allow us to wean ourselves off the primary source of pollution and enable everyone to sell back to the grid any excess production for a profit."

"Senator Channing?"

Channing looked at James and sneered.

"You're still taking a local approach to a global problem. Even if your ambitious plans worked in the United States, how will this curtail the remaining three-quarters of the world's greenhouse gas emissions? Your two-legged stool is looking very shaky, Congressman."

James didn't wait for an invitation to respond. He smiled at the senator, realizing that Channing wasn't forewarned about the most powerful component of his climate change policy.

"I couldn't agree more, Senator. Which is why the *third* leg of my platform encourages other countries to follow suit. Instead of relying on a non-binding treaty to impel these countries to reduce carbon emissions, my program will include punishing tariffs and surcharges on any imported products that cannot certify they're at least as green as equivalent American goods."

James turned away from addressing Senator Channing and faced the audience.

"The United States economy is still twice the size of any other nation's, including China. The world's largest polluters depend on trade with the U.S. to uphold their standard of living. My plan is the only one with the teeth to hold everyone accountable for excessive climate change emissions, while also encouraging consumers and producers to switch as quickly as possible to renewable energy sources."

James paused for a moment, then looked into the camera.

"For two hundred and fifty years, the United States has been the world's technology and economic leader, and under my plan it will also be the world's *clean energy* leader. We can no longer leave our planet's destiny in the hands of large corporations and other countries. I will empower the people to take matters into their own hands and let the law of supply and demand solve this problem in the American way."

The audience rose to its feet and cheered enthusiastically. From the back of the room rose a new and rising chant, as young people formed the letter M for Marshall with their arms and hands.

"*EM-power, EM-power, EM-power,*" they shouted.

James formed a heart-shaped *M* with his fingers and smiled out into the audience. Channing and Harper could do nothing but sneer disdainfully in his direction.

28

Georgetown Waterfront Park, Washington DC

January 15, 2:00 p.m.

J ames walked through the packed crowd assembled in Georgetown Waterfront Park, chatting and shaking hands with excited fans. Even though temperatures were below freezing, thousands of followers had traveled from throughout the Mid-Atlantic states to attend his first rally. With campaign contributions surging since the last debate and his switchboard swamped with people asking how they could support his campaign, Nick had scheduled the rally to capitalize on his momentum ahead of the Iowa caucus.

A band played upbeat songs from an elevated stage at the southeast corner of the park, where volunteers served free hot dogs and warm cocoa to attendees under a large tent. As James ambled through the throng, adoring fans swelled to get closer to their favorite candidate. Many of them pumped signs reading *Marshall for President*,

Empower the People, or simply *M-Power*—which had become his unof-
ficial campaign slogan.

His security team had expanded their presence at the event, and
three large men traced his path, watching every person that
approached him to ensure they weren't brandishing a weapon. Four
more stood on the raised platform controlling access to the stage,
scanning the sea of civilians for any danger signs. But for James, this
was barely a passing thought, as he soaked up the adulation of his
supporters. The entire span of the park between Whitehurst Freeway
on the east side and the Potomac River on the west was packed.
Across the street, curious onlookers in highrise condos stood on their
balconies, gawking at the raucous crowd.

James slowly worked his way toward the stage, trying to shake
everyone's hand along the narrow wedge that his handlers made for
him. When he finally reached the platform and bounded up the
steps, the crowd broke into a giant cheer as everyone saw their leader.
Julie and his two children stood behind and to his right, while Nick
and a few campaign volunteers stood clapping to his left. In the background, the band played God Bless America.

James raised his right arm and waved at the crowd. It was a sunny
day, and the light sparkled across the Potomac River. To his right, he
would see the Washington Monument and the Capitol Building
rising above the rooftops of downtown DC. Further south, along the
edge of the river, sat the John F. Kennedy Center for the Performing
Arts. It was a perfect patriotic setting for his first live public address
to the people.

As the song wound down and James prepared to speak, the
crowd's cheer escalated in volume. He smiled and turned his head,
trying to make eye contact with individuals across the park. After a
few minutes, he held up his hand, asking the crowd to let him speak,
and the din subsided.

"Welcome," his voice boomed out over the huge speakers, "to our
little hot dog roast."

The crowd roared to signal the strength of their assemblage.

"First, I'd like to thank everyone for coming out on this chilly day to lend your support. I hope the hot cocoa is at least keeping your *insides* warm."

A cheer rose from the crowd, as they raised their styrofoam cups in appreciation.

"I'd also like to thank the millions of supporters who've contributed their hard-earned dollars to our campaign. We appreciate every single donation, no matter how small. Since the beginning of our campaign, we've refused individual donations greater than five hundred dollars. This is our way of showing that we'll never be beholden to large corporations or establishment money. We serve the people—*all* of the people."

James smiled as another loud roar emanated from the crowd. He turned behind him and motioned to his campaign staff.

"I'd also like to thank the many volunteers who've so generously offered their time and talent to support my campaign. They've been invaluable in helping get our message out and taking calls from the thousands of people who've called and written in with their suggestions and support. Special thanks to Nick Garcia, my chief of staff, who's been with me from the start, when I was just a dewy-eyed, unknown congressman."

Nick nodded toward James as the crowd cheered.

"Finally," James said, turning to his family. "I'd like to thank my wife and two children, without whose love and support I could never have found the strength to enter and prevail in this contest."

James paused for a moment and looked skyward.

"And to our dear and precious Breanna—you are always in our hearts and prayers. May your light continue to shine down upon those who know and love you."

The crowd suddenly became quiet in deference to James's murdered daughter.

James looked back into the crowd and smiled.

"I know that I'm not the only one who has endured hardship and heartache. *All* of us experience trials in life, and we all need support from our loved ones and our broader community to thrive. This is why I've chosen to become your candidate for President. To help

remove the barriers stopping us from being everything we want to be
—*to improve lives.*"

The assembly cheered and pumped their placards.

James paused as his expression turned more serious.

"Our founding fathers said that everyone is created equal, with
the unalienable right to pursue happiness. But too often our government has installed laws and barriers which only serve to *impede* our
liberty and progress. We've come to rely on our government to dictate
our mores and protect us from ourselves. How is this different from
the monarchy we sought emancipation from two hundred years ago?"

A loud chant of *EM-power, EM-power* rose from the crowd.

"Our country is filled with smart, industrious, and good people,"
James continued. "People who've advanced the quality of life and the
standard of living, not just for Americans, but for people around the
world. Americans invented electricity, the computer, the mobile
phone, and the Internet. With the right kind of support, we can send
people to the moon, and beyond."

Another loud cheer filled the park.

"But a slow and insidious cancer has spread across our great
nation since our founders' simple vision. A century ago, nearly all
government regulations were based on common-law crimes such as
murder, rape, and theft—things that everyone knows are wrong."

James scanned the crowd and saw many nodding faces.

"Now, there are so many laws covering every facet of our lives that
many people break them without even being aware. Our ever-
increasing regulatory code is slowly suffocating the quality of life and
the initiative of everyday Americans. We have only four percent of
the world's population, but we house *twenty-two* percent of the
world's prisoners. Are Americans less moral than the people of other
countries?"

"Nooo!" came a loud shout from the audience in unison.

"Of course not," James said, emphatically. "We simply have more
oppressive *laws*. These are not just restricting the freedoms envisaged
by our founding fathers," he said, as his voice rose in intensity.
"They're creating a whole new class of violent criminals who are

growing rich bypassing the system. It's time to reclaim our moral rights and our safe neighborhoods!"

"*Free-DOM, free-DOM, free-DOM,*" chanted the crowd.

James paused as he waited for the clamor to subside.

"We can start by legalizing recreational drugs. Whatever you want to do in the privacy of your own home that doesn't hurt anyone else is *your* business, not the government's. We'll help those with addiction disorders by using the taxes from the free trade of these substances to create rehabilitation programs and safe-use sites. And we'll take the supply and distribution of these substances out of the hands of drug gangs and return the profit from its legitimate trade to responsible suppliers. By so doing, we'll simultaneously reduce the number of overdoses, drug-related HIV infections, and felons overpopulating our prisons."

As another cheer rose from the crowd, the distinctive odor of marijuana smoke permeated the park.

"There are *other* ways we can make our world a safer place," James continued. "It starts by acting more responsibly with what we pour into our oceans and air. Our overreliance on fossils fuels is slowly destroying our planet. We must find new ways to convert to renewable energy that doesn't suffocate our atmosphere."

James paused to look at individual audience members.

"Each of us has the ability to generate our own power and sell it back to the grid to reduce our reliance on large municipal power plants. My clean energy plan will provide rebates to offset the cost of installing solar panels and other sources of renewable energy within your own homes. Those who continue to be carbon hogs will be heavily penalized—including other countries who try to sell us dirty goods. We have the power to produce clean energy, and we must hold everyone to account to make our planet a safe and habitable home!"

"*EM-power, EM-power, EM-power,*" chanted the audience.

"What else can we do to make our planet a safer and less stressful place?" James asked. "There are more immediate external threats, which need equally affirmative action. The United States has increasingly become the target of foreign aggressors, who are taking escalating military action. We cannot stand by while these countries and factions grow stronger and become increasingly belligerent. We have no quarrel with any group or nation that wishes to practice its faith or political ideology peacefully. But if you threaten the United States or its allies, we will not stand idly by."

"*USA! USA! USA!*" chanted the crowd.

James raised his voice to speak over the throng.

"We will cease trade with any country that threatens the United States. Nor will we share our spoils with any country that supports a rogue regime. You are either *with* us or against us—there is no middle ground. Any direct acts of aggression will be returned in kind. We have the strongest, bravest, and most technically advanced army in the world, and we will not hesitate to use it to protect our freedoms and quality of life."

As a large roar filled the park, James noticed a familiar figure pushing through the crowd toward the front of the stage. It looked like one of the thugs who had cornered him at the restaurant in Virginia. He stepped back from the microphone and turned toward Mike, who was standing behind him.

"Red shirt, two o'clock—twenty feet from the stage," he said.

Mike motioned to another bodyguard, and they stepped down the platform in the direction of the man.

James returned to the mic and refocused his attention as he looked out over the cheering crowd.

"There is still more we can do at home to improve the quality of life for Americans," he said, as the crowd hushed. "Our healthcare system has become an albatross that can no longer carry its weight. By virtually every measure—from access, to cost, to quality of care— the American system is failing. We pay more than twice as much for our healthcare, yet our mortality rates from preventable illnesses trail other developed nations, while more than thirty million Americans cannot even pay for any care."

James scanned near the front of the stage to see if he could find the man in the red shirt. Mike stood at the side of the stage looking up, shaking his head, indicating they'd lost the mark. No matter,

James thought. He wouldn't have been able to accomplish much in this dense crowd, anyway.

"This can be easily corrected," he continued. "It starts with the way healthcare providers are paid. The current system pays too much for invasive tests, drugs, and surgery, and not enough for good old-fashioned doctoring. My plan will rebalance these payments and encourage your doctor to spend the necessary time in the examination room to properly diagnose your condition so you can heal quickly and naturally. And you can rest assured, knowing you will never again be hit with a health bill that forces you into bankruptcy."

"Jim-Mee, Jim-Mee, Jim-Mee," the crowd shouted.

James looked out into the audience and waited for their chants to recede before continuing his speech.

"Finally, there are still far too many Americans who are living in poverty or without jobs. This is unacceptable in the richest nation on Earth. Unfortunately, we are not only the *wealthiest* country but also the most *unequal* in terms of income disparity. Almost one half of our nation's wealth is concentrated in the hands of the top one percent. It is indefensible that the average ratio of CEO pay to that of the median worker is more than two hundred to one. How many of you think your boss's job is two hundred times as valuable as yours?"

"Boooo!" came the loud reply from the crowd.

"I can't dictate how much everybody should be paid by privately-owned companies. But I can sure as hell control how much corporate and individual tax they pay. When I become President, I will immediately require every federally funded agency to rebalance their pay scales so that the top executive earns no more than three times the average salary of its workers. That includes the office of the President. Any private company that exceeds this ratio will be subject to progressive corporate taxes matching the severity of their imbalance. We will return America's wealth to the hardworking middle- and lower-income classes."

"EM-power! EM-power! EM-power!"

James smiled as he saw the audience enthusiastically pumping their signs and yelling in excitement. He waited a full minute before raising his hand, asking the crowd to let him speak.

"There's one *other* neglected economic class in America," he said. "And that is people of color. Blacks and Hispanics still earn significantly less than whites for equivalent work. This is inexcusable and can also be corrected. I would expand the federal Equal Pay Act to expand discrimination based on gender to include race and ethnicity. In this country, *all* men and women are created equal, and I will ensure all are given equal rights and treated equally."

He paused for a moment, then raised his fist in the air.

"Diversity doesn't divide and separate us—it brings us together and makes us *stronger!*"

"*Jim-MEE! Jim-MEE! Jim-MEE!*" the crowd chanted.

James paused for a moment to bask in the adulation, then turned to motion his family to join him at the front of the stage.

Just as he turned, a loud crack rang out from across the park and the wooden floor of the platform splintered just to the left and behind him. Within seconds, four men in black suits surrounded the candidate and hustled him and his family off stage.

Someone in the crowd screamed, and everybody stampeded for the exits.

29

J Edgar Hoover Building, Downtown DC

January 15, 5:00 p.m.

James slumped in his chair in the interview room at the FBI headquarters building, as Mike and Nick looked silently away. It had been almost two hours since the attempt on his life at the waterfront rally, and he was still shaking. He wasn't thinking about his own life as much as that of his family. The bullet that had narrowly missed him could have easily struck his wife and children standing only a few feet behind him.

What the hell was I thinking? he thought. *I've needlessly put my family in danger again. For what? To boost my ego—just to be President? I've already lost one member of my family. I'm being reckless and selfish. This has to stop—today.*

Regardless of the outcome of the attempted murder investigation, he'd already decided to drop out of the presidential race.

Because the case involved a high profile political figure, the investigation had been turned over to the FBI. Anthony Marino, special agent in charge of the DC field office, had called for James's chief of security and his chief of staff to join the congressman at his office for questioning. They'd been waiting for a few minutes when a tall, lean man wearing a dark suit walked into the office and closed the door behind him.

"Congressman Marshall?" he said, holding out his hand to James. "I'm Special Agent Anthony Marino. I'll be heading this investigation."

James shook the agent's hand, then Nick and Mike stood to introduce themselves.

"Please, have a seat," Marino said. "Can I get you a coffee?"

"I think I'm plenty enough jacked up already, thanks," James said.

Nick and Mike shook their heads, taking James's cue.

Marino appraised the other two men's demeanor as he sat down.

"These sorts of things can be pretty unsettling. I understand this wasn't your first incident?"

James nodded.

"This is actually the third time someone's tried to take a shot at me. If you include the roughing up in the public restroom."

"What was the second time? How did that go down?"

"That involved a lone gunman. I caught him trailing me back to my office. I drew him into an alley, and we had a little scuffle. I managed to get the better of him that time."

Marino raised an eyebrow at the congressman's chutzpah.

"Were they brandishing guns in each case?"

"In the restroom incident, there were three men. I didn't see them carrying any weapons. I think they meant the confrontation as a warning. In the second case, it was one lone man who drew a pistol."

"Was any warning given the second time around?"

James shook his head.

"He was a man of few words. I don't think his intention was to *talk* to me."

"Did you recognize any of your assailants?" Marino asked.

"No. It was a different man in the second incident. But I recognized one of the thugs from the restroom incident standing in the crowd near the stage shortly before the shot was fired at the rally."

"Do you think he's the one who took the shot?"

James shrugged as he looked in Mike's direction.

"Our security detail tried to apprehend him when the congressman brought the man to our attention," Mike said. "But the shot seemed to come from across the freeway intersecting the park. And the position of the bullet strike behind the podium indicated it came from pretty high up. I don't think the man Congressman Marshall saw could have gotten into that position that quickly."

Marino nodded at the bodyguard's assessment.

"Was your team providing security at the other two incidents?"

"Only the second one. The congressman hired us to protect him and his family shortly after he received the first threat."

"How did he manage to get the jump on Congressman Marshall the second time?"

"He ambushed me from behind with a pipe. It won't happen again."

Marino narrowed his eyes as he stared at Mike. He knew the FBI's training wouldn't allow a federal agent to be so sloppy, but it wasn't his place to criticize a private operator's methods.

"The second assailant," Marino said, turning to James. "You said he was apprehended? Was he turned over to DC police?"

James nodded.

"What did they find?"

"Nothing, to my knowledge. Whatever his intent was, or whoever he was working for, he wasn't spilling any secrets."

"Did you provide a sketch of the assailants to the local police?"

James seemed detached from the conversation, as if he no longer cared about the outcome.

"Yes," he said, impassively.

Marino looked at him quietly and nodded.

"We'll follow up with the local authorities to combine the intel, then run it through our database."

The agent paused for a moment.

"It sounds to me like someone—or some group of people—want you out of the way, congressman. Can you think of anyone in particular who might hold a powerful grudge against you?"

James looked at the agent as if he had two heads.

"I'm a *presidential candidate*, Agent Marino. There are a lot of people who disagree with my policies."

"Enough to want to *kill* you?"

"Let's put it this way. If I became President and passed my proposed legislation, there are plenty of people I'd be putting out of business."

Marino understood James's meaning fully. He'd been following the congressman's campaign, and he admired his courage and conviction.

"Let's talk about the venue for today's rally," he said, looking at Nick. "Did you select the location?"

"Yes," Nick said. "In consultation with the congressman, of course."

"If you don't mind my saying, it seems like an unusual place to hold a rally. Such a narrow park, wedged between the freeway and the river, with no clear evacuation routes. Did you know how many people would be attending?"

"Because this was our first rally, it was hard to estimate," Nick said. "We were surprised by the turnout and were frankly overwhelmed by the size of the crowd."

Marino glanced in Mike's direction.

"Did you consult with your security team regarding the choice of venue?"

"Not until after the arrangements were made," Nick said. "Then Mike's team scoped out the property and took the necessary precautions."

Marino paused for a long moment. It was obvious to him that the congressman's team had given only superficial attention to the potential threat.

"We'll sweep the rooftops of buildings with a line of sight to the platform, but whoever took the shot is probably long gone. Maybe we'll get lucky and find some clues to the assault weapon from the slug we recovered at the scene. In the meantime, I recommend you keep a low profile, congressman. I'll be in touch if we find anything."

James looked down and shook his head. He didn't have any more confidence that the FBI would make progress finding his assailants than the local police had. But it didn't matter. He handed the agent his card and scribbled a number on the back.

"I plan to keep a very low profile, Agent Marino. I'll be announcing my retirement tomorrow. You can reach me at my home number if you need me."

As James stood and shook hands with the agent before taking his leave, Nick and Mike looked at one another in shock.

Neither had any warning of James's intentions.

30

Marshall Residence

January 15, 9:00 p.m.

James placed his key in his front door lock and stumped over the threshold. As he turned to hang his overcoat in the closet, his daughter scampered over the tiled floor and swung her arms around her father's midsection.

"Daddy! Are you okay? Did they catch the bad man?"

James kneeled down to hug his daughter.

"Not yet, baby. But don't worry—he won't be coming after me anymore."

Julie and Heath joined them in the lobby, and they all stood hugging each other for a long time.

"At least *somebody* thinks you've got a serious shot at being President," Heath joked, as they separated.

"They won't have to worry any longer," James said. "I'm going to announce my withdrawal from the race tomorrow."

Julie looked at her husband with sad eyes. She knew how much this meant to him and how hard this decision had to be.

"You must be hungry," she said. "There's still plenty of roast beef warming in the oven."

"I'm not hungry, hon. I'd just like a little brandy and relax in the study, if that's okay."

"Of course, Jim. How about a piece of pie, at least. I made your favorite—key lime."

James smiled at Julie and pulled his family close again. It felt good to know that everybody was safe.

"Sure," he said. "Maybe that'll help settle the butterflies still fluttering in my stomach."

Brooklyn looked up at her father with a puzzled look.

"Why are the bad men trying to hurt you, Daddy?"

James picked up his daughter and carried her to the study, where he sat her on his lap on the sofa.

"I guess they don't like some of the things I was trying to change, sweetie."

"But you said you wanted to be President to *help* people. Why are they so angry?"

James leaned back and held his daughter's head against his chest.

"Everybody has different ideas about what's best for the country. You can't make *everyone* happy in this business, pumpkin."

Julie walked into the study and placed the pie plate on the coffee table in front of James.

"Come on, little one," she said. "It's time for you to go to bed. I think Daddy needs some rest too. I'll tuck you in."

Julie took Brooke's hand and led her upstairs to her bedroom. A few moments later, Heath appeared at the entrance.

"How are you holding up, Dad?" he said.

"I'm alive, and nobody in my family was hurt. All things considered, I feel pretty good."

James stood up and walked over to the bar. He picked up a crystal decanter and poured two glasses of brandy.

"Join me?" he said, holding up a glass.

"Sure."

Heath took the glass and sat on the couch beside his father. They each took a long, slow sip.

"Crazy day, huh?" Heath said, breaking the awkward silence.

James crossed his legs and leaned back.

"You could say that."

"The strange thing is that before the rally was interrupted, you had the crowd in the palm of your hand. It was a great speech, Dad."

"Thanks, son. I guess I only have one more of those to worry about now."

Heath looked at his father for a long silent moment.

"Are you sure you want to do this, Dad? I mean, you're so close now—it's actually within reach. You'd whip Templeton in the final run-off. This is your chance to really make a difference—"

"If I *made* it that far," James sighed. "Somebody's determined to stop me, no matter the consequences. I'm more concerned about you and the rest of my family. That bullet came far too close..."

Heath wrinkled his forehead, looking puzzled.

"Aren't there *other* precautions you can take? What about the Secret Service? The leading candidates had protection in the last election. Surely they can protect you too?"

James shook his head.

"This is the third time someone's sent me a strong message. There's still over a year to go before the next President takes office. I can't put my family at risk any longer. I'd never forgive myself—"

Julie had been hesitating behind the study entrance listening to the conversation and walked in.

"You haven't touched your pie, James," she said looking at his plate. "You could do with a little sweetness to purge the bad thoughts from your day."

She looked at Heath.

"Can I have a few moments alone with your Dad?"

"Of course, Mom." Heath leaned over and gave his father a hug. "I love you Dad. I'm proud of you no matter what."

"Thanks, son," James said. "Ditto."

When Heath left the room, Julie picked up the plate and handed it to James. She smiled at him as he took a bite of the pie.

"You know he's right," she said. "You've almost got the nomination in the bag. And Templeton's approval ratings have been sliding."

James put his fork down and set his plate on the coffee table.

"None of that matters if I'm not around to execute my plans. Somebody wants me out of the way, and they've threatened my family. Today was the last straw. It's too easy nowadays to take someone out. After Bree—"

Julie reached out and placed her hand on James's.

"That was different. There was nothing we could have done about that. But you're in a position of power now. You can mobilize the entire strength of the Secret Service to protect you. Why don't you ask—"

"They still said they could only protect the two of us, remember? What about the *kids*?"

"I can homeschool Brooke for a few months. As long as she's with me, she'll be safe. We can keep Mike on with some of his private detail to keep a watch on Heath. It's just you they're targeting, anyhow."

James leaned back and rested his arm on the sofa.

"*So far*. What about the timing? The Director said we're not eligible for coverage until after the first or second primary. That's still weeks away. I don't want this cloud hanging over our heads—"

"Under the circumstances, they might be willing to make an exception. Now you're leading in the polls. A lot of things have changed since your last discussion with the Director."

James frowned.

"What about Channing and Akerman? They'd have to sign off on it, and they're not exactly eager for me to stay in the race. This is the easiest way to get me out of their hair."

"They wouldn't dare. If it became public that they refused the leading presidential contender Secret Service protection, they'd look like hypocrites. Channing can't afford to risk losing any more ground to you—he has to take the high road."

James paused and took another sip of his brandy, then looked into Julie's eyes.

"What about you, hon? What do *you* want? Nothing'll be easy if we stay in this race—"

Julie squeezed James's hand and crinkled her eyes.

"I know how much this means to you, sweetheart. You know how I feel. You've come so far—now is not the time to quit. Call the Director tomorrow morning and schedule a meeting. If they agree to provide protection, I'm in this all the way with you."

James looked at Julie and smiled.

"Let me sleep on it."

Ten miles away, a quiet tap sounded on the door of an apartment in Silver Spring, Maryland. A man in a red shirt picked up his Ruger semiautomatic pistol off the side table and tiptoed toward the entrance. He peered through the pinhole and recognizing one of his colleagues, he dropped his pistol to his side and opened the door.

The man on the other side suddenly raised a gun with a long barrel to the red-shirted man and fired two shots into his head. As the red-shirted man crumpled to the ground, his assailant turned quietly and exited the building via the stairwell.

Inside the apartment, a large map of DC sat pinned on the wall, with red *X*s marking targets of interest. Taped to the wall beside it, lay photos of each member of Congressman Marshall's family.

31

Secret Service Headquarters, Washington, DC

January 19, 10:00 a.m.

James sat in the Director's office tapping his foot impatiently. It had been three days since the assassination attempt at Georgetown Park, and he'd kept a low profile while awaiting word on Secret Service protection. He'd called the Director the following day and was told they would expedite the request. But James was growing weary of skulking around at home under the watchful eye of his private security detail. He was eager to get an answer so he could get on with his life.

Director Richardson came into the office and closed the door.

"Sorry for the delay, Congressman. I was just talking with the Secretary of Homeland Security. Good news—you've been approved for expedited Secret Service protection."

James nodded impassively. He still wasn't sure he was ready to get back in the presidential race with the extra pressure swirling around his campaign.

"Can you clarify who exactly will receive coverage and in what manner?"

"The regulations stipulate protection for the candidate and his spouse. The number of agents assigned will depend on the assessed degree of threat and the amount of travel you and your spouse engage in. Our team will cover you wherever you go, even outside the country."

"What about my children?"

"Unless there's a specific credible threat, the regulations only provide for protection for the presidential candidate and his spouse."

"But I've already received a direct threat."

"Did it pertain to your children?"

"I believe their exact words were: 'drop out, or some very bad things are going to happen to you and your family.'"

"When was that, exactly?"

James thought back to when he'd taken Julie to the restaurant in Virginia.

"Around mid-October."

Richardson leaned back in his chair and crossed his arms.

"That was almost three months ago. Since then, you've received two personal attacks and no further threats toward your family?"

"No, but—"

"In our experience," Richardson said, "most of the risk toward presidential candidates occurs at public events such as rallies, primaries, and conventions. The best thing you can do to keep your family safe is to minimize their interaction at these kinds of affairs, where passions run high and it's harder for our team to control the variables. Obviously, when you're together, everyone falls under our umbrella. As an extra precaution, we'll station a full-time detail outside your personal residence."

James looked directly at the Director as he remained silent.

"What are your children's ages?" Richardson said, shifting uncomfortably in his seat.

"I have a seven-year-old daughter and a son attending George-town University."

The Director paused, as he processed the logistics.

"That's spreading our resources too thin. We can't assign additional agents to track school-age children unless there's a more direct threat. Our mandate is to focus on the primary target. If you're still concerned about their safety, I'd advise you to arrange supplemental private security."

James paused as he pondered the proposal.

"Do you still want to proceed?" the Director asked. "If so, I'd like to introduce you to your lead agent, who can begin making the necessary arrangements."

"I suppose so," James sighed. "Let's get the ball rolling."

32

Marshall Campaign Office

January 21, 9:00 a.m.

J ames walked into his campaign office amid a hushed staff, as
two Secret Service agents wearing earpieces assumed position
outside the front door. Everybody stopped what they were
doing and followed the congressman's stride toward the rear office.
They'd all seen the news coverage of his assassination attempt and
been briefed by Nick about the attack. As he closed the office door,
they looked at one another uncertainly, then returned to their
computers and phones.

"Glad to see you back in the game," Nick said, standing up to
greet James.

"If I'd known it was going to be *this* rough," James joked, "I probably wouldn't have signed up. College football was tiddlywinks
compared to this racket."

Nick glanced at the agents by the front door.

"I see you've added a few cheerleaders."

"We're going to have to get used to it. Now we've got the *big* guns covering our every move."

Nick nodded in approval. Not only did it elevate the congressman's image in the public eye, it also made the chief of staff feel more important. He pointed to a graph on the wall.

"If it's any consolation, that latest stunt gave you a nice kick in the polls. You're up another five points. Whether it was your stirring speech or a sympathy boost, I can't be sure."

"Well, if it's *that* easy, maybe we should just arrange a few more assassination attempts."

"Something tells me your new security team won't be on board with that," Nick chuckled.

James sat down and crossed his leg.

"So, what's on the schedule for the coming week? Because I'm pretty pissed and ready to tackle anyone or anything that gets in my way."

Nick smiled as he looked at his computer.

"The rally gave us a nice bounce. You're looking good going into Iowa. Our ads are drawing good focus group feedback, and campaign contributions are continuing to climb. The first caucus is ours to lose."

"That's what I'm worried about," James said. "You know how fast things can turn around in an election campaign. I don't want to take any chances."

Nick scanned his screen to review the upcoming schedule.

"I've got you slotted for some more press interviews to keep you in front of the voters. A visit to some high-profile factories might also provide some good PR."

"Good idea. How about a solar panel producer? That aligns nicely with my clean energy program. And what about a military base? Some of the biggest response at the rally and in the debate were in response to my foreign policy statements."

"I like it," Nick said, tapping his keyboard. "How about an aircraft carrier? The Gerald Ford is scheduled for commissioning next week at Norfolk. That would make you look very presidential."

"And *safe*," James laughed. "No one would dare take a shot at me surrounded by six thousand sailors."

James looked out the office window at the campaign staffers working quietly at their desks and noticed Emma resting her head on her hand. He opened the office door and stepped into the anteroom, placing his hands on his hips.

"Who died in here?" he said. "It's gonna take more than some crazy guy with a rifle to knock this candidate out of the race. What happened to my happy campaign team?"

Everyone stopped what they were doing and turned around. As loud applause filled the room, James looked toward Emma, who radiated a giant smile.

33

Rojas Villa, Charambira, Colombia

January 29, 5:30 p.m.

Carlos Rojas rested on his oversize sofa watching the evening news, surrounded by his lieutenants and bodyguards. It had been a surprising first few months in the Democratic presidential campaign. No one, least of all the drug lord, expected Congressman Marshall to make such a strong and convincing run at the Presidency. Even more worrisome to Rojas, had been the candidate's uncanny ability to rebound from repeated obstacles placed in his way. The congressman was proving to be a far more formidable adversary than he anticipated.

On TV, Wolf Blitzer was chatting with his chief political analyst, John King, about the upcoming Democratic presidential caucus.

"John, with only two days to go before the first Democratic caucus, Congressman Marshall has proven surprisingly resilient.

How is he looking in the latest polls, and what are your current projections for the Iowa caucus?"

A bright graphic appeared on the large glass screen beside King.

"Among registered Democratic voters nationwide, our latest poll shows Congressman Marshall with 35% of the vote, Senator Channing with 30%, and Governor Harper with 15%. The remaining twenty percent are still uncommitted. In the state of Iowa, the race is a little tighter, with only two points separating the front-runners."

"How are the candidates polling on the major issues?"

King nodded and turned back to the glass panel.

"On the subject of climate change, Marshall's clean energy initiative gives him a strong eight-point lead over Channing, with Harper trailing far behind. On the healthcare issue, Marshall's single-payer plan is trailing Channing's support for the Affordable Care Act by five points. But on foreign policy, Marshall's tough stand on the North Korea situation places him in a commanding ten point lead over Channing."

"What about the controversial drug legalization issue?"

"Surprisingly," King reported, "Marshall's been steadily rising in the polls when voters are asked this question. He's risen from less than five percent of Americans supporting full drug legalization to over thirty percent in the latest polls."

"Is that among registered Democrats?" Blitzer asked.

"That's among *all* voters—Republican and Democrat. Among registered Democrats, he holds a forty percent approval rating."

Blitzer paused as he appraised the numbers.

"Do you anticipate continuing gains in Congressman Marshall's numbers based on the recent trends?"

King nodded.

"His numbers have risen consistently since he entered the race in September. His strongest gains have been around his centerpiece program of drug legalization. Americans seem to be accepting his arguments that it will lower gang-related crime and not cause an increase in drug use."

"In spite of some early stumbles," Blitzer said, "you could say he's won each of the first three debates. He seems to be connecting with the voters."

"He's a charismatic and passionate speaker," King agreed. "Plus, he's considerably taller than the other candidates, and you know how American's like a tall President."

Blitzer chuckled.

"Are you saying he has a strong chance at going all the way to the White House?"

King turned to point at the screen.

"It's looking to be a close race, but among Democratic voters, Marshall has a strong lead over his nearest opponent, Senator Channing. In a direct match-up, Marshall is running neck-and-neck with President Templeton as America's choice for President, while Channing trails six points behind. If Marshall can beat Channing in the Iowa caucus, he'll be hard to catch."

Blitzer turned back to face the camera.

"Thanks, John, for your insightful commentary. It will indeed be a very interesting Iowa caucus. Watch our full coverage of the event here on CNN this Thursday, starting at six p.m. Eastern time."

Rojas picked up his TV remote and turned off the broadcast, then flung the remote to the other side of the sofa.

"This Marshall politician still has a tough battle ahead, no, boss?" one of the lieutenants said to the drug lord.

Rojas nodded pensively.

"He has at least three challenges to overcome, Diego. First, he has to beat this Channing candidate in the upcoming election, then he has to rack up enough votes in the other state elections to win his party's nomination for President. Finally, he has to beat the current President from the other party, in November."

"That's three to one odds," another bodyguard said. "I don't like his chances. We still want Templeton to remain President, no?"

Rojas nodded.

"Si, Tomas. The bigger the fight they put up to block our product, the greater our profits. But this Marshall character will take down all the barriers. Then we'd be competing with every tiny operator between Peru and Canada. We must find a way to ensure this candidate does not have a chance to implement his policies."

"But he's proven harder to eliminate than our other adversaries," Tomas said. "Our *teniente* in Washington now says he has the Secret Service protecting him and his family. How will we get him out of our way?"

Rojas paused as he looked out his window over the dark expanse of Pacific Ocean.

"We'll have to step up our game and enlist the aid of some people closer to Mr. Marshall."

Rojas turned toward his lead *sicario*.

"Diego, I think it is time for you to make a trip to the United States."

Rojas picked up his phone and tapped the screen to place a call.

"I will begin laying the groundwork for our next move."

———————————

Three hours later, two furtive figures met in a dark, cold alley in the Navy Yard neighborhood of Washington, DC. One of the individuals loomed over the other and held the smaller one with both hands by the shirt. He pressed his face in close and pumped his head forcefully while he spoke, while the other person stood limp with his hands by his side.

After harassing the quivering figure for many minutes, the tall man stepped back and reached into his pocket. He pulled out a thick white envelope and stuffed it into the other man's hand. Then he wagged his finger in the man's face as if reinforcing an important point. As the tall man disappeared around the corner, the other man stuffed the envelope in his pocket. Then he briskly walked in the direction of the nearest Metro station.

34

Marriott Hotel, Des Moines, Iowa

February 1, 9:00 p.m.

James sat in his hotel room with his wife watching the election results for the Iowa caucus, while his daughter curled up asleep next to them on the sofa. He'd spent an exhausting day shuttling between the state's big cities delivering last-minute speeches and was happy to rest his feet. Both rooms on either side of theirs were reserved for his Secret Service detail, as two agents stood watch outside his door. Downstairs in the hotel's main conference room, a large group of supporters awaited the congressman's appearance after the votes were finalized.

On TV, Wolf Blitzer announced that the polls had just closed.

Julie squeezed James's hand.

"Are you nervous?" she said.

"*Relieved*, more than anything," James replied. "I'm just glad I can stop campaigning for a moment and see some results for my efforts."

"You've done everything you can, sweetheart. It's amazing how far you've come."

James looked at Julie with a wry smile.

"Remember way back in September when you said I was crazy to enter this race?"

Julie pushed away, feigning insult.

"I thought some of your ideas were a bit too extreme for mainstream America. But I always thought you'd be a fabulous President."

"I remember you being a little less enthusiastic than that," James teased. "I think your exact words were that I was committing political suicide."

Julie punched her husband playfully on the shoulder.

"Well, you almost *did*, in more ways than one."

James wrinkled his brow and looked at Julie apologetically.

"Sorry to put you through all that, babe. But it looks like smooth sailing the rest of the way, with the A-team now keeping a close watch over us."

Julie huffed.

"If this is any indication of how our lives are going to be for the next four years, that's not the *only* thing that will be quieter around here. We can barely make love without worrying about the guards hearing us in the next room and outside the door."

"I'm sure they've heard worse," James chuckled.

"Are you saying I'm not *expressive* enough," Julie said, rubbing her shoulder against James.

Brooklyn suddenly stirred on the sofa and sat up. She looked at the TV and squinted at the graphic displaying on the screen behind the political analysts.

"What does that the strange colored map mean, Daddy?"

"That's a map of Iowa, honey. The light blue patches show where Daddy is leading, and the dark blue indicates where my opponent has the lead."

Brooke lowered her eyebrows and frowned.

"It looks like the bad man is winning."

"Not necessarily," James said, appraising the graphic more closely.

"The dark blue patches are mostly in rural counties, where the population is lower. Your dad's leading in the big cities, which have more delegates. See the numbers on the side of the graph? That shows me with twenty delegates and Senator Channing with eighteen, so I'm slightly ahead."

"What do the white patches mean?" Brooke asked.

"That's where the county polling stations haven't yet begun reporting their votes."

Julie squirmed on her cushion.

"Those numbers are a little too close for my comfort. I've seen the count swing back and forth a number of times."

James paused to listen to John King comment on the electoral map.

"We're still waiting for Cedar Rapids to report," he said. "That's six more delegates. If the night's trend hold's up, most of those should go to me."

"Why are you so much stronger in the metropolitan areas?" Julie asked.

"The demographics of the cities lean toward a more educated and ethnically diverse makeup. They're generally more liberal than the conservative farm belt, and they align more closely with my policies."

Blitzer asked King something about superdelegates, and the analyst pointed to another graph showing the overall delegate count.

"What's a superdelegate?" James's daughter asked. "Are they stronger and more powerful than the regular ones?"

"In a way, I suppose they are," James chuckled. "They get to cast their ballots for their favorite candidate based entirely on their *own* opinions, rather than on the votes cast by the people in these local elections."

"That doesn't seem fair," Brooke said. "Isn't America a democracy?"

James smiled at Brooke's innocence.

"It is, sweetie. It's just that certain parts of the electoral process are complicated."

"Actually," Julie said. "I'm a little confused about this whole superdelegate thing, too. Who exactly are these people, and why do they have special privileges?"

"They're mostly comprised of high-ranking Democratic politicians, including members of Congress, governors, and a few former Presidents. A few election cycles back, the party vested them with special votes to counterbalance the possibility of a populous candidate stealing the nomination and keeping the Democrats out of the White House."

"You mean a populous candidate like *you*?" Julie said.

She listened as John King explained how the majority of the superdelegates were siding with Senator Channing.

"I agree with Brooke—that doesn't seem fair. That's another seven hundred delegates you have to make up in the primaries."

"It's been an uphill battle so far," James said. "Why should it be any different the rest of the way? We'll just have to show the party establishment that I'm the people's favorite and hope they vote with their conscience at the convention."

Julie turned back to the television where Wolf Blitzer was preparing to make an announcement.

"Based on the percentage of accumulated votes across all precincts," he said, "CNN is now projecting Congressman Marshall as the winner of the Iowa Democratic caucus. The final delegate count is twenty-five for Congressman Marshall, and nineteen for Senator Channing."

"Great," Julie said, "Forty-four delegates down and only forty-seven *hundred* to go."

An hour later, James and Julie entered the hotel's conference room to raucous applause. As James glad-handed his way to the podium, supporters pumped campaign signs and cheered loudly.

James two-stepped the stairs to the top of the stage and thrust his arms above his head in a touchdown salute. The room roared in approval. He walked up to the microphone and prepared to speak, but was drowned out by the crowd. After about two minutes, the clamor finally began to dim.

"That's one small step for the Marshall campaign—" he said, "and one giant leap for the American people!"

The room burst into another loud cheer as his supporters grinned and pumped their signs.

"We still have a long journey ahead of us to achieve our goal," James continued. "But tonight, the people have spoken. And we should *all* take pride in our achievement. This couldn't have happened without the support of all of you and the many Iowans who turned out to cast their votes. To you, and to the people of Iowa, I'm immensely grateful."

Someone in the room pointed to a television screen where another network was calling the Iowa win to Channing, citing the seven Iowa superdelegates who were siding with the senator.

A loud boo filled the room as more supporters saw the result.

James held up his hand and called for calm.

"It looks like our party *insiders* are going to need a little more convincing," he said. "But there are five times as many pledged delegates who cast their votes with the people than there are unpledged superdelegates. Let's redouble our efforts for the New Hampshire primary and win it going away. Let's show the political elite how grass-roots activism can take back America!"

As chants of *Jim-Mee* and *EM-power* filled the room, James smiled at Julie.

This won't be the only raucous room in the hotel tonight, he thought.

35

Civic Arena, Manchester, New Hampshire

February 8, 8:00 p.m.

In the week following the Iowa caucus, the superdelegate controversy dominated the news. Even though James had won the caucus and held a sizable lead over Senator Channing in the national polls, most superdelegates continued to pledge their support for the senator. The opposing camps had become increasingly combative, with loud protests and shoving matches breaking out at each candidate's appearances. Many supporters from the Marshall team were accusing the Democratic National Committee of rigging the nomination process in favor of the establishment candidate. James had called for calm, imploring his followers to express their concerns peacefully. But inside, he was seething as well.

On the evening before the New Hampshire primary, he prepared to speak before a large group of supporters at the Civic Center in

Manchester. Inside the hall, twelve thousand screaming fans pumped campaign signs and chanted the familiar Marshall campaign slogans. His Secret Service detail had scoped the facility ahead of time and secured all exits except the main entrance, where private security guards used detection dogs and handheld wands to check the incoming flow of attendees. Inside the arena, more guards patrolled the arena floor, while Secret Service agents scanned the bleachers with binoculars. At the lead agent's insistence, James had foregone his usual crowd walkthrough, as he stood quietly backstage with his wife and daughter reviewing his notes.

At eight p.m., James walked out onto the stage amid rapturous cheers. It took a full ten minutes before the din abated enough for him to step up to the mic.

"Good evening, *super-supporters!*" he yelled into the mic, making a thinly veiled reference to his opponent's special band of followers.

For another five minutes, the frenzied crowd hollered and cheered for their favorite candidate. James noticed a few signs for Senator Channing sparsely interspersed among the ubiquitous Marshall campaign banners. But instead of pumping up and down, they appeared to shift erratically side-to-side, as if being jostled by adjacent fans.

When the cheers finally subsided, he stepped back up to the microphone.

"We stand here today on the eve of another momentous vote for the future of our country. A week ago, the people of Iowa cast their ballots for the Democratic nominee for President, and we were fortunate enough to win a majority—"

James paused, as loud cheers filled the arena.

"And, tomorrow, the good people of New Hampshire lend their voices to the rising tide of support."

The many hometown fans in attendance hollered in approval.

"We've been truly blessed," James continued, "by the many Americans who've lent support in the form of campaign contributions, encouraging letters, and—yes—with their votes. But none of this would be possible without the hundreds of volunteers who've so selflessly contributed their time and energy to this campaign. And for this, I give my sincere thanks."

James paused, as his expression turned more serious.

"But there's a serpent lying in the grass—an insidious force waiting to snatch our victory away from us. A band of insiders, who hold special privileges in the final nomination process, to be held this summer at the Democratic convention. These so-called *superdelegates* have been vested with powers to override the people's choice and decide for themselves who should lead our party in the presidential election."

The room erupted in loud boos and catcalls.

"Thirty-five years ago," James continued, "after another anti-establishment candidate went on to capture the White House, party insiders decided to change the nomination rules so that the Democratic presidential nominee would no longer solely be determined based on local primary elections. They felt that giving the power to individual voters, who were too easily persuaded by populist candidates, would lead the party away from its mainstream roots. In other words, they decided that *they* knew what was better for the party and the country than the people they were elected to represent!"

The sound of boos filled the arena.

"Do *you* think the political old-guard is smarter than you?!" James cried.

"Nooo!" came the loud and harmonious response from the crowd.

"Do *you* want a bunch of party insiders to choose your presidential candidate for you?"

"Nooo!"

James paused to underscore his next point.

"Unfortunately, the Democratic Party has chosen a very undemocratic process for nominating your choice of President. The deck was stacked against us even before we started. Seven hundred and twelve party insiders will make the final decision as to who will lead our country. And ninety percent of these special delegates have said they will vote for Senator Channing at the convention—regardless of the vote count in the primaries."

"*Shame! Shame!*" the crowd chanted.

"After many debates, months of public advocacy, and millions of votes cast in state primaries across the country, your future will lie in the hands of a small clique of insiders. Insiders who are committed to maintaining the status quo and supporting the political old guard. *One* of whom just happens to be Senator Ken Channing."

As the crowd seethed and roared its disapproval, James noticed a group of people turn on a Channing supporter, wrenching his sign out of his hands and trampling him to the ground. Three members of James's security team quickly converged on the commotion and began escorting the Channing supporter toward the exit.

James raised his arm above his head and opened his hand, asking the crowd to quiet down.

"In the true spirit of democracy," he said, "some of my opponents' supporters are in attendance here today—"

"*Booo!*"

James held up his hand again.

"Let us not criticize our fellow countrymen who are exercising their constitutional right of free speech and assembly. These individuals deserve our respect and admiration. We welcome *all* legitimate voices within our party. In a few short months, we will need to come together to fight a bigger and tougher adversary. If you want real change for your country, we must form a *united* front to remove the real embodiment of the political status quo: President Templeton!"

James smiled as the crowd began cheering again.

"Do not hate, do not put down, do not silence your fellow Americans. Embrace them as equals. Engage them in dialogue. Link your arms together and walk as one. Each of us is a drop of water that can make only a ripple in the ocean. But together, we can create a tidal wave that can overcome any barrier. Tomorrow, we will send a signal to those who stand in our way that Americans want change. And that *no* one can stop us from returning this great country to the people!"

As the arena filled with chants of *EM-power*, James stepped away from the podium and was joined at the front of the stage by Julie and Brooklyn.

Today, at least, he felt the power to change the world.

36

The Source Restaurant, Washington DC

February 10, noon

"You're sure moving up in the world," Ray said, taking a seat opposite James at Wolfgang Puck's famous restaurant at the Newseum, next to the Capitol.

"*Inching*, possibly," James huffed. "With two percent of the delegates in the bag, I've still got a hell of a mountain to climb."

Ray noticed minority leader Akerman sitting with three other senior congressmen three tables away, looking in James's direction.

"I think you're being a little hard on yourself, Jim," he said. "You picked up almost twice as many votes as Channing last night in New Hampshire. At this pace, you'll walk away with the nomination before half the states are counted."

"That's not what the pundits are saying," James frowned. "When you include the committed superdelegates, the senator still has a commanding lead."

"You know how fickle these guys are," Ray said, smiling at his colleagues. "They're just going with the safe candidate until the needle swings far enough in the other direction. Everyone loves a winner. If you keep racking up decisive wins in the primaries, eventually they'll swing to your side. They're not fools—when you show them you can win the White House, they'll jump on the bandwagon."

James picked up the menu to scan the food selections.

"I hope you're right, Ray. It's a matter of optics. With most of the media adding in the superdelegates, it looks like I'm badly trailing. I'm afraid it'll influence the voters. I just wish there was more I could do to bring the superdelegates over to my side."

A buxom waitress appeared at their table and pulled an order pad from her pocket.

"Good afternoon, gentlemen. My name's Jennifer, and I'll be your server. Have you had a chance to review the menu?"

"Do you have something *special* to offer us today, Jennifer?" Ray said, smiling at the waitress.

"The specials today are potato-crusted halibut and wild mushroom risotto," she said, ignoring Ray's thinly veiled pass.

"The halibut sounds delectable," Ray said.

"I'll have the risotto, thank you," James said, handing the menu to the waitress.

"Would you like anything to drink?"

"Vodka martini, straight up," Ray said.

"A glass of the house Pinot for me," James said.

"Excellent," said the waitress. "I'll be back in a few minutes with your drinks."

James shook his head as the waitress headed off to the bar.

"You're incorrigible."

"Hey—only *one* of us is married here. Have you forgotten how to flirt?"

James cocked his head.

"Is that what that was?"

James looked around the room and caught Akerman glancing at

him. He nodded at the minority leader and smiled. Akerman held his gaze for a brief moment then returned his attention to his colleagues.

"You know," Ray said, noticing the awkward exchange, "one thing you could do to get these guys on your side is socialize with them a little more often. You don't have to worry about *me*—I'm already in your corner. You should be over there with Akerman, wining and dining with the other party mavens."

"Even though he can barely contain his disdain for me?"

Ray shook his head.

"These guys are like a first date. You just have to show a little love to win them over."

"You don't think that runs contrary to my whole anti-insider platform? I'd look like a bit of a hypocrite if some reporter posted a picture of me kicking back with one of the mainstays of the Washington establishment."

The waitress returned and placed their drinks on the table.

"This lone wolf thing can carry you only so far," Ray said, sipping his martini. "Even if you win the White House, you won't be able to advance your agenda without supporters in the House and Senate. There are two sides to this equation, and you're placing all your cards with the general public."

Ray took a moment to survey the room.

"Look around this place," he said. "Half the eyes in this restaurant are focused on you. You're the *it* guy right now. You have to take advantage while the iron is hot. Nobody actually *likes* Channing and Akerman. You just have reach out and share that sparkling personality of yours. I've got a feeling most of these superdelegates are looking for a good excuse to switch sides. Once you get these guys in your corner, you'll steamroll your way to the White House."

James looked around the restaurant and smiled as he made eye contact with some familiar faces.

Maybe Ray was right. It wouldn't hurt to be a little more inclusive.

He saw his two Secret Service agents dining quietly at a table by the front door and was reminded how much he'd sheltered himself from the outside world.

I can't do this alone, he thought.

37

House of Representatives, Capitol Building

February 12, 10:00 a.m.

J ames took a deep breath before entering the assembly room. It had been many weeks since House members had voted on a bill, and today's bill struck particularly close to home. The Marijuana Decriminalization Act had bounced back and forth between floor debates and committee amendments three times over the past two years. Each time, the revised bill had been voted down by the Republican majority, supported by a large number of Democrats. Today's debate and vote was viewed as a last gasp for the fledgling bill.

The bill proposed to remove marijuana from the Controlled Substances Act and transfer regulatory authority from the Drug Enforcement Agency to the Bureau of Alcohol, Tobacco, and Firearms. By so doing, it would eliminate criminal penalties for anyone who manufactured, distributed, or possessed the drug. James suspected the timing of the newly amended bill was meant as a rebuke of his drug legalization platform, with the intent of publicly shooting it down once and for all. Even though the odds were stacked against him, he saw today's debate as another opportunity to influence opinion in both the public domain and in the legislative assembly.

But as he stepped into the hall and began walking down the aisle, something unexpected happened. Many members on the Democratic side began clapping as the junior congressman passed. James slowed his pace and shook hands with the members who congratulated him on his recent victories. Apparently, he'd found a new measure of respect and admiration among his colleagues.

As he passed Ray's seat, his friend leaned over and whispered in his ear.

"Knock 'em dead, buddy!"

The Republican side of the assembly remained conspicuously silent, but everyone followed his path to the speakers' box. As James took his front row seat, he glanced at Minority Leader Akerman sitting behind him in the next row.

"Good morning, Tom," James said.

Akerman's lip curled in a sinister smile.

"*Live* by the sword, *die* by the sword, Congressman," he said, suggesting today's vote would be a litmus test for his presidential aspirations.

James was the only designated speaker sitting on the Democratic side of the speakers' box. The one Republican speaker was Eugene Stevens, the majority whip.

They're bringing out their heavy gun to deal me a fatal blow, James thought.

The Speaker recognized the Republican member first, and Stevens strut confidently to the podium.

"Mr. Speaker," he began. "This bill has been tabled three times, and in each case, it has failed to gain a majority. It's obvious to every member in this chamber that recreational drug legalization doesn't carry widespread support. It's time to put this issue to rest once and for all. The reason it has failed to gain support is simple. Legalization of marijuana will only increase its availability and use, and create significant new health and safety risks."

The Republican side of the room stamped their feet and hollered in support.

"Congressman Marshall's assertion that decriminalization will reduce organized crime is misguided," Stevens continued. "Legalization will only increase the number of suppliers scrambling to gain their share of the lucrative trade of this dangerous substance. Our streets will be overridden with a whole new gang of junkies and drug-dealers that will be impossible to contain."

Another enthusiastic round of applause came from the right side of the assembly.

"But mostly, the passage of such a bill sends an inappropriate message to our constituents that we are tacitly endorsing the use of this hallucinogenic substance. Let us continue to act as responsible legislators and outlaw this substance for what it is: a dangerously addictive and mind-altering drug. Our job as legislators is to create laws that protect the public, and that is precisely what we will do here today."

Stevens swiped his finger across his neck in a cut-throat gesture.

"Vote *no* on the Marijuana Decriminalization Act!"

As the Republican side of the assembly rose to their feet and cheered, Stevens walked past James and sneered. As far as he was concerned, the matter was closed. By supporting a lost cause, James was just going to dig himself a deeper hole.

James walked to the podium and paused for a long moment to look out at the assembled members. Everyone was silent and looking at him expectantly. His reputation as a powerful orator had grown since he'd entered the presidential race, and they knew he wouldn't go down without a fight. It was political theater, at the highest level.

"It's *true* what Congressman Stevens said," James began, to a hushed audience.

"Our job as legislators is to create laws that serve the people. Not to *protect* them, because that's what the army and police are for."

James paused. All eyes were locked on him.

"Rather, the purpose of laws is to *enable* the people. To channel their passions and energies toward endeavors that increase their collective enjoyment and reduce their pain, within a set of guidelines that ensures fairness and security for all. That is exactly what our founding fathers did when they created the U.S. Constitution, which vested every citizen with the unalienable right to pursue happiness, unencumbered by the tyranny of law. This document has guided our way of life for over two hundred and fifty years and enabled us to become the wealthiest and most proudly independent people in the world."

As James heard a loud cheer from the Democratic side of the hall, he panned over the Republican contingent. Many were nodding in approval.

"But our constitution," he continued, "*also* stated that when the form of government becomes destructive to these ends, it is the right of the people to alter or abolish it. I propose to you, my fellow members, that this is what today's bill represents: the dismantling of an arbitrary law that restricts the simple right of the people to pursue happiness."

James could hear the level of applause in the room growing in volume and number.

"Marijuana is no more dangerous than cigarettes or alcohol, and it has been proven to reduce the suffering of those who are in pain. We've seen what decades of prohibition has done. It's done nothing but build a worldwide crime syndicate while simultaneously filling our jails with people who are merely practicing their right to pursue happiness at no threat to their fellow citizens."

James paused, as he locked eyes with Congressman Stevens.

"It's *true* that passage of this bill will send a powerful message to your constituents. It will send a message that you respect their right to seek enjoyment in whatever form they please as long as it doesn't harm others, and that you will no longer place artificial barriers in their way. Vote *yes* for freedom of expression, *yes* for freedom from pain, and *yes* for freedom over drug lord tyranny!"

Almost every member from the Democratic side of the hall rose instantly from their seats, cheering loudly. The Republican side remained seated in a show of party solidarity, but James caught many nodding faces, betraying their true sentiments.

As he stepped down from the podium and walked back to his regular seat at the back of the hall, he glanced at Akerman. The minority leader was also applauding and nodding as he followed James's path up the aisle.

Twenty minutes later, the final vote appeared on the display panel above the press gallery. The count was two hundred and twenty-five to two hundred and ten, against. James had lost the battle but won the war. Seventy percent of the Democrats had sided with him, together with a sizable number of Republicans.

The block of unpledged delegates had started swinging his way.

38

Longworth Building, Congressman Marshall's Office

March 1, 8:00 a.m.

James propped his feet up on his desk while he sorted through a tall stack of mail. This first hour of his workday was often the most rewarding because it gave him a chance to catch up with constituent correspondence. Most of the mail was positive, complimenting him for his firm stance on the issues and encouraging him in his campaign for the Presidency. Even the negative mail was often informative, as it revealed inconsistencies in his platform or ways in which his messaging wasn't resonating. Occasionally, he'd receive blatant hate mail filled with obscenities and name-calling, but he considered that a normal part of being a high-profile public figure.

Since he'd entered the race to become President, his volume of daily mail had steadily risen. Normally, he directed it to his campaign office, where his growing staff of volunteers vetted the large mass of correspondence. But today, he had a little downtime before a scheduled meeting with his chief of staff, and he'd picked up an unopened stack for some quiet reading.

He flipped through the mail looking for something personal and stopped when he saw an unusual brown envelope. The hand-written address had his title misspelled, with only one 's' in Congressman. This wasn't unusual since many of his fans came from lower-income, less-educated households. But something about this letter made the hair on the back of his neck stand up. The postage stamp was of a higher denomination than required for regular domestic mail. He turned the envelope over and saw that it had no return address. Flipping it over again, the postmark showed it was mailed from San Diego two days ago.

James's eyes narrowed as his face tightened.

Something about this letter didn't feel right. He pinched the package gently and noticed the top edge near the flap was slightly thicker, with a strange spongy feel. Against his better judgment, he raised the envelope to his nose and took two short sniffs. Nothing smelled out of the ordinary. He turned the letter over and carefully inspected the perimeter of the enclosure flap. It was tightly sealed all the way around and puckered, as if someone had used a damp cloth instead of licking it shut.

James put the envelope down on his desk and opened his door to motion to one of the Secret Service agents sitting down the hall.

"Sorry to bother you, Gene," James said, as the agent trotted up to his door. "It's probably nothing, but I received a suspicious package today and wanted your opinion. Can you take a look?"

The agent nodded, and James pointed to the envelope on the near side of his desk. Gene looked at the envelope for a few long seconds then pulled a pen from his pocket and used it to flip the package over. He waved his hand behind his back, motioning for James to step away. Then he lifted his wrist to his mouth and spoke into his hand-held microphone.

"Suspicious package in Maverick's office. Send hazmat team asap."

The agent turned around and held out his arm as he walked toward James.

"Please exit the room immediately, sir. We'll need you to keep away from this office until it's been swept and cleared. As a security precaution, please wash your hands and face thoroughly with soap and water. Let me know if you experience any unusual symptoms."

James looked at the agent confused.

"How long will this take?"

"We need to send the package to our chemical analysis lab," Gene said. "We should know within a few hours if there's a problem."

James began to feel his muscles twitching involuntarily as he realized the gravity of the situation.

"Am I contagious? Should I be quarantined?"

"At this point, there's no sign of open release or direct contamination. Just to be safe, I recommend you wait outside on the Capitol grounds with at least ten feet of separation between you and anyone else. We'll be standing nearby and advise when everything is clear."

As James headed toward the restroom to clean up, two individuals wearing full-body suits and plexiglass face masks rushed past him.

Jesus, he thought. *Just as everything was coming together...*

39

Longworth Building, Nick Garcia's Office

March 2, 9:00 a.m.

"Any news?" Nick asked as James walked into his chief of staff's office the next morning.

"The lab results came in positive," James nodded. "They found a packet of VX nerve agent rigged to explode when the envelope was unsealed."

"VX?" Nick said, with a puzzled look. "Never heard of that one."

"It's the same stuff agents used to assassinate Kim Jong-un's brother in Malaysia. They tell me it's one of the deadliest poisons ever created. Even a tiny amount can be absorbed quickly into the skin, causing the muscles to violently contract, suffocating the victim within seconds."

Nick shook his head incredulously.

"That's crazy. I thought there were procedures in place to catch this sort of thing. After the anthrax scare a few years back, didn't the Capitol Police institute a protocol for screening congressional mail?"

"There is. Every package addressed to the White House, Congress, and other federal agencies goes through a special irridation process intended to neutralize any poisons. Incoming mail to the Capitol receives an additional visual screening for unusual external signs before being forwarded to the recipient."

"How did this one get through?"

"This letter was addressed to my campaign office, instead of the Capitol. I picked it up personally with a bunch of other mail and brought it here to read. I was just lucky to detect something suspicious before opening the package."

Nick wrinkled his forehead.

"*Lucky* is the operative word. We get thousands of pieces of mail delivered to the campaign office every day. How can we be sure—"

"I know what you're thinking," James said. "The postal service has placed a hold on all mail addressed to me until the elections are over. It's simply too risky. We're not going to subject our staff to any unnecessary threat."

Nick looked at James with a worried expression.

"This is what—the *third* attempt on your life since you entered the presidential race? I'm worried about you, Jim."

James nodded and placed his hand on his chief of staff's shoulder.

"Don't worry about me, Nick. Every time they try to eliminate me, we close more loopholes. They're running out of ways to get to me," he chuckled.

James leaned back in his chair as his expression turned more serious.

"But there *is* something else we can do to ensure my legacy is preserved. That's why I wanted to see you today. Do you mind if we use your office? They're still sweeping mine to ensure there are no traces of the poison."

"Of course. What did you have in mind?"

"It's time to choose a running mate. We're climbing in the polls, and the superdelegates are beginning to defect to our side. We need to have a unified ticket to present at the convention and for the final leg of the campaign this fall."

"I agree," Nick said. "I've already been thinking about suitable candidates."

"Same here. But I want to go about this the right way. This is way too important to base only on our gut instincts. I wanted to clarify our objectives first, then evaluate the qualifications of our short list for VP."

Nick smiled at his boss's familiar approach to tackling the issues.

"I'd expect no less," he said. "I'm guessing you'll want someone with a fair amount of experience?"

"Definitely. We need to counterbalance my deficiency in that area. Preferably someone who's held an executive position in political office—not another congressman."

"Like a *governor*, maybe? Carol Chase's second term in coming up for reelection in January. That would be perfect timing."

"Yes..." James nodded. "And I like the idea of having a woman as my running mate. That might help us capture the female vote. Same thing with a person of color. We need more Latinos, Asians, and African-Americans in high-profile executive positions."

Nick thought for a moment.

"What about Joelle Rivera, governor of Texas? She hits most of the bases: female, Hispanic, and executive experience managing a big state."

James paused as he contemplated the option.

"She has most of the qualifications, but she leans pretty far to the right on the issues. If something happened to me, I'd want someone who's reasonably aligned with me idealistically. I'd like to have confidence my running mate would carry the torch forward in the implementation of my main programs."

Nick walked over to a large map of the United States hanging on his wall that he'd been using to keep track of the state primary count. He held his hand in the air and waved it slowly from left to right, slowing moving down. He stopped suddenly in the middle section of the map.

"*Maggie Castillo*," he said, swinging around. "She's biracial, speaks Spanish, and she's starting her second term as governor of Colorado. Plus, she's been a big supporter of the marijuana decriminalization initiative in her state."

James nodded as his eyes lit up.

"I've been a big fan of hers ever since she was a first-term congresswoman. She's articulate and passionate about many of the same issues we're building our platform on. She'd be perfect."

"And she's pretty easy on the eyes," Nick smiled. "You two would make a hell of an attractive ticket."

James paused as he rubbed his jaw in thought.

"But she'd have to resign her governorship mid-term. She doesn't strike me as a quitter."

"She's got a strong lieutenant governor in Neil Johnson, who could hit the ground running. Besides, Vice President of the United States is a big step up, and it positions her to take the top job in a few more years."

Nick paused for a second.

"As long as she doesn't mind ducking a few bullets standing next to you."

James snapped his head as he looked up suddenly at Nick. His chief of staff was only half kidding. Any VP running on his ticket would indeed be placing herself in a precarious position. If anything happened to him, she'd be the next one in the line of fire.

"There's only one way to find out," James said, picking up Nick's office phone. "Let's see if she's up for the job."

40

Oval Office, The White House

March 15, 9:30 a.m.

President William Templeton sat at his desk reading a briefing on his Democratic presidential competition. With a little over nine months until the general election, it was time to turn his attention to securing a second term in office. Although he had a favorable approval rating and good prospects for winning reelection, he knew nothing was guaranteed in American politics. With a number of concerns on his mind, he'd arranged a meeting with his chief of staff, Royce Hyland, to discuss their campaign strategy.

The Democratic race had narrowed to two front-runners: Senate Minority Leader Ken Channing and first-term Congressman James Marshall. Channing was a known entity, with a long and consistent record of taking safe, middle-of-the road positions on most of the issues. Although he was widely respected on both sides of the political aisle, he lacked charisma and was viewed by many as a Capitol Hill lifer.

But Congressman Marshall was an enigma. Coming out of nowhere, he'd captured the lead for the Democratic nomination in only two short years. A dyed-in-the-wool anti-establishment candidate, his radical ideas flew in the face of traditional American values. Although most people had written him off as a hopeless dreamer with no chance of winning the Presidency, his youthful enthusiasm and strong oratorial skills had gained him increasing currency across the political spectrum. Most worrisome to the President, the congressman had an uncanny ability to overcome repeated challenges and setbacks to claw his way to the front of the race.

This renegade could be a dangerous adversary, he thought.

Templeton's thoughts were interrupted by a tap on his door.

"Come in," he said.

"Good morning, Mr. President," his chief of staff said, closing the door behind him.

"Royce, have a seat. I've been reviewing these briefings and wanted your input on how we can best position our campaign against these candidates. I don't want to leave anything to chance leading up to the November election."

Royce leaned back on the couch and crossed his legs.

"I don't think you have too much to worry about, sir. Your approval ratings are strong, and the Democrats have fielded two weak candidates."

"That's not what the polls are saying," the President said, holding up the report. "They're showing this Marshall character running neck-and-neck with me in a presidential run-off."

"That's just because he's a new face garnering lots of media attention right now. This honeymoon effect will start to dissolve once he faces a real contender."

The President peered at his chief of staff over his reading glasses.

"I'm not so sure. We've seen it before, where a relative unknown captures the public imagination and steamrolls into the White

House. This guy reminds me of JFK. He's young, handsome, and full of fresh ideas. The public has taken quite a shine to him."

Royce sat forward and leafed through his briefing.

"But his policies are very left-wing, attracting mostly young voters and potheads. This drug legalization thing is a non-starter, and the public will never go for socialized medicine. We need to position him as a radical extremist, someone who'll pull the country away from its conservative values."

"I thought so too," the President said. "But every time he steps in front of a microphone, he pulls more and more people onto his side. He's able to back up his positions with some strong facts. He's even begun to swing a sizable number of moderates within his own party."

"We're still talking *Democrats*, Mr. President. Even if he captured the majority of registered Democrats in the general election, his support among Republicans is even more lopsided in the other direction. Among blue-collar and rural white males, you're killing him in the polls."

The President dropped the report on his desk with a loud plop and pushed back in his chair.

"I don't want to rely on the redneck vote to win the election. Besides, Marshall's platform isn't *all* left-wing. He's a strong free enterprise advocate and a foreign policy hawk. And he's always going on about how we need to stop the government from meddling in everybody's private affairs. That's our base. Once he captures the nomination and gets voters from the other side of the spectrum paying attention to him, he could easily begin stealing votes from our constituency."

Royce paused again to flip through his report.

"His Achilles' Heel is his lack of experience. He's putting two years of junior legislative experience up against your twenty-plus years of executive experience at the state and federal level. I can't see the conservative electorate taking a chance with an unproven candidate being their commander in chief."

The President nodded as he put his feet up on his desk.

"I agree it's his biggest weakness. But his announcement last week of Governor Castillo as his running mate helps to offset this. She has a strong record pulling her state out of the last recession, and she's got almost as much executive experience as me."

"With respect, sir, running a state isn't the same as running the country. Neither candidate has any foreign policy experience, nor experience putting troops on the ground. The American people are going to want a proven leader."

The President paused as he looked out his window.

"The strange thing is, these public attempts on his life have actually made him look presidential. He's gained a certain amount of sympathy and admiration from the public for his decision to stay in the race in the face of all this adversity. I think we need something more on this candidate."

Royce looked at the President with a puzzled expression.

"What did you have in mind?"

"He's too clean. Everybody's got a skeleton in the closet, some fatal flaw. We just need to find it. I want you to delve into Marshall's past with a magnifying glass. If we can't find any dirt on him, we'll manufacture some of our own."

Royce paused, as he contemplated the President's meaning.

"I'll see what I can dig up, sir."

41

Starbucks Coffee Shop, George Washington University

April 10, 8:00 a.m.

E mma stood lost in thought as she waited for her barista to fulfill her morning coffee order. She'd noticed a recent change in Congressman Marshall's attitude toward her, but she couldn't quite place it. She'd been thrilled to be invited with a few others to help him prepare for his second debate, and she was confident he'd found her input helpful. But she'd been inexplicably shut out of the second round of debate preparations, with no explanation. Since then, the congressman seemed unusually aloof around her. Something didn't add up, and she was feeling hurt and confused.

When her order was called, she took her coffee to a table in the corner and stared out the window.

"Do you mind if I sit here?" a well-dressed man asked, interrupting her thoughts. "All the other seats are taken."

"Yes...of course," she said, shifting her chair to give herself a little extra space.

"To be honest," the man said as he sat down, "I noticed you were looking a bit...*contemplative* this morning. I thought maybe you could use a little company."

Emma's eyes darted across the man's face suspiciously. As a pretty GW coed, she'd had her share of unwanted advances from unsolicited admirers. But there was something about this man's countenance that seemed unusually professional, that made her feel safe.

"Is it that obvious?" she chuckled.

"I hope it's nothing too serious," the man said. "You're far too young to be carrying the weight of the world on your shoulders."

"Other than my huge student debt, you mean?" Emma joked.

"Well if that's your biggest problem, that can be easily enough fixed."

Emma turned her head suddenly toward the man and narrowed her eyes.

"How do you mean?"

"What would you say if I could make that disappear?"

"Look, mister," Emma said, reaching for her purse and beginning to stand. "I don't know what your game is, but I'm not that kind of girl."

The man reached out his hand and placed it gently on Emma's wrist.

"Please. Hear me out. I assure you, I don't have any designs on you. I'm just offering to help."

"Why?" Emma said, pausing on the edge of her seat. "You don't know me. Why would you make such an offer to a complete stranger?"

"Don't you work for Congressman Marshall?"

Emma's eyes flared as it suddenly became apparent what the stranger's agenda was. She glanced behind the counter to catch the attention of the cashier. She was no longer feeling safe, and she was ready to call for help if the man tried to detain her any longer.

"Just give me one minute to explain," the man said, holding up his palms in defense. "We're in a public coffee shop. Nobody's going to hurt you. If you don't like what I have to say, I'll leave and you'll never see me again."

Emma paused for a moment to consider her options. She didn't want to make a scene if it could be helped, plus she knew it would be safer staying within the confines of the coffee shop than wandering out in the open where she'd have less control.

"You're treading a very thin line," she said. "I'll give you thirty seconds. Then if you don't leave me alone, I'm calling the cops."

The man nodded, then lowered his voice.

"I've been asked to make you a proposal," he said.

"What kind of proposal? By whom?"

"A monetary reward. A *sizable* monetary reward."

"What kind of reward? For doing what?"

"Paying off your student loans. *All* of your student loans."

"How could you possibly do that?"

"Let's just say I know people in very high places."

Emma could feel the hair rising on the back of her neck the more she listened to the stranger. Part of her wanted to run or scream for help, but another part remembered how much she'd been worrying recently about carrying a six-figure student loan with no full-time job prospects upon graduation.

"Who?" she asked.

"I'm not at liberty to say. We need to maintain plausible deniability. You understand."

Emma nodded. She understood fully what he meant.

"People don't make these kinds of offers unless they expect something illegal or immoral in return," she said. "What exactly do you want me to do?"

"I'm not asking you to do either of those things." The man looked around the room to make sure no one was listening. "We're just looking for some dirt on your favorite congressman."

Emma smiled, recognizing the familiar DC campaign game. Since the dawn of democracy, it had been a time-honored strategy to search for unflattering personal details of one's political opponents in the hope of exposing it in the theater of public opinion to dash their political aspirations.

"Good luck with that," she said. "He's as unspoiled a politician as you'll find in this town."

"*Everyone's* got demons or skeletons in their closet. Surely you've lived long enough to know that."

"What makes you think I can help you?" Emma said. She almost felt like someone else was uttering the words coming from her mouth. But she'd felt betrayed by the loss of confidence of Congressman Marshall, and this looked like a viable opportunity to settle her debt quickly. "I'm just a part-time volunteer at his campaign office."

"We've noticed that you have his ear—if not his *eye*."

Emma's face suddenly tightened.

"Have you been *watching* me?"

"Just him. We only see you when you enter his line of vision."

"Yeah, well, I seem to be out of his favor these days. So it looks like you've got the wrong girl."

"Come now—" the man said, allowing his gaze to drift below Emma's neckline. "With your ample assets, surely you can find a way to distract him?"

"What do you want me to do—*sleep* with him?"

"That won't be necessary. A kiss, a grope, even a convincing *leer* might be enough to do the trick."

Emma scowled at the man as his intentions became clear.

"And how exactly do you propose to *use* this, in the unlikely event I'm successful in this act of subterfuge?"

"Let *us* worry about that. You just set the trap—we'll be sure to capture his fall."

"What if he doesn't take the bait? He's a married man, after all."

The man laughed at Emma's naivety.

"If he's as pure as you think he is, you have nothing to worry about. And your student loans will remain in no danger of being paid off anytime in the next ten years."

Emma paused for a long awkward moment. She could hardly believe she was giving serious consideration to the offer.

"How will I know when you're ready?"

The man handed Emma a blank card with a handwritten number on it.

"We're *always* ready. Watch for a message from this number."

Emma looked at the card and shook her head.

"How can I trust that you'll fulfill your end of the bargain?"

"You can't. But you're getting a very large gift for a very small sacrifice. If you're successful in drawing him out as we've asked, you'll be able to verify your loan balance is paid off the next time you sign on to your student aid account. All we're asking you to do is a little flirting in return for a six-figure payout."

Emma's face twisted in anguish, undecided how to proceed.

"You're asking me to betray my personal beliefs and the confidence of a man I admire."

"Look at it as a test of his *integrity*. If he doesn't take your bait, you'll have proof he's everything you thought he was. But if he *does*, you'll know your confidence was misplaced. Wouldn't you like to know either way?"

Emma exhaled and nodded slowly.

"Can you give me a few days to think about it?" she said.

"I'm sorry—this is a limited time offer. There are a lot of pretty girls in this town who'll do a lot more for a lot less."

"Fine," Emma said, standing to leave. "We'll find out soon enough who holds the higher moral ground. Do you have a code name or something I should use to contact you?"

"That's so old school," the man said. "We don't do that cloak and dagger stuff. Don't try to contact me—you'll hear from us when the time is right."

42

Marshall Campaign Office

May 15, 11:00 a.m.

On a rainy Saturday morning, James pulled up in front of his campaign office in a black SUV. He'd grown accustomed to being driven around by his security detail and had finally made peace with it. He found it relaxing to sit in the back seat and get caught up on briefings and correspondence while being chauffeured between his many campaign stops. Best of all, he never had to flag a ride—the Secret Service was always ready and waiting for him whenever he needed to go somewhere.

Today, he decided to stop in his campaign office and thank his staff for all their hard work. His campaign was firing on all cylinders, with successive state primaries falling one-by-one to his side of the ledger. Contributions were continuing to climb, and his pledged delegate lead over Senator Channing was widening. After the scare at the

Capitol, everything was back on track, and James once again felt safe under the protection of his elite security team.

As he opened the office door, the staffers stopped what they were doing and looked up. For the many volunteers, James was the center of their universe, and the planets were lining up. Everybody loved a winner, and there was plenty of love to spread around. James stopped to chat with each staff member, asking them how much they were enjoying working on the campaign and if there was anything he could do to make their job easier. Nobody complained—they were happy to be part of what they considered history in the making.

When he made his way to Emma's desk, the student volunteer seemed especially ebullient. She was wearing a tight pink cardigan sweater that hugged every inch of her shapely body. She smiled a toothy grin and thrust her chest out as James approached her chair.

"Good morning, Emma. How's my special debate advisor? Any new events lined up at GW?"

"Yes..." Emma stammered, her dilated pupils betraying her excitement. "The Yale debate team is visiting our school to address the subject of gun control. I don't suppose you've got any tips you can share—"

"I'd love to help," James said. "In fact, why don't you join me for lunch today, where we can exchange ideas? I need to hone my message in that area too. That subject hasn't come up in any of my debates yet."

"*Really*?" Emma chirped. "Thank you so much, sir...I mean, Congressman."

"*James* is fine," James laughed. "We're pretty informal around here. I've got a few things to go over with Nick. Will noon work for you? I hope you don't mind tagging along with my security team. Goes with the job, now, I'm afraid."

Emma looked at the black truck parked outside the window, with the two Secret Service agents stationed under the awning. She could hardly believe that she was going to be escorted by the future President in a Secret Service vehicle to a private meeting.

"My god, yes," she said. "I'll be waiting."

An hour later, James and Emma scampered out of the SUV through pouring rain into the front lobby of the Capitol Grille.

"Wow," Emma said, peering around the luxury restaurant. Amid rich mahogany wood paneling and framed art of famous American politicians, hushed diners conversed quietly in weighty discussions.

"I've never been here, but everyone says it's *the* place in DC to be seen. I hear all the heavy hitters come here for lunch."

"We might bump into a few famous faces," James laughed "Present company excluded, of course."

"I didn't mean..." Emma apologized. "I mean—it won't be long before you're the most powerful man in the world."

James chuckled as the hostess led them to a table near the back of the restaurant.

"Do you mind if I freshen up?" Emma said. "I'm a little wet from the rain..."

"Of course," James said, noticing Emma's sweater clinging tightly to her bosom. "It's the weekend. There's no rush."

When Emma returned, he saw that she'd taken her sweater off and applied a bright shade of red lip gloss. She hung her sweater over the back of her chair and sat down opposite James. When she placed her phone down on the table, James noticed she had a recent text thread open.

"I hope you don't mind," Emma said. "My sweater needs to dry. Am I dressed okay?"

James quickly glanced at Emma's outfit. She was wearing a white silk blouse and a knee-length skirt. Other than her shirt being open one more button more than normally prudent, she looked very professional.

"Yes..." he paused, "I think you fit right in."

Emma's phone vibrated, and she quickly picked it up. She tapped on the screen for a few seconds, then placed it into her purse.

"Sorry, it's my mom. Always the mother hen—checking up on where I am and what trouble I'm getting into."

James's face turned introspective as his thoughts turned to his daughter Breanna.

"Parents can never be too careful these days. It's a dangerous world out there..."

"I'm sorry. It must be difficult for you sometimes—"

"I'm fine. It's just that you remind me a little of my daughter. She'd be close to your age..."

Emma noticed the pain on James's face and reached her hand out to touch his fingers holding the base of his water glass.

He pulled his hand away quickly and lifted his glass to take a drink.

"Are you excited about your upcoming debate?" James said, changing the subject.

"Yes, but I'm feeling a little out of my element. This isn't a subject I have much familiarity with. I haven't heard you talk much about gun control, other than tangentially with regard to drug legalization reducing gang activity. What's your position on the issue?"

"Honestly, I don't understand America's obsession with guns. The Second amendment seems an anachronism of a bygone age. I think the founding fathers added it with the King of England's oppression still fresh in mind. Even the wording is out of date: 'a well-regulated militia, necessary to the security of a free state.' We've got an open democracy and a professional army now. Gun ownership is no longer something that needs to be entrenched in the constitution."

"So you'd abolish the Second Amendment?"

James paused to place his lunch order with the waiter.

"No," he said after the server walked away. "That would be political suicide. But I think there needs to be more checks and balances. Gun violence is out of control in this country. As a minimum, I'd introduce legislation requiring every gun purchase to be registered. But I think we need to go further than that. There should be a federal database carrying the ballistic fingerprint of every registered weapon. If someone intends to use their gun for legitimate purposes, they shouldn't be afraid to have it traceable for illegal use."

"That's another strong policy position," Emma said. "Do you think you can sell it to the public?"

"Everybody said the same thing about legalizing drugs. But the American people are slowly coming around. I think when I've built up a bit more political capital, we can introduce some of these new policies."

Emma looked at James over her heavy mascara.

"You know, a lot of my friends think you want to legalize drugs because you're endorsing their use. Just to set the record straight —*are* you?"

"Quite the opposite," James said. "I'm actually a bit of a square. I've never even experimented with marijuana."

"Not even in college?"

"Not even in college."

Emma's phone buzzed again, and she pulled it out of her purse to look at the display. James noticed her breathing became uneven as she furrowed her eyebrows reading the message.

"I can't picture you as a *prude*," Emma said, placing her elbows on the table, revealing her cleavage. James instinctively glanced downward, then immediately back up.

Emma slid her foot forward under the table and caressed James' leg with her toe.

"You must have experimented with *other* things in college?"

James's expression suddenly turned serious.

"Emma," he said, withdrawing his foot. "I think maybe you've got the wrong idea about me. I'm sorry if you thought this was anything other than a professional courtesy."

He motioned to the server to bring the check.

"I think it's time we ended this. I don't want you coming into the campaign office anymore. We won't be needing your services any longer."

The server brought the restaurant bill, and James slipped a hundred dollar bill in the check-fold. As he stood and walked toward his Secret Service detail waiting by the front door, he noticed an unusual expression on the face of a lone diner sitting at a nearby table. The man sneered and nodded as James passed by.

Good Lord, James thought. *What now?*

43

Marshall Residence

May 16, 9:00 a.m.

The following morning, James slept in, feeling more tired than usual. When he woke up, Julie wasn't in bed, so he put on his bathrobe and walked downstairs. There was a faint phosphorescent light coming from the kitchen, but no sign of activity. He tiptoed toward the light, hoping to surprise his wife with a gentle hug. But when he entered the room, Julie was standing by the island, looking straight at him. Her face was drained of color and and locked in a stony expression as if she'd just seen a ghost.

"Honey," James said, leaning in to hold her. "Is everything okay—"

Julie flinched at his touch and nodded toward the island, where a tablet lay face-up on the counter. A newspaper story displayed on the screen, with a picture of Emma and James at the Capitol Grille.

Congressman Caught With Intern, the headline read.

James groaned.

"What the hell is *that*?" Julie said, crossing her arms.

"It's not what you think—"

"You're staring at her *tits*, for Christ's sake!" Julie screamed. "While she's *fondling* you under the table!"

James stepped back and shook his head in shock.

"Honey, it was a setup. I was caught completely off guard. There's nothing...I have absolutely no interest—"

"That's not what it *looks* like," Julie said, nodding toward the tablet.

James looked at the photo and sighed.

"I'm sorry. I shouldn't have looked...it was an impulse reaction when she leaned over the table—"

"Was it an impulse reaction to take a scantily-clad intern to lunch?"

"She wasn't dressed like that when I took her," James backpedaled. He could hear himself digging a deeper hole the more he talked. "She works in the campaign office and wanted help preparing for a college debate tournament. It was raining, and she took off her wet sweater—"

"To reveal her perky breasts?"

James closed his eyes and shook his head. He knew he'd crossed the line, even if he *had* cut off the engagement when the situation began to spiral out of control.

"You're right. I shouldn't have even gotten myself into this situation. I'm sorry, honey. I swear to you—there's nothing going on."

He nodded toward the news photo.

"I was guilty of being led on, in an obvious case of entrapment. You know me. This isn't the man you married."

Julie stood ram-straight, searching James's face for any sign of deception, darting from one eye to another. After a few seconds, James leaned in and put his arms around her.

"Baby, I'm so sorry you had to see this. I'll never make a mistake like this again. You're the only one I ever wanted..."

Julie pulled her head back and looked at James with tears streaming down her cheeks.

"Do you still find me attractive? I mean, I can't compete with that..."

James placed his hands beside her waist and hoisted her onto the island.

"Are you kidding me?" he said, with a big grin. "You're more attractive than ever. No one can hold a candle to you."

He leaned in and kissed Julie passionately. She spread her legs as James pressed against her.

Suddenly, Julie grabbed James's hair and pulled his head back.

"If I ever catch you even *glancing* at another woman—" she threatened.

"You won't. Now shut up and let me make love to you."

44

Longworth Building, Congressional Office

May 17, 9:00 a.m.

James leaned back in his office chair, rubbing his forehead as he thought through the previous days' events. He hadn't slept well worrying about how the restaurant exposé would affect his public image. He couldn't believe he'd been stupid enough to have fallen for such an obvious trap. As he pinched his tired eyes, he heard a light tap on his door.

"Come in," he sighed.

"Rough night?" Nick asked, poking his head in the door.

"You could say that," James said, motioning for Nick to come in.

He held up a copy of the newspaper, with the restaurant picture prominently displayed on the front page.

"Not exactly the way you want your wife to find out about these things," James said.

"Is there something I should know about?" Nick asked, taking a seat on the couch.

James shook his head.

"No. It was an unfortunate mistake. Nothing happened beyond what you see in the photo. She obviously had a hidden agenda. I dismissed Emma as soon I realized she wanted something more than a professional relationship."

Nick picked up the paper and studied the photo.

"The optics are bad—"

"It can't be any worse than what I had to deal with yesterday with my wife."

"I can imagine," Nick said. "Is everything patched up?"

"I think so," James nodded, then he paused. "So, how do we get ahead of this?"

"I think you have to come clean and be honest about what happened. Let's get you a press interview lined up asap—preferably *today*. Just tell them it was a professional meeting that went somewhere you didn't want. Explain that nothing further happened and that you're no longer working together."

James paused for a moment and nodded.

"Do you think this will affect our campaign?"

Nick shook his head.

"Clinton survived a far worse scandal and managed to serve out his Presidency. Yours was a minor indiscretion that will soon be forgotten. The important thing is to have your wife by your side at future appearances. Once the public sees that she's fine with it, they'll be fine with it."

"How are our numbers holding up?" James asked, still worried about a possible ripple effect.

Nick opened his portfolio and handed James a graph with three lines on it. One dotted line starting at zero was labeled 'Marshall'. Another dotted line labeled 'Channing' started 500 points higher, but was climbing more slowly. Across the top, a solid line simply labeled 2,383 ran straight across the page.

"As you can see," Nick said, "you've been climbing at a faster pace than Channing since the Iowa caucus. With almost half the primaries behind us, you're scheduled to pass him in another few weeks."

James eyeballed the two dotted lines and drew a mental picture of where they'd cross.

"That crossover point is looking awfully close to the 'need to win' number. He's still carrying the majority of the superdelegates going into the convention. I'm not sure there'll be enough to assure the win."

Nick leaned back and rested his arm on the sofa.

"Remember, those superdelegates are still officially unpledged. They've been slowly swinging to your side over the past few weeks. If you keep racking up decisive wins in the primaries, most of the delegates will come around by the convention. They won't be able to vote against you in good conscience when they see the voting public has clearly sided with you."

"I hope you're right, Nick," James said, looking at the graph. "I hate leaving the final result until the last second."

"Just keep your eye on the prize the rest of the way," Nick said. "And *off* young interns' breasts."

45

Spectrum Center, Charlotte, North Carolina

July 26, 6:00 p.m.

The Spectrum Center was charged with excitement as the Democratic National Committee Chairwoman took the stage. After three days of speeches by prominent party politicians at the party's national convention, it was time to tabulate the final vote count. Although the pledged delegate numbers from the state primaries and caucuses were already known, the final superdelegate votes were still to be revealed by live roll call.

Although James had a commanding lead among the pledged delegates, the majority of the superdelegates were still publicly endorsing Senator Channing, giving the senator a small lead of fifty points coming into the convention. Among political pundits and news analysts, there was rampant speculation about how many superdelegates might switch their votes at the last second to side with the people's favorite.

Normally, they sided with the candidate they believed had the best chance of winning the general election against the incumbent President. But even though most polls showed James having a stronger chance than Channing in the final run-off, most superdelegates were still throwing their support behind the senior senator.

Many analysts believed this was a result of secret backroom deals between party leaders, who thought that Congressman Marshall was wrenching the party away from its traditional values. Still, nobody wanted to end up on the losing side, as the new President would command tremendous power in setting the new legislative agenda. All House seats, and one-third of the Senate seats were up for reelection in November, and there was considerable fear among delegates that if they sided with the wrong candidate, they could lose their seats in a popular backlash.

On the arena floor, thousands of supporters from both sides stood shoulder-to-shoulder pumping placards for their favorite candidate, loudly chanting their names and campaign slogans. Periodically, a shoving match would break out between the opposing camps, and security would rush in to break the two sides apart. There'd been escalating discussion in the news media about the unfairness of the superdelegate system, and a motion was tabled by the Marshall camp to disqualify their block of votes ahead of the convention, but the DNC voted it down with a strong majority.

As the DNC Chairwoman stepped up to the mic, she was greeted with an equally loud chorus of cheers and boos. Whatever happened at the convention, it would be difficult to repair the friction between the two sides and present a unified front against President Templeton.

"Good evening Democrats," she yelled over the bedlam, "and good evening America!"

The balance of cheers and hoots tilted only slightly more in a positive direction.

"After many months of debates and state primaries, we've finally reached the moment of truth, where your elected delegates will choose our new leader."

The dissonant cry in the arena escalated to a fever pitch. Even though both the pledged and unpledged delegates were elected, the chairwoman chose to ignore the fact that only *some* were sworn to cast their vote for the nominee based on ballots cast by the voting public.

"We will tabulate the final delegate votes for each state by verbal roll call," she continued. "The presentation will be by alphabetical order. The first state to report is Alabama." The chairwoman paused as she looked out over the delegations. "Alabama—how do you vote?"

As each state representative announced their allocation of votes, a large screen behind the chairwoman kept a running total. Everyone in the room knew the magic number was 2,383—representing a simple majority of the total delegate count, including superdelegates. The final superdelegate numbers would be revealed in the combined count presented by each speaker.

As the state representatives revealed their vote allocations amid much fanfare, James and Maggie sat with their families in a private booth in the stands. On James's lap lay a pad of paper. He'd drawn a line down the center of the page, with the number of preliminary superdelegate endorsements for each state on opposing sides. As the final state numbers were revealed, James crossed out the provisional numbers and penciled in the updated count.

Julie watched her husband keep track of the accumulating totals while his left knee nervously bumped up and down.

"How are we doing?" she asked after the first five states had reported.

"Only a few defections so far," James said, referring to the number of superdelegates who'd switched their support to his side. "We've captured eleven swing votes. It's going to be close."

Heath was sitting on the other side of James, doing his own math. He knew that including the US territories and the District of Columbia, there were a total of fifty-seven districts to report.

"You only need forty more, Dad," he said. "With less than ten percent reported, it's looking good."

James smiled at Heath. He was happy his son was taking such a strong interest in the electoral process. It was a nice bonding moment for the two of them.

"Thanks, son," he said, trying to sound confident. But underneath, his arm muscles were twitching involuntarily, and his stomach was churning.

As the numbers continued to roll in, Julie noticed James's hand was shaking, and his writing was becoming increasingly erratic.

"There's no need for *two* of you to be killing yourselves," she said, taking the pencil from James's hand. "Why don't you let Heath keep track while you listen to the proceedings? You're missing all the action."

She pointed to the giant video monitor beside the stage, showing his live image.

"See? You look all tense and distracted. Show your people some love!"

James looked at Julie and sighed. She was right. He was torturing himself focusing on the end result and not enjoying this once-in-a-lifetime moment. He sat back and clasped Julie's hand, exhaling deeply.

As the roll call continued moving through the states, many territories added personal commentary along with their vote count. When the call reached James's home state of Maryland, the speaker was especially complimentary.

"The state of Maryland casts thirty-three votes for Senator Channing," the speaker announced, "and *sixty-two* votes for the champion of the people, the protector of American freedoms, and the savior of our planet, Congressman James Marshall!"

Julie squeezed James's hand as he proudly beamed over the huge monitor.

"Isn't this more fun than doing arithmetic?" she whispered in James's ear.

James squeezed Julie's hand three times.

When it came down to the final state of Wyoming, the tally on the board showed only seven votes separating the two candidates. James couldn't help glancing down at Heath's notes. The state had a total of eighteen delegates up for grabs, but fourteen were already locked in from the primary.

Heath scribbled some quick numbers. James had secured ten of the pledged delegates to Channing's four from the state primary. That brought the new accumulated count to 2,382 to 2,379. Unbelievably, it had come down to the final four unpledged superdelegates. James needed all four to win.

Heath looked up at his father.

"This is it, Dad," he said.

As the Wyoming representative stepped up to the floor mic, Julie squeezed James's hand so tightly his fingertips started to turn blue.

"Madam Chairwoman," the speaker began, "The great state of Wyoming is the state of many firsts. The first national park, the first state to guarantee women the right to vote, and the first state to elect a woman governor. Tonight, we are proud to be the last state to cast our votes."

She paused as the entire room held its collective breath.

"For Senator Channing, we cast—"

Someone stepped up behind the speaker and tapped her on the shoulder. James could see from the monitor that it was Governor Harper, the candidate who'd thrown his support behind Senator Channing after losing the November debate. The speaker stepped away from the mic and turned to confer privately with the governor. Their silent conversation was displayed to the entire arena on the giant monitor at the front of the stage. After what felt like an eternity, she nodded her head and seemed to mouth the words 'are you sure' to the governor. The governor nodded, and the speaker scribbled something on a notepad, then she lifted the microphone up to her mouth.

"The state of Wyoming," she announced, "casts *four* votes for Senator Channing—"

Somebody in the arena screamed as she realized what was happening.

"...and *fourteen* votes," the speaker said, "for the next President of the United States—Congressman James Marshall!"

The display on the vote board toggled over to 2,383 for Congressman Marshall, as the entire arena exploded in pandemonium. James's supporters jumped and cheered, pumping their placards deliriously. The camera cut to a live feed of James, who was holding his wife in a tight embrace, while his son and daughter leaned over, swinging their arms around their parents.

After a few seconds, everyone in the booth stood up, and James and Maggie waved and blew kisses to their followers.

Half an hour later, after Senator Channing finished his concession speech, the DNC Chairwoman returned to the stage to introduce the winning ticket to their waiting fans.

"Time for you to address your adoring subjects," Julie said, poking James in the side.

"Not without my running mate," he said, grabbing Julie's hand and leading his family toward the stage.

"I thought *Maggie* was your running mate," Julie said.

James looked at his wife and smiled.

"I told you there was no other woman for me, didn't I?"

46

Marshall Campaign Office

August 1, 9:00 a.m.

A week after securing the presidential nomination at the Democratic National Convention, James walked into his campaign office with Maggie Castillo by his side. As soon as the staff saw the couple, they rose out of their seats in a standing ovation. While James paused to soak up the applause, he noticed Heath standing at the back of the room, joining in the celebration with Nick. He held up his hand to settle the group, then turned toward Maggie.

"Good morning, everybody," he said. "As you probably noticed, we've added a new member to our team. Governor Castillo brings a wealth of experience to our ticket, and I'm proud to have her as my running mate."

James paused, as he looked around the room.

"I want to thank all of you for your hard work these past few months. Without you, none of this would have been possible, and the two of us are deeply grateful for all your dedicated effort. But now the really hard part begins, as we face a new, more powerful opponent. If we truly want to make a difference, we have to capture the big prize three months from now. So keep making those calls, keep organizing those rallies, and keep collecting those campaign contributions. Because now it's going to get *really* interesting."

As the office broke into spontaneous chants of *EM-power*, James turned to Maggie.

"Meg, do you mind if I take a couple of minutes to chat with my son before we get started?"

"Of course not. Just send me the signal when you're ready. I'll use the time to get to know your campaign team."

"It's *our* campaign team now," James smiled. "Join me in the back office in ten minutes?"

"Deal."

James walked to the back of the room toward Nick and Heath. He hadn't seen his chief of staff since the last day of the convention, and he wanted to thank him personally.

"Nick," he said, "I can't thank you enough. Can you believe how far we've come? It seems like only yesterday when we were kidding about your title." James turned and motioned toward the busy office staff. "Now you've got over a *hundred* people to boss around."

"I'm just happy to be part of history," Nick said. "I wouldn't want to be anywhere else."

James turned to Heath, who was standing beside Nick wearing a proud smile.

"I'm a little surprised to see *you* here today, Heath. I thought you and Olivia were heading to California to visit her family before the fall semester resumes?"

"I was going to, but after the convention, I realized how much I want to help your campaign. I've actually been thinking about it for quite a while. After the close call in Charlotte, I figure one extra helping hand could make the difference between winning and losing."

"Good point," James nodded. "Besides, I kind of like the idea of you staying close to the fold, where my security team can keep a closer eye on you. At least until September. I don't want this to interfere with your studies."

"Great," Heath said. "How can I get started?"

James looked at Nick then back toward his son.

"I was going to do a little strategizing with Nick and Maggie in preparation for the presidential debate in a few weeks. Would you like to join us? I could use another fresh perspective."

Heath's eyes widened in excitement.

"Really, Dad? I'd love to!"

James motioned to Maggie, and they all went into the back office.

"Maggie," James said, "you remember my son, Heath? He's asked to join our campaign team, and I thought the best way to bring him up to speed is for him to be a fly on the wall during our strategizing. Do you mind if he sits in for a few minutes?"

"Of course not," Maggie said, extending her hand. "Welcome to the team, Heath."

"Where should we start?" James said, turning toward Nick. "I thought maybe we could begin by listing Templeton's policy positions on the whiteboard to compare our strengths and weaknesses."

Nick picked up the TV remote control and clicked on the office monitor.

"Unfortunately, Templeton's already jumped the gun on us. He's wasted no time starting attack ads on the major networks. This will give you a good idea of where he thinks we're weakest."

Nick tapped the remote, and a video clip started to run.

Congressman Marshall thinks he's the best candidate to lead our country, the clip began, showing an empty hall in the congressional building, with the sound of crickets chirping in the background.

Yet he barely has two years' experience as a junior congressman, where his biggest accomplishment is voting yes to a failed drug legalization bill.

The camera cut to a scene of vagrants smoking pot on a busy downtown street.

We've made great strides recovering from the last economic recession, the clip continued, showing an image of the President signing bills in the Oval Office, surrounded by senior members of Congress. *Unemployment rates are at the lowest levels in four years, and economic growth is back on track. Now is not the time to experiment with an unproven leader.*

The clip cut to images of North Korean missiles rising into the sky and terrorist bombs exploding in European cities.

We live in precarious times, with threats from many sides. This November, vote to protect America's values and protect America's future— reelect President William Templeton. Paid for by the—

Nick clicked the remote and turned off the TV.

"That's what we're up against," Nick said, turning to James and Maggie. "At least according to the other side."

James nodded.

"That's pretty much what I expected. He's hitting on his biggest perceived strengths: the economy, foreign policy, and his leadership experience."

"It's only a matter of time before his next ad disparages your healthcare and energy plans," Nick said. "We need to hit back hard on his failed climate change and drug enforcement policies—"

"You know I'm not a fan of negative ads, Nick," James said. "That's fine for the other guy, but I think we need to stand on our own merits. We're bringing new ideas to the table that the American public is beginning to rally around. Let's focus on our strengths, not the other guy's weaknesses."

James swung his chair around to Maggie.

"What do you think, Meg? What kind of ads have you found effective in the gubernatorial races?"

"I'm with James on this one," Maggie nodded. "Negative ads work, but they send the wrong message. If we go negative, it makes us look weak and defensive. Let's champion our strengths and show the public how our policies will improve their standard of living."

"Alright then," James said, turning to the whiteboard. "Let's identify our differences and highlight our strengths." James picked up a marker and handed it to Heath. "Would you like to do the honors, Heath?"

"Um...okay," Heath said, hesitating. "What exactly do you want me to do?"

"Draw a line down the center of the board and write Templeton at the top of the left column and M-C at the top of the right. As we go through the issues, just record our respective positions. If you've got some ideas on where you think we can improve our position, feel free to speak up any time."

"Let start with drug enforcement," Maggie said. "Since this is an area where Templeton clearly thinks he has an advantage."

"Good idea," James said. "Templeton's approach is all about longer sentences and increased enforcement around the current criminal justice system. But it's been proven not to work. He's just throwing away money on ineffective interdiction, putting more non-violent users in jail, and building a worldwide crime syndicate."

"Whereas drug legalization has been proven to reduce overdoses, HIV infections, and drug-related gang activity," Maggie said, finishing James's sentence. "And we can *prove* this from the experience with marijuana decriminalization in my state. This is an area where the facts speak for themselves."

"I agree," James said, nodding at Heath as his son summarized the points on the board.

"What about foreign policy?" Nick said. "Based on Templeton's ad, this is another area he's going to suggest our side is lacking."

"On the positive side," Maggie said, "you've got to give him credit for keeping America relatively safe during his term as President. While Europe and the rest of the world have suffered through numerous terrorist attacks, we haven't had a single foreign-sponsored attack since 9/11."

"True," James said, leaning back in his chair. "But you could also say he's been asleep at the wheel while our enemies have been rapidly militarizing and threatening neighboring countries. He did nothing to stop Russia from annexing Crimea or North Korea from lobbing repeated test missiles in our direction."

Maggie nodded.

"I think your plan to isolate them via trade policies is bold, but it's not without risks. We can't afford to alienate the one buffer keeping North Korea from launching an all-out war. If China perceives a U.S. trade embargo as a threat to their economic health or sovereignty, that'll put two million more soldiers across the DMZ."

James nodded, pondering Maggie's comments. He was impressed with her breadth of knowledge on foreign policy, and she wasn't pulling any punches. She'd be an invaluable advisor and second-in-command.

"Good points, Maggie," he said. "I think we need to tighten our policy on this subject. I don't want to be caught with my pants down at the first debate."

James turned to his son, who was standing quietly by the whiteboard.

"What do *you* think, Heath? Have you been keeping abreast of these geopolitical developments? There must be a lot of discussion on campus about the North Korean standoff."

Heath paused for a moment, then nodded.

"It's a tough situation, Dad. If we provoke North Korea too strongly, they could annihilate twenty million South Koreans within seconds. On the other hand, if we do nothing, it won't be long before they have the capability to send nuclear missiles all the way to the U.S. mainland."

Heath's eyes darted between his father and Maggie as he pondered the issue.

"What if you implemented a *phased* trade embargo? See if the Chinese would be willing to cut off fuel supplies and other critical logistic support as long as Kim refuses to dismantle his nuclear program. If they *are*, we might be able to starve him into submission. Our navy can protect other non-essential material getting in or out of the country via a blockade. If the Chinese continue to be uncooperative, then we can begin turning the screws on them. Eventually, one or the other side will realize it's a no-win scenario."

James stared at Heath for a long moment, then glanced toward Maggie.

"We might be looking at our future national security advisor," he joked. "That's very impressive thinking, son. Get that up on the board. That's something we can sink our teeth into."

For the next two hours, the four of them moved through the remaining issues, bouncing ideas back and forth about how they could differentiate their message from President Templeton's. By the end of the meeting, James was satisfied that they'd established a strong enough platform to present a compelling alternative. Equally important, he felt that he'd chosen a strong and insightful leader in Maggie Castillo as his running mate. And he was glad to have Heath back in the fold, where he could use him as a sounding board while keeping a closer eye on him.

James turned his wrist to look at his watch.

"It's been a productive morning," he said. "I think we've got more than enough material to prepare for the debates. What do you think, Maggie? Will this help in the VP debate?"

"Definitely. Let's compare notes in another week and to make sure we're aligned on the key talking points. But I'm feeling good."

"Nick," James said, turning to his chief of staff, "can you talk to our ad agency? Have them put together some TV spots for our review. I want to be crystal clear in our messaging. We'll focus on one issue per ad. The line of separation between us and the other guys should be as clear as that solid line on the board."

"On it, boss," Nick said.

"And you, young man," James said, turning toward his son. "I'm thrilled that you've joined our campaign team. Keep contributing like that, and you may be President *yourself* some day!"

47

Meany Hall, University of Washington, Seattle

September 26, 6:00 p.m.

James stood behind his lectern, assessing the audience for the first cross-party presidential debate. Although the theater at the University of Washington was more intimate than the venues used for the Democratic presidential debates, the television audience for tonight's event was twice as large, with almost a hundred million viewers tuning in to watch. The news media had built up the debate as a David vs. Goliath battle between ideological extremes. To most political pundits, President Templeton represented the far right, with Congressman Marshall symbolizing the radical left. For the first time in generations, many believed the ideological future of the United States lay in the balance.

James swallowed hard as he realized what was at stake.

The theater hushed as Fox News Anchor Chris Wallace began to explain the debate rules. Although Fox News leaned to the right on the political spectrum, James felt any questioning bias would be canceled out by the left-leaning audience. Washington was a perennially blue state, and most of the attendees had been chosen by lottery from the host university's students and faculty. He'd be surrounded by a mostly supportive crowd.

"Tonight's debate will be divided into six segments of fifteen minutes each," Wallace stated, "with each segment dedicated to one issue. Each candidate will be allotted two minutes to speak on each issue, followed by ten minutes of open discussion. Based on a coin toss, President Templeton will speak first."

The moderator paused, then looked up at the stage.

"President Templeton, there's been much heated debate in this country in recent years on the subject of immigration. On the one side, many people argue that the influx of foreigners into the United States has stolen jobs from native-born Americans and has eroded the country's traditional values. On the other side, proponents argue that immigration brings much-needed diversity and facilitates economic growth. If you win a second term, how would you manage this contentious issue?"

"Thank you, Chris," the President responded, "for raising this important question. For more than two centuries, America has been a beacon of light for people looking to improve their lives, and for two centuries, America has welcomed immigrants from other countries onto its shores."

Templeton smiled and paused for the viewers to absorb his sound bite.

"But we live in a different world, with a new set of challenges. Escalating ideological wars and advanced technology have made it far too easy for disaffected newcomers to disrupt our hard-fought freedoms and security. The last successful terrorist attack on American soil was carried out by nineteen Islamic militants who should never have been allowed entry to the United States. We must be far more vigilant in protecting the citizens of this country from foreign threats. In my second term of office, I will introduce a bill that blocks entry into the United States from any citizen of a country that sponsors terrorism. As commander in chief, my number one priority is to keep the American people safe. We will not have another 9/11 on my watch."

"Congressman Marshall," Wallace said, "how do *you* plan to keep America safe?"

James looked up from some notes he'd scribbled and peered at the moderator.

"I think we're confusing two issues here, Chris—immigration and national security. The militants who attacked our country on 9/11 were not *immigrants*—they were holders of temporary visas. The United States had the capability then, and has the capability now, to identify and block suspicious travelers from crossing our borders. The 9/11 attacks occurred as a result of an intelligence agency miscommunication, which has been subsequently corrected. It is the careful oversight of these agencies that has kept America free from terrorism, not our immigration policies."

The audience politely applauded.

"But the President's right about *one* thing. America is indeed a beacon. It is a beacon for those who have the temerity and the skills to start a new life in a foreign land. Immigration has expanded our economy and created the largest peaceful melting pot of cultures in the world. Immigrants and their children founded forty percent of America's Fortune 500 companies. These companies generate over four trillion dollars worth of revenue—larger than the economies of all but the four largest countries in the world. Immigration makes our country *stronger*, not weaker."

The audience clapped more enthusiastically.

"I would start by expanding the current quota for new immigrants into the United States by twenty percent," James continued. "I would also pass the DREAM Act that paves a path to citizenship for the millions of undocumented immigrants who came to the U.S. as children—"

"Even from countries that patently sponsor terrorism?" President Templeton said, interrupting the positive crowd response. "What will keep your *melting pot* from becoming a boiling cauldron of inter-culture conflict and terrorism, as we've seen happen in France and Britain?"

James turned to address the President directly.

"A blanket blockade of immigration from select countries defeats the whole point of immigration. Which our own Immigration and Naturalization Act says is to permit the reunification of families, the admission of valuable skills to the US economy, the protection of qualified refugees, and the promotion of diversity. Many of the people seeking to leave these conflict-ridden states are exactly the kind of people who'll work hardest to create a positive future for themselves and the rest of the American public. Steve Jobs, who created the largest and wealthiest company in America, was himself the son of a Syrian political refugee—one of the countries on your terror watch list. If we followed your immigration policies, we'd be stifling one of the most powerful engines of economic and technological growth in the United States."

The high-tech-oriented audience from Seattle roared in approval.

"And your so-called *dream* act?" Templeton fumed. "By giving carte blanche citizenship to every illegal alien, you're encouraging every Mexican drug-dealer and jobless person to sneak across our border, putting an even greater strain on our welfare system."

James smiled as the President continued to dig himself a deeper hole.

"The DREAM Act focuses on giving citizenship rights to young people who simply came to the United States to be with their families," he said, looking at Templeton.

Then he turned to face the camera.

"Birth rates in the United States are now below the sustainable population level, and it's projected that within two generations there will be more seniors in this country than people of working age. We need young immigrants to sustain our economy and enable the United States to maintain its status as the largest wealth-creating country in the history of the world. You're making a critical error in judgment, Mr. President—immigrants are *makers*, not *takers*."

A hearty cheer from the audience drowned out President Templeton's attempt at rebuttal.

"Our time is up for this subject, gentlemen," the moderator said. "In keeping with your kitchen analogy, let's jump from the frying pan to the fire with another contentious issue: drug legalization. Congressman Marshall, you've proposed the full legalization of all drugs. Can you clarify the difference between decriminalization versus legalization, and how legalization will benefit the nation as a whole, not just the relatively small number of drug users?"

James smiled.

"Yes, Chris, this can be a confusing issue. In short, decriminalization removes crimes for the possession and use of illicit drugs. Legalization goes one step further, permitting their lawful use, as well as their manufacture and distribution. Decriminalization only solves *half* the problem, by permitting consumption but not controlling where the drugs are coming from. It strengthens the trafficking syndicates that are waging a bloody war on the streets of America and south of our border. The bottom line is that full legalization reduces drug overdoses, drug-induced infections, and drug-fueled organized crime, while generating taxes from the legitimate trade of psychoactive substances that can be used to help rehabilitate addicts—"

This time Templeton interrupted before the audience had a chance to respond.

"Congressman Marshall throws these statistics around like so much *salt*," he said, practically spitting out the words. "There is no evidence whatsoever that legalization reduces organized crime or drug usage rates. This is simply an irresponsible plan that will drag America into the dark ages of opium dens and hookah cafes. Even his own *running mate* was smart enough to hold the line at the decriminalization of marijuana."

James smiled as he scribbled some notes on his notepad, then he turned to the President.

"Marijuana represents only a small percentage of recreational drug use in America. Much of the impetus for decriminalizing this drug has been based on its proven medicinal pain-reduction properties. Nonetheless, the Colorado experience has already proven the economic and health benefits of legalization. Marijuana use is actually *down* among teens, and the state economy has improved faster than most others since pot use was legalized."

James turned to face the audience.

"We've seen how Portugal's extension of this program has produced the lowest incidence of fatal overdoses and the fewest cases of HIV and AIDS among drug users in the entire European Union. But if the President *really* wants to see the benefits of a progressive drug policy, he need look no further than our neighbors to the north. Just one hour's drive north of this location, the city of Vancouver, Canada, operates safe injection sites that have reduced overdose deaths and improved the average life expectancy of hard drug users by over ten years."

"So you'd transform our downtowns into magnets for drug users by spending public money injecting hard drugs *for* these addicts?" the President asked.

James shook his head at the President's ignorance. He looked into the camera with sympathetic eyes.

"The people who are charged with possession offenses are often those with mental-health issues, the poor, and those who can't control their addiction. This is not a criminal justice problem—it's a *social* justice problem."

The audience began clapping again.

"It's time to stop stigmatizing as criminals users who need our help. Current drug-repression policies are rooted in prejudices, unfounded fears, and closed-minded ideological hegemony. The war on drugs has clearly failed. It's time to free our people from the tyranny of oppressive drug policies and free our resources to where it can do the most help. There is only *one* candidate who has the vision and the courage to fix this broken system. As your next President, I will respect your right of expression, the sanctity of your bodies, and welcome everyone who comes to us for help."

As the crowd rose to their feet in a standing ovation, James glanced to his side. President Templeton was tearing up his speaking notes and glaring at the young congressman.

Maybe it wouldn't be so hard to topple the giant after all, James thought.

48

Rojas Villa, Charambira, Colombia

September 26, 9:00 p.m.

Carlos Rojas shifted uncomfortably on his sofa as he watched the post-debate political analysis on CNN. Most of the analysts were saying that Congressman Marshall had won the debate, making President Templeton look bumbling and coldhearted. Wolf Blitzer had even suggested that Marshall looked *presidential* behind the lectern. With just over a month until the general election and the two candidates running neck-and-neck in the polls, many people were saying the impossible was now within reach. The young congressman could very well capture the popular vote and lead the country in a radical new direction.

Rojas picked up the remote control and pressed it angrily to turn off the TV. His lieutenants looked at one another nervously, recognizing the gravity of the situation. They were less worried about the potential impact on their business than the consequences of their failure in stopping the candidate. They both noticed the conspicuous absence of Diego, who had mysteriously disappeared soon after the failed letter attack.

Rojas looked out his window as he pondered his options. After a few minutes of silence, he finally spoke.

"This candidate is one persistent son of a bitch. He has the gift of *La Tunda*. No matter what obstacles get put in his way, he seems to have a magical ability to defeat his adversaries."

"Maybe he's just been lucky so far," his bodyguard Tomas said. "It has to run out sometime, right, boss?"

The muscles in Rojas's jaw rippled as he stared at Tomas.

"Was it *luck* when he ambushed our *sicario* in the alley? Was it *luck* when he intercepted our poison package? Was it *luck* when he made the most powerful man in the world look like a fool?"

Rojas leaned back and exhaled deeply.

"This man is not *lucky*. He's smart, strong, and *careful*. And now he is making *us* the ones who look like fools. We're running out of time to remove this thorn in our side."

"What else can we do, don Carlos?" his lieutenant Miguel asked. "He's surrounded himself with Secret Service protection, and soon he'll be living in an impenetrable fortress. How can we stop him?"

Rojas looked out the window at the blackening sky.

"We must stop him *before* he gets to the White House," Rojas said. "We have one more ace in the hole. It's time to buy some insurance. We will hit him where he is weakest. And you two will take care of it personally."

Rojas removed his nickel-plated Beretta pistol from his waistband and placed it menacingly on the sofa beside him.

"I don't think I need to remind you what the consequences of failure are."

"No, don Carlos," Miguel said.

"It will be taken care of," Tomas nodded.

49

Georgetown University

November 5, 3:00 p.m.

One week before Election Day, the capital was bristling with the latest developments in the presidential race. President Templeton and Congressman Marshall were running neck-and-neck in the polls, and ads from both sides were ramping up the rhetoric about who would make the better commander in chief.

Receiving almost as much attention, were the close contests for House and Senate seats. Whoever won the Presidency would need a majority in both houses to have any chance at implementing his plans. James had campaigned tirelessly alongside the key swing candidates, and polls were projecting a near-tie in both legislative chambers. It was shaping up to be one of the closest and most exciting elections in decades.

At Georgetown University, the political debate had reached a new level of fervor. Everybody had an opinion about who was the best candidate, with heated arguments breaking out in dorm rooms and classrooms across campus. The fact that Congressman Marshall's son was a student at GU only heightened the debate, and the closer it got to Election Day, the more attention Heath received. He tried to keep a low profile, but his pervasive security detail made him stand out all the more. On Friday afternoon, after classes ended for the day, he and Olivia strolled along the Jesuit Cemetery footpath toward their dorm rooms.

"You seem a little preoccupied today," Olivia said, noticing Heath's pensive mood.

"Sorry, Liv. It's this election craziness. It's the only thing anyone wants to talk about. I'm having a hard time finding any peace and quiet. Everybody wants a piece of me, whether it's the right-wing whack jobs who view me as their personal punching bag or the left-wing zealots who view me as some kind of savior."

Olivia glanced behind her, recognizing two serious-looking men in suits tracing their path.

"Well, you *have* acquired a dedicated following."

"No kidding," Heath said. "It's like I'm living in a fishbowl, and everybody's eyes are on me. I'm sorry if I haven't been myself lately. I'm just beginning to feel closed in."

As they crossed the lawn opposite Copley Hall, Olivia turned her head toward the river.

"How about we take a little break for some ice cream? You know, go to our favorite place down by The Harbour? You won't be as recognized there, at least."

"I dunno," Heath said, holding up. "Dad doesn't want me to stray too far off the campus grounds. He's paranoid about my safety, after the latest threats."

"How much trouble can you get into with these two goons looking over your shoulder? Let's live a little!"

Heath hesitated for a moment, then he smiled at Olivia.

"You're right. A little side excursion can't do us any harm. Thanks for being patient through all this, Liv."

"It's not *your* fault you just happen to be the son of the most polarizing political figure in this town in generations."

Heath stopped and looked at Olivia.

"Is *that* what you think of my father? I thought you were on board with his policies?"

"I am. But you have to admit, he's steering the country in some radical new directions. It's inevitable that *some* people are going to react negatively."

"Nobody makes meaningful change without ruffling a few feathers."

"You sound more and more like your father every day," Olivia laughed. "So what happens if your dad *wins*? Won't your fishbowl get even smaller? Will you move into the White House?"

The couple slowed up approaching the corner of 37th Street and Prospect, as the crosswalk counter counted down to zero.

"*God*, no!" Heath said. "Nothing will change, at least for me. I'm still going to live in residence here at GU, and you're still going to be my *first lady*. We'll just have a different security team following us around everywhere we go."

Olivia glanced behind her to see how far back the bodyguards were, then suddenly grabbed Heath's hand.

"Come on," she said, pulling Heath through the yellow light. "Let's live dangerously for a few hours."

As they ran laughing across the intersection, the two bodyguards pulled up on the other side of the street, motioning for Heath to wait for them. Within seconds, a gray panel van screeched to a stop beside Heath and Olivia, and the side door slid open. Two heavy-set swarthy men jumped out of the vehicle and pushed Olivia to the sidewalk, then they grabbed Heath's arms and pulled him into the van.

As Olivia looked up in shock from the sidewalk, she saw a frantic look on Heath's face as he held his hand up to his ear in a calling motion. Seconds later, just before the van disappeared around a corner, she saw Heath's cell phone flying out the side window onto the pavement.

PART III

TAKING ORBIT

50

Route 29, Georgetown

November 5, 3:30 p.m.

Heath awkwardly pulled himself to a sitting position on the floor of the panel van. After the two thugs dragged him into the van, they pulled a canvas bag over his head and bound his hands behind his back with plastic tie-strips. A few seconds later, he felt someone reach into his back pocket and remove his phone, followed by the sound of a window opening and closing. He had only a few moments to appraise his surroundings before everything went black. Along with the two goons, there was a driver, all of them appearing to be dark-skinned Latinos. The van had no rear seats or windows and was clad in bare steel on the sides and floor.

Whoever these guys were, Heath thought, they weren't fooling around.

"What do you *want* with me?" he yelled. "Where are you taking me?"

"Shut up!" someone directly across from him said with a heavy accent.

Heath could hear two men speaking Spanish from the front seats. Their accents were thick, not like the American or Mexican Spanish he was familiar with, and he had trouble following what they were saying from his limited high-school classes.

"*Toma a puente*," the man in the passenger seat said. Something about a bridge.

Heath could feel the van turn to the right, followed a few seconds later with the hollow echo sound of the wheels rolling over an elevated surface. With Heath's vision blacked out, his other senses were heightened. He could hear the familiar echo of the car's passage over the Potomac River below and the faint smell of salt from the tidal estuary.

The Francis Scott Key Bridge, he thought. *They're taking me south.*

He knew it was pointless to ask his captors what they wanted with him. There was only one possibility. After the repeated attempts on his father's life and his warnings to Heath to stay on campus, it had something to do with his presidential bid. His father had often mentioned how many people stood to lose if he made it to the White House. It was obvious to Heath that his abductors planned to use him as ransom to force his father to withdraw from the race or stop the passage of his laws.

Heath's memory flashed back to the image of Olivia lying helplessly on the sidewalk while he was thrown into the van. He knew she'd be torn up with guilt for trying to run away from his protection detail, and his heart raced thinking of her. The best thing he could do to help his loved ones and survive this ordeal was to remain calm. He took a few moments to breathe in and out deeply. At least the thick weave of the canvas bag was porous enough to give him some air, he thought.

Heath shuffled his hands trying to relieve the pressure of the tie-strips digging into his wrists and realized he still had one small advantage. His abductors had taken his phone and thrown it out the window, but they hadn't yet noticed his *watch*. The Apple Watch that

Olivia had given him on his last birthday had a GPS and cellular tracking feature. If he could hide it from his captors, he might have a chance to call for help. Even if he couldn't call, the location of his watch could be tracked using the Find My Phone feature on his iPhone.

But what if no one finds my phone? Heath thought. *Did Olivia see it thrown out the van window? Would someone else find it and bring it to the police?*

There were simply too many variables left open to chance, he thought. Heath knew he'd have to do everything in his power to save himself.

Suddenly, the van slowed down, then banked to the right and accelerated. The sound of the wheels under the thin metal floor indicated they were traveling at highway speed.

Now they're headed west.

It had only been a couple of minutes since the sound of the van traveling over the bridge stopped and they moved onto solid ground. Heath knew there were only two highways that close to the bridge. He strained to listen to the sounds from outside the van. He couldn't hear the familiar echo from the river. That meant that they hadn't turned north onto the George Washington Memorial Parkway, running adjacent to the river. They were on Highway 66.

Heath thought back to the many weekend road trips he and his family took in his youth. If he could trace their general direction by keeping track of the turns and timing of their route, he'd have a good idea where they were taking him. But it had been at least ten minutes since they'd picked him up and counting one-one-thousands wouldn't last very long. Then he remembered the watch on his wrist.

It has a stopwatch feature! he thought. *If I can just start it, I'll have a pretty accurate record of how far we've traveled.*

Soon after receiving the watch, he'd fumbled with learning how to use its various features but had only tried the stopwatch function a couple of times.

Do I tap the side button two or three times? Think, Heath!

He closed his eyes and tried to flash back to when he followed the online tutorial.

Press once to bring the utilities to the main screen, then press twice to enable the stopwatch function. Then press the big crown on the side to start the timer.

Okay—but I have to do this carefully, so the guard doesn't catch on to what I'm doing. If he notices that I'm fiddling with my watch, he'll throw that out the window too.

Heath pushed himself up against the sidewall of the truck and slowly moved his right thumb over the surface of the watch until he felt the side buttons. He pressed the small button once, then again twice quickly in succession. Then he pressed the crown until he felt it click.

Let's hope I remembered it right, he thought. *Now I just have to pray there aren't too many turns.*

For the next hour or so, the van stayed on the highway, moving at a constant speed. Eventually, it slowed and took an off ramp onto another road. Heath listened to pick up any clues to their location. The sound of the tires on the ground was more muted, indicating they were on a slower road. Now and then, he'd hear the sound of another car passing by them traveling in the other direction.

We've moved from a four-lane highway to a two-lane road, he thought.

After a few minutes, he heard the sound of the engine revving and his body weight shifted toward the back of the van.

Now we're climbing.

About twenty minutes later, he felt pressure building in his ears and the sound of the van reverberating from both sides of the road.

Higher elevation. A heavily forested road. We're going over the Appalachians into West Virginia. It's amazing how much you can sense just from your hearing, he thought.

They traveled another thirty minutes or so, then the van pulled over onto the gravel shoulder and stopped. The man in the passenger seat got out of the van and swung the side door open. He and the man in the rear compartment pulled Heath out of the van, and they carried him about twenty feet along the shoulder. Heath could smell the fresh scent of spruce trees and hear the sound of birds chirping in the forest.

Then he heard a short beep followed by the sound of a trunk door opening on a car. The two men lifted Heath up by his arms and dropped him into the trunk. He tried to keep his watch covered with his other hand, but one of the men reached in and pulled up his sleeve.

"*Que Demonios?*" he said.

Heath felt one of them hastily unfasten his watch, then the two men spoke in agitated Spanish for a few minutes.

"Make a sound, and we shoot you," the man from the back of the van eventually said, and the trunk door slammed shut.

Then the two men entered the car, one in the front seat and one in the rear. As the car drove off, Heath heard a cell phone ringing from the back seat. The man in the back seat answered the phone and began to speak in Spanish.

"*Si*," he said. "*Lo tenemos estamos en el parque.*" We have him. We are in the park.

Heath could hear another man's voice speaking in Spanish on the other side of the conversation. He pushed his ear to the backrest of the seat and struggled to make out what he was saying. It was muffled, but there was something about his tone that sounded vaguely familiar.

So this is an inside job, Heath thought. *I've got to find a way to contact my father.*

As the car swerved through the twisty mountain pass, Heath's mind began to wander to what his abductors planned to do with him. He knew they'd be using him for ransom, but beyond that, he didn't know if he'd ever see his loved ones again.

51

J. Edgar Hoover Building

November 5, 5:00 p.m.

James and Julie walked into the FBI interview room escorted by Agent Marino. Olivia was huddled in one corner, her eyes red from crying, with her arms wrapped around her legs propped up on the chair. Mike sat in the opposite corner, looking sheepish and sullen. Julie sat beside Olivia and put her arms around her shaking shoulders.

"I'm sorry, Mrs. Marshall," Olivia cried. "It's my fault this happened. It was my idea to steal Heath away from his bodyguard. If I hadn't—"

"Hush, Olivia," Julie said. "Don't be so hard on yourself. It's only natural—"

"Can you tell us what you saw?" James said, sitting on the other side of Olivia, placing his hand over hers.

"It all happened so fast. We'd just crossed the street when a van stopped in front of us. Two big guys came out and pulled Heath inside. They disappeared so quickly—"

"Did you get a good look at the men? What did they look like?" James asked.

"They just looked big. And dark-skinned."

"African-Americans?"

"No. Hispanic—but darker than most."

Agent Marino slid two pencil portraits across the table toward James and Julie

"Olivia already supplied our artist with a rough description. Do these men look familiar to either of you?"

James and Julie shook their heads.

"I've never seen them before," James said.

"Did Heath say anything before they took him away?" he asked Olivia.

"No, but he made a motion with his hand just before they closed the door. He held his hand up to his ear, like he wanted to call me or something."

James turned to Agent Marino.

"Have you tried tracing his phone?"

Marino pulled an iPhone with a cracked screen from his pocket and placed in on the table.

"We found this on the sidewalk where the van was last seen. Olivia said they threw it out the window before they turned the corner. Can you confirm this is your son's phone?"

James picked the phone up and clicked the home button. The passcode screen displayed four blank digits.

"I don't know his code," he said, looking inquisitively at Julie.

"Try 5484," Olivia said. "It's the phone digits for Livi."

James tapped the numbers onto the cracked glass, and the home screen appeared. He tapped the phone icon and the contacts list came up.

"It's Heath's phone alright," James said. "It showing his number assigned to the phone."

"May we hold the phone for a few days?" Marino said. "It's a longshot, but there might be something on it that might give us a clue as to who took him and where. Did Heath know anyone that meant him harm?"

James looked at Marino with a puzzled expression.

"Isn't it obvious what this is about?" He glared in Mike's direction. "They couldn't get to *me*, so they took the closest person they could get their hands on."

"Have you received any ransom demands?" Marino asked.

"Not yet, but I'm expecting one anytime. There's only one reason they would want him..."

James turned toward Julie and shook his head.

"I'm sorry, baby," he said, reaching out to hold her hand. "I should have dropped out when I had the chance—"

Julie looked at Mike.

"Did you notice the license plate?"

"I got a partial," Mike said. "Just the first three digits: T2T—"

"What's the protocol for tracking the van?" James asked Agent Marino. "Don't you guys use street cams and satellites for this sort of thing?"

Marino nodded.

"We've already accessed the street cams in the vicinity of the abduction to track the van's direction. We placed it heading west on Highway 66, then lost track of it."

"What about satellites?" James asked. "Can't you track it from the air?"

"It's been almost two hours. Highway 66 only runs for one hour from DC to its terminus. From there, they could have headed in any direction. We're still scanning, but there's a lot of gray vans on the highways in this area—"

James's phone suddenly rang, and he looked at the screen. It showed an unknown caller. He tapped the screen and held it up to his ear.

"Is this James Marshall?" a man with a Spanish accent asked on the line.

James tapped the speaker button and placed it on the table in front of Agent Marino.

"Yes, how can I help you?"

Agent Marino pulled a digital recorder out of his pocket and placed it beside James's phone.

"We have your son. If you want him back alive, withdraw from the presidential race immediately. If not, we will mail him back to you one piece at a time."

"Yes, I will comply," James said. "How can I arrange to have my son returned—"

"We will be in touch. We will look for your announcement shortly."

There was a click on the line followed by silence.

"*Hello? Hello?*" James said. "How will I know—"

Agent Marino held up his hand, indicating the line had gone dead.

"What now?" James said. "Can you trace the call? How can we arrange the swap—"

Marino reached over and picked up James's phone.

"First, we'll trace the number. But these guys look like they know what they're doing, so they're probably using a disposable burner phone. We've put out an all points bulletin to local police in the tri-state area. Our best chance is to locate the van with the indicated plate numbers."

James shook his head as he looked at Julie.

"Like you said. There's a lot of gray vans plying the roads of southern Virginia. They could be anywhere by now. It's obvious there's only one way to get my son back. I'll announce my withdrawal from the presidential race immediately."

Marino paused for a moment.

"You have every right to do so, Congressman," he said. "But you should know this will not guarantee you'll get your son back. In our experience, the odds of the hostage being returned are less than ten percent after the abductors get what they want. Honestly, I think your best bet is to stay the course and let us tap your phones so when they call again, we have a better chance to place their position. As long as you're still holding some bargaining chips, you've got a better chance to come out of this whole."

James paused to look at Julie and Olivia. Olivia looked back at him with pleading eyes. Julie simply nodded.

"Tell me how you'd like me to proceed, Agent Marino," James said. "You'll have all of my resources at your disposal."

He glanced toward Mike.

"Except my private security team. I won't be needing *their* services any longer."

52

Cranberry River Wilderness Area, West Virginia

November 5, 10:00 p.m.

Heath sat shivering on the dusty wood floor of a dark shipping container, rubbing his sore wrists. It had been many hours since his abductors switched getaway vehicles and thrown him in the trunk of the second car. Without his watch, it was impossible to know how much further they'd traveled, but the roads had grown increasingly twisty and rough, until they finally stopped somewhere near a river. The two men in the car then pulled him out of the trunk and dragged him to the container, where one of them released his tie-straps and canvas hood before locking him inside the metal crate.

He'd had only a few seconds to appraise his surroundings before the heavy steel doors enclosed him in pitch-black darkness. He noticed the property was heavily forested, with a small wooden shack positioned about fifty feet from a shallow river. Judging by the transition of roads in the final hour from paved to gravel to pot-holed dirt, he figured they were many miles from any town or adjacent property. The only other possibility for human habitation in the area might be the odd fly fisherman looking for a quiet spot to catch rainbow trout. Heath knew from his own experience camping with his family in the remote regions of the Appalachian mountains that the chances of crossing paths with another person in this part of the country were extremely small.

As his eyes adjusted to the darkness of his surroundings, Heath looked around. There was a small opening in the far corner of the bin near the ceiling, with vertical steel bars spaced six inches apart. It was dark outside, but Heath could see a few stars poking through the canopy of trees rustling in the cool evening breeze outside the window. He stood up and walked in the direction of the faint light, tripping over a plastic bucket resting on the floor. He picked it up and sniffed in the open end and grimaced. It smelled of stale urine and feces.

Great, he thought. *I guess this is going to be my bathroom while I'm stuck here.*

He carried the bucket to the end of the container where the small window was and upended it on the floor. Then he stepped up on the underside of the bucket and tried to peer out the window. It was still almost two feet above his head. He reached up and grasped two of the metal bars and pulled himself up, pressing his feet against the plywood walls for support. The only thing he could see was a dense thicket of trees and a thin sliver of the moon about forty-five degrees up and to his right. He closed his eyes and tried to remember when he last saw the celestial body. Two nights ago, he and Olivia had gone for an evening stroll through the Georgetown University Commons. She'd remarked how bright the moon was in the southwest sky.

Given the regular eastward trajectory of the moon, that means I'm looking to the south, he thought. *Which means the cabin is positioned to the west of me along a river flowing southwest. Which doesn't help me much, without my phone or watch. I have no idea where I am, other than somewhere in the mountain wilderness of West Virginia.*

As he strained his muscles to hold himself up by the opening, he turned his head and listened. The only sound he could hear was the soft gurgling of the river a hundred feet away and the occasional hoot-hoot sound of owls in the forest.

Heath's head fell forward as he slumped against the wall.

So this is going to be my home for the indefinite future, he thought. *A dark, fetid steel box, with no one to keep me company, save a few lonely owls. I wonder how long I'll have to stay here, or if I'll ever see the full light of day again.*

As he pondered his predicament, he heard the sound of steel bolts sliding on the outside of the container door. He scampered down off his stool and returned to his sitting position near the door. The doors swung open, and he squinted through the darkness to see the two men who'd thrown him into the container a few hours earlier. One of them pointed a handgun at him while the other held a paper bag in his hand. The man with the bag reached into the sack and threw three items onto the floor beside Heath: a sandwich wrapped in plastic, a bottle of water, and a roll of toilet paper.

Lava tus manos antes de comer, the man said, before closing the doors and bolting them shut. Don't forget to wash your hands before eating.

Heath scooped up the items and began unraveling the sandwich as he listened to the laughs of the two men fade off into the distance. He hadn't realized how hungry he was; it had been almost twelve hours since he'd eaten anything. As he bit into the stale sandwich, he noticed a trickle of foul liquid inching down the floor from the direction of the moonlit window. Quickly standing up, he shifted to the elevated side of the compartment.

Laugh while you can, assholes, he thought. *My Dad and I don't give up easily. We'll see who ends up with the dirtiest hands.*

53

Marshall Residence

November 6, 6:00 p.m.

J ames shifted uneasily on his living room sofa as he watched the
evening news. His son's abduction had been picked up by all
the news agencies and instantly gone viral. Analysts and
armchair detectives had begun speculating on the motivation for the
kidnapping and projecting how the sudden turn of events might
affect the presidential campaign. Most people believed it had something to do with the congressman's divisive campaign platform, and
social media was humming with conspiracy theories involving North
Korean leader Kim Jong-un, Big Oil, and disaffected doctors.

At least they're showing his captors' faces, James thought, as CNN
displayed the police sketches on the screen, asking the public to
contact the FBI with any tips.

His house, already surrounded by the ever-present Secret Service
detail, was now swarming with FBI agents eager to pounce on new

clues about his son's abductors. All of his phone lines had been tapped, as Agent Marino kept a close watch with his team from the adjacent study, ready to intercept any incoming calls. Julie had taken Brooke upstairs in an effort to keep their daughter insulated from the frightening lockdown. James hadn't heard from the kidnappers for almost twenty-four hours, and he'd become increasingly worried for Heath's safety.

His eyes narrowed as he saw Agent Marino pass by the living room.

"Are you *sure* this is the only way to deal with these kidnappers?" he asked. "I don't see why we can't just give them what they want. It seems so straight-forward, to do a simple trade—"

Marino entered the room and sat on an adjacent chair.

"You'd lose all your leverage if you dropped out of the presidential race. It's the only thing keeping you tethered to them. Once they get what they want, they have no reason to return your son. He's already seen them up close and probably has some idea where they've taken him. This is the best chance to see your son alive again."

James looked at the agent with a sickening feeling in his stomach. He was rapidly losing faith in law enforcement ever capturing the criminals. First Bree, then the attempts on his own life, and now Heath. In every case, they couldn't stop the bad guys from getting close to him and his loved ones.

Even the Secret Service, he thought. *Could they have saved Heath if they'd extended their coverage to the rest of his family?*

As he seethed over the way the Director had denied his request to include protection for his children, his cell phone suddenly vibrated atop the glass coffee table. The screen read Unknown Caller. He looked up at Agent Marino, who sat down beside him. Marino held up his right hand and slowly counted down with his fingers, as he motioned for his team to trace the call. When he gave the signal, James tapped the Answer button, then pressed the speaker button for everyone to hear.

"Hello?" he answered.

"Do you want to see your son alive again?" the caller said, with a Spanish accent.

"Of course I do," James said.

"Why are you stalling, then? We're not the kind of people you want to want to play games with, Congressman. If you want to see your son in one piece, you have twenty-four hours to meet our demands. After that, we will begin mailing his body parts back to you."

James looked at Agent Marino and shook his head, confused as to what he should say. Marino held his index finger horizontal and turned it in a circle, motioning for James to keep the caller on the line.

"Alright, I'll do it. I'll do anything. Just don't hurt my son—"

"You have twenty-four hours. This is your last warning."

The screen showed the call ended and James turned to Agent Marino. Marino looked at his assistant, who was peering at his computer screen while he spoke with the cellular operator.

"They identified the base tower," his assistant said. "But we only got a partial trace on the adjacent towers. There wasn't enough time to triangulate the power levels on all the receivers. But we've identified that it's coming from the Washington National Forest Preserve in West Virginia. We have it down to a five-mile radius."

James looked at Agent Marino hopefully.

"That's pretty good, right? You can send a team and close in on them from outside the circle."

"It's not quite that easy," Marino said, shaking his head. "That's a thirty-mile perimeter, encompassing almost a hundred heavily forested square miles. We simply don't have the manpower to cover a search zone that large. Plus, these guys know what they're doing. They're probably calling on the move, so we can't triangulate a fixed position."

Marino nodded to his assistant.

"Nonetheless, we'll send a helicopter team out right away to see if we can find anything suspicious."

James shook his head in frustration.

"So what now? Wait until they start sending pieces of my son back to me in the mail?"

"I'll position a team in the area we traced. We'll just have to wait for the next call and see if we can keep them on the line longer—"

"If there *is* a next call. What part of *last warning* didn't you understand?"

Julie had been listening from outside the room and sat down beside James.

"Brooke's sleeping," she said, squeezing her husband's hand. "Keep the faith, James. Our boy will come back."

As they rested their heads on each other's shoulder, the doorbell rang. Agent Marino motioned for James to stay seated, and he approached the door slowly. He looked through the peephole, then swung the door open. Olivia was standing on the front steps, escorted by a Secret Service agent.

""Olivia," Julie said, walking up to greet her. "Are you all right? What are you doing—"

"His watch!" Olivia said, breathlessly. "I was trying to make sense of the signal Heath sent before his captors closed the van door. He wasn't motioning for me to *call* him. It was his *left* hand he was holding up to his ear! He has an electronic watch on his left wrist!"

"Come in," Julie said, placing her arm around Olivia's shoulder, leading her to the living room. "This is Agent Marino with the FBI. Tell him everything you know."

"His Apple Watch," she said, darting her eyes between Agent Marino and Heath's parents. "I gave it to him as a gift on his last birthday. It can be traced via the onboard cellular and GPS chip. Maybe they didn't notice he was wearing it—"

Marino nodded as he listened to Olivia.

"GPS is more precise than cell tower triangulation for tracking a signal. If he's still wearing it, we can trace his location to within a few hundred feet. But it would have to be paired—"

"Yes," Olivia said. "We did it together after he unpacked the gift. Do you have his phone? We can do a trace using the Find My Phone feature."

James reached into his jacket pocket and pulled out the phone with a cracked screen. Agent Marino had returned it to him earlier in the day, and he'd kept it close knowing it was the last thing his son touched.

"Here," he said, placing the phone on the coffee table. "Show us how."

Olivia picked up the phone and pressed the home button, then quickly tapped in Heath's lock code. Then she swiped her finger across the screen and typed *Find My Phone* in the search box. A spinning compass appeared on the screen, followed by a satellite map with a glowing blue beacon.

"But we already know where his phone is—" James began.

Olivia shook her head as she tapped the bottom of the screen.

"He paired his devices. This app shows where *all* of his connected products are."

She tapped the link for Heath's Apple Watch, then spread her fingers over the satellite map to zoom in on his location.

"There! That's where his watch is! Near this building in this forested area—"

Marino took the phone from Olivia's hand and pinched his fingers over the screen to zoom the picture out. The beacon appeared close to the junction of highways 48 and 259.

"Billy," he said to his assistant. "Take this to the helicopter flight crew. I'm going to send a SWAT team to investigate. Proceed with extreme caution. We don't want to alert them to our presence."

"Will do."

Marino turned to James and Julie.

"Let's hope it's still attached to his wrist. We may have just caught a lucky break."

For the next hour and a half, James, Julie, and Olivia waited anxiously to hear back from the SWAT team. When Agent Mario's cell phone rang, they hugged each other hopefully.

"Yes?" Marino said, speaking into his phone. "Did you search the surrounding buildings and terrain? What about the adjacent properties? Did anyone see any sign of a gray van or anything suspicious? Keep two men on the ground, searching the area. I'll contact them as soon as we get another call."

Marino tapped his phone to end the call, then looked at James and Julie with a frown.

"They found the watch, but no sign of your son. It appears that his abductors threw the watch in a field when they noticed it. Unfortunately, they most likely have long since cleared from the area. But we're narrowing in. We'll find him, I promise you."

James looked at Julie and Olivia and pulled them close.

Stay strong, son, he thought. *We're coming for you.*

54

Washington National Forest, West Virginia

November 7, 9:00 p.m.

H eath stood atop the rancid waste bucket peering outside his container window. In the two days since he'd been locked in the holding cell, he'd filled his time plotting his escape. But his options were severely limited. He was surrounded on all sides by half-inch thick corrugated steel and a locked metal door. The only non-steel material in the box was the plywood floor, bolted to the subfloor with heavy screws.

He'd considered trying to overpower his captors when they visited his trailer twice a day with food provisions, but he knew it would be impossible with one of them training a gun on him at all times. His only chance of escape was through the wood floor. He'd tapped the entire length of the floor with his knuckles and using the hollow echo sounds, determined that the joists under the plywood were spaced one foot apart. If he could somehow wedge the plywood panels from the underlying structure, he might be able to dig a tunnel in the dirt and slip away under cover of darkness.

But what could he use to cut through the wood and create a wedge? He didn't have anything sharp enough to dig into the half-inch thick hardwood. The only thing that might work were the steel bars on the windows. If he could remove one, he might be able to use it as a chisel to chip away at the wood. His captors probably wouldn't notice one missing bar, since the opening was too thin for him to squeeze through. But how could he separate the bars that were welded to the window frame? He'd already tried to shake them loose with his hands, to no avail.

After much consideration, it finally hit him. He might be able to leverage them loose with a makeshift tourniquet. He unbuckled his leather belt and wrapped it around two adjacent bars, then knotted the open ends around one of his shoes. Then he slowly turned the shoe, tightening the belt around the bars. After hours of painstaking effort, he managed to bend one the bars enough to create a crack at one of the welding joints. Then he banged the bar with his shoe until it detached from the frame.

Wonderful, he thought, holding the crooked bar in his hands. *I just need to chisel away at the floor and tunnel myself out of this god-forsaken place. Now I know how those guys in the movie Great Escape must have felt. Except I don't have months to dig my tunnel. The presidential election is in only a few days. I won't be much good to these guys after that. I've got to work quickly.*

Heath set to work immediately, trying to cut a hole in the floor. Using the sole of his shoe as a hammer and the rough end of the steel bar as a chisel, he began chipping the wood away at the corner of one of the panels. He knew if he could get the bar under the panel and use it as a lever against the support joists, he might be able to wedge it free from the bolts.

The strategy worked better than he hoped. It didn't take long to dig a small hole in the board, and using his foot to exert extra pressure on the bar, he was able to lift the wood up a few inches. Every few seconds or so, he stopped and listened for the sound of approaching footsteps or voices. So far, his captors hadn't heard his clumsy burrowing sounds.

Heath reached into the small opening and scratched the earth with his fingers. It was soft and damp.

Good, he thought. *It's not frozen. I can use the bar as a pick and my shoe as a bucket to collect the dirt, then empty it outside my window. It'll take a while, but it looks doable.*

Thanks for showing me the way, Steve McQueen.

As he continued prying the plywood panel up from its fasteners, he heard the sound of voices approaching. He collected his bucket and placed it over the hole in the floor, then sat down near the door. Had his captors heard the unusual noises from inside the container and come to investigate? It was past his customary feeding time— why else would they be coming to see him?

As he crouched against the wall, he slipped the metal bar into the front of his pants. If he got a chance, he wouldn't hesitate to use it as a shiv.

Heath heard the outside latch lifting and the sound of bolts turning to unlock the door. Then one of the panels swung open, and the two thugs stood in the moonlight sneering at him.

"What do you *want* from me?" Heath shouted. "You'll never beat my father. After he becomes President, he'll hunt you down like the dirty rats you are!"

The men looked at one another and laughed.

"Your father will never be President," the man from the back of the van said. "Not as long as we still have pieces of you to trade."

The two men climbed into the back of the container and approached him menacingly. While one of them kept a pistol pointed in Heath's direction, the other one pulled out a long knife. Heath backed up slowly toward the back of the container. When he reached the back wall, he reached into his pants for the metal bar.

It's now or never, he thought. *I guess the bed and breakfast routine is over.*

He waited until the man with the gun got within three feet, then he placed his right foot against the back wall and thrust forward with all his strength. As he lunged toward the man, he swept his left arm in front of him, knocking the gun out of the man's hand, then plunged the metal bar as hard as he could toward his face. He missed the man's eye but opened a huge gash on his cheek. As the man hollered in pain, Heath made a mad dash for the open door. But just before he reached the exit, someone grabbed him by the ankles, and he fell face down.

Someone climbed on his back, pinning him to the floor using a knee on his spine. The other man held his legs down, yanking his hands behind his back. Heath had only a second to see the shiny glint of a metal object beside his head, before he felt a searing pain in his right ear. Seconds later, he felt a warm sticky feeling in his open ear canal.

The men climbed off him and threw a towel on the floor.

"Use this to stop the blood," one of the men said. "We need you alive for a few more days."

As Heath lay writhing in pain on the cold plywood floor, the door slammed shut, leaving him in agonizing darkness.

55

Marshall-Castillo Campaign Office

November 8, 9:00 a.m.

O n Election Day, the campaign office was quiet, except for a
few leftover staffers taking phone calls. Most of the campaign
team had moved downtown to the Willard-InterContinental Hotel to
prepare for the anticipated victory celebration. But the polls were still
too close to call, and Nick didn't want to leave anything to chance. He
knew many voters made up their minds on the last day, with final
impressions potentially making the difference between victory and
defeat in key swing states. He'd arranged a meeting with James and
Maggie to discuss last-minute strategy.

James sat in the back office gazing out the window, past his Secret
Service team and his new ever-present security minder, Agent
Marino. He could hear Nick and Maggie talking in the background,
but his mind was hundreds of miles away in West Virginia. His heart
was no longer in the presidential race, and he'd already decided to

step down regardless of the outcome as soon as Heath was safely returned.

"What do you think, James?" Nick said, pointing to some figures on the whiteboard. "Should we focus our efforts on advertising, media appearances, or factory visits on our final day?"

"What?" James said, snapping out of his fog. "I suppose...advertising has the best reach." He knew he didn't have the stomach for another public appearance. "Yes—let's step up the ads."

Maggie and Nick paused as they looked at James. It was obvious that his son's abduction was weighing heavily on his mind, and neither wanted to press him when he was in such a fragile mood.

"I'd be happy to step in for you, James," Maggie said. "If you need to take a little time..."

"That's much appreciated, Maggie. Sorry—I guess I've been a little preoccupied lately."

"We completely understand," Maggie said, placing her hand over James's. "How are Julie and Brooklyn holding up?"

"As well as can be expected, under the circumstances. We're trying to keep Brooke insulated from the situation. It's been pretty hard, with the FBI crawling all over the place."

"Have they made any progress finding Heath's captors?" Nick asked.

"Just a couple of false alarms. The van they took him in was last seen heading toward West Virginia. The FBI traced the last call to a wilderness area in the Appalachians, but they don't know if he's still there."

"So his abductors have made contact?"

"Yes," James nodded. "They're holding all the cards. We just have to wait for their next call—"

"What are their demands?" Nick asked.

"Same as before. They want me to withdraw from the presidential race. But their threats have grown more extreme, and now they have Heath for leverage—"

"Are you considering—"

James sighed and looked down.

"The FBI says his abductors will have no reason to return Heath if I capitulate. Besides, I can't do this to the American people at the eleventh hour. Nor to you, Maggie. I dragged you into this thing. I'd just be throwing you to the wolves at this late juncture—"

Maggie leaned forward and squeezed James's forearm.

"Don't worry about me, James," she said. "Nobody could have seen this coming. I'll land on my feet no matter how things turn out tonight. Everybody will understand if you want to be with your family in this time of need."

James looked at Maggie with soft eyes.

"Thanks, Maggie. Would you and Matías join Julie and me tonight to watch the election returns at my place? I'm a bit housebound with the FBI tapping all my phones."

"Of course, James. We'd be honored. I can't think of anything I'd enjoy more than celebrating our victory together."

James nodded, then looked at Nick.

"Nick, if you can coordinate things at the InterContinental, Maggie and I will come down to address the campaign team after the results are announced."

"Definitely," Nick said. "We'll be waiting for you. Have you got your acceptance speech finalized?"

"I do."

It just might not be what everybody's expecting, James thought.

56

K Street NW, Foggy Bottom

November 8, 1:00 p.m.

James stared out the window of his Secret Service escort vehicle, watching a light drizzle roll across the glass. As he watched the streetscape pass by in a blur, he wondered where Heath might be at this moment and what he was thinking. Surely he'd be afraid, not knowing what his captors planned to do with him. He must have figured out that his seizure had something to do with James's presidential bid, and that he was likely being used for ransom. But he couldn't know his father's intentions, or if his abductors would honor the terms of any trade. The more he thought about it, James felt increasingly boxed in, with only one viable exit.

His mind raced ahead, trying to piece together the clues to his son's abduction. The FBI had traced the accent of the caller to the Valle del Cauca region of Colombia, a known hub for cocaine production and distribution. If a drug cartel was behind this, he thought, they'd stop at nothing to protect their interests. James knew better than anyone what was at stake. If he successfully legalized cocaine use, its street price would plummet overnight, and every coca grower in South America would have easy access to the U.S. market. The handful of syndicates that currently controlled the illegal trade of the drug would be quickly marginalized.

James also knew the reputation of the Colombian cartels for brutality. He had no doubt about the legitimacy of their threats concerning Heath. Anyone who stood in their way was either bought off or eliminated. No one was immune from their reach. Whether it was the police, army, or high-level Justice officials, no one could compete with their vicious methods and unlimited supply of cash. Virtually everybody succumbed eventually, in one form or another.

Even the leading presidential contender in the most powerful country in the world.

James's breathing grew more and more labored as he pondered his predicament. The symbol of his murdered daughter, and the entire reason for his presidential bid, was about to win. Either he'd be forced to quit the race and give up his dream of making the streets safe from drug gangs—or his son would be killed and dismembered.

Agent Marino, who was sitting beside him in the back seat, turned his head, sensing James's distress.

"This must be hard for you, with so much going on right now," he said. "I know it must look like an impossible situation—"

"Damned if I do, and damned if I don't," James said. "Now it's down to the wire. The ironic thing is that just as I'm on the cusp of achieving everything I dreamed, I might lose everything I hold dear."

Marino's lips tightened as he looked at James.

"It might be hard to stomach, but the closer we get to the deadline, the more pressure they have to deal. If you win tonight, they'll be even more motivated to negotiate."

"Or *cut the cord*," James said. "Remember, they said there'd be no more warnings. I'm afraid in this case, winning might really mean losing. If they don't contact us again today, I only see one way out of this."

"With respect, congressman, I don't think you'd be serving your own or your son's interests if you were to quit. Besides, who's to say that if you dropped out of the race that your successor wouldn't pick up the baton and finish what you started? You've captured the imagination of the country with your ideas. The next candidate would be foolish to throw away all that accumulated political capital."

James smiled at the FBI agent.

"And what do *you* think, Agent Marino? As a law enforcement officer, I'm guessing you're not exactly a fan of the Marshall plan."

"It's hard to get behind the idea of pardoning the sins of ruthless criminals who've killed and poisoned so many Americans. But I have to admit, there's a certain logic to your proposal. I'm a fan of the free enterprise system, and I believe in the law of supply and demand. Your plan simply removes the artificial barriers driving up the price of drugs and limiting the competition to supply them. I just hope you're right that once the market opens up, we won't have a new epidemic of junkies flooding the streets."

"What about your job? Aren't you worried that if I remove the source of half the violent crime in this country that you'll be out of work?"

"A few of my friends at the DEA might be crying in their soup, but I'm pretty sure *my* job is safe. The world will always be filled with angry and greedy men. We still need cops to protect the rights of law-abiding citizens and hold those who don't respect our laws to account."

James looked outside again. The rain had stopped, and passersby had put away their umbrellas and pulled out their phones, checking messages.

"There's one thing I still don't understand," he said. "How did these guys get my private cell phone number anyway? My congressional office number is a matter of public record, but only a few close family members and associates know my mobile number."

Marino raised his eyebrows and shrugged.

"It's not hard to hack someone's private contact information these days. It might be as simple as someone lifting one of your acquaintance's phones while he wasn't looking and checking the contact list. Maybe they forced it from your son or got it from his phone before they threw it out the van."

"Maybe. But I can't even remember my own *wife's* cell number, with it always just one tap away. And his phone would have been locked if it was in his pocket—"

James's phone buzzed. He pulled it out of his coat and looked at the screen.

"Unknown caller?" Marino said.

"It says the White House."

"That's *one* number you don't easily forget."

James tapped the screen and held the phone up to his ear.

"James," a familiar voice on the line said. "It's President Templeton. I just wanted to call and tell you how sorry I am to hear about your son. If there's anything you need, please don't hesitate to let me know. I'm prepared to place the full resources of the federal government at your disposal to help bring him back alive."

"Thank you, Mr. President," James said. "But I've got a very determined FBI agent sitting beside me who's already doing everything possible to find him."

"Well, please let me know if there's anything else you need. And good luck tonight."

"And to you, Mr. President. May the best man win. One way or the other, I'm sure we'll be talking again later this evening."

"Yes, I suppose we will."

"Goodbye, Mr. President."

James placed his phone back in his pocket and stared out the window.

Maybe there'll be no winners tonight, he thought.

57

Marshall Residence

November 8, 6:30 p.m.

On election night, the Marshalls and Castillos rested uneasily in James's living room, watching the returns on television. Adding to the drama of the year-long presidential race coming to a close, everybody was on edge awaiting news about Heath. While the FBI team waited in the adjoining room for another call from his captors, the Secret Service locked down the residence. Nobody wanted to take any chances with so many high-profile targets under one roof.

Wolf Blitzer had announced the first polls were closing, and the electoral map was starting to fill in with the familiar colors of the U.S. political quilt. The analysts were projecting a close race down to the wire, with the outcome depending on a few key swing states. Of equal importance, were the four hundred plus congressional seats up for grabs. Whichever party won the Presidency would also need a majority in the House of Representatives and the Senate if they hoped to have any chance at advancing their legislative agenda. The Republicans had gone into the election with a narrow lead in both houses, but it was widely expected that the party that won the Presidency would pick up many new seats on the coattails of the more popular candidate.

Shown beside the electoral map on the large CNN glass display screen were two graphics representing the floors of the two legislative chambers. The opposing colors of the two parties straddled the middle aisle, with a vertical needle representing the tipping point between the two sides.

Brooklyn sat beside her father looking at the TV with a confused expression.

"Why is the map painted in different colors this time, Daddy?" she asked. "Are you still blue?"

"Yes, pumpkin," James smiled. "Daddy's blue. But this time my opponent leads a different party, so he's shown in red."

Julie laughed. She was glad her daughter had broken some of the tension.

"Where did they ever come up with that color scheme, anyhow?" she asked.

"As best I can tell," James said, "it was purely accidental. As the story goes, *The New York Times* originally chose red for the Republicans because they both started with the letter R, and because blue was on the opposite side of the color spectrum, they chose it to represent the Democrats. I guess all the other media outlets followed them."

Maggie smiled, happy for the distraction.

"Here I thought it was because the Republicans always seem to be angry and we Democrats are always holding our breath," she said.

"That's as good an explanation as any," James chuckled. "Except tonight, it looks like *everybody* will be holding their breath."

As the couples watched the election results start to trickle in, James glanced back and forth to his phone, lying face up in front of him on the coffee table. He hadn't heard back from Heath's captors in almost forty-eight hours, and he was growing increasingly concerned for his safety. If he could speak with Heath to confirm he was safe, James was ready to meet their demands. He just needed to hear his son's voice.

"Look Daddy—you're winning!" Brooke said, noticing the election map starting to turn blue.

James hugged his daughter.

"That's just the first few states, sweetie. The ones in the northeast are usually blue, so that's no surprise. As you see the colors fill in towards the bottom and spread west, I expect you'll see plenty of red states. We've still got a long way to go before anyone's declared a winner."

"It's funny how the distribution looks pretty much the same in every election," Maggie said. "It's almost as if voters choose their candidates the same way they buy their cars—based on whatever Dad preferred."

"That could be part of it," James said, looking down at his phone again. "But Americans have grown far more mobile over the last few decades. I suspect it's more a city-country effect. The coastal states with the big cities usually vote Democrat, whereas the states with higher farm populations vote Republican. I bet if we laid a satellite map of the country lit up at night, we'd see a pretty high correlation between the lights and the colors. East of the Mississippi, especially in the northeast, the Democrats light the way, while the darker states west of the Mississippi are mostly Republican. Except the three Pacific states, of course."

"Plus Colorado," Maggie said. "I'm counting on *my* state being a blue beacon in that sea of red tonight."

James's mind wandered as he thought of Olivia's attempt to locate Heath using his phone.

"Can you excuse me for a moment, Maggie?" he said. "I need a little fresh air."

He opened the french doors leading onto the backyard deck, then closed them behind him so as not to let the cold draft into the living room. It had begun to snow, and he leaned on the elevated rail, looking out into the pitch blackness.

A Secret Service agent patrolling the yard noticed James and called up.

"Everything all right, Congressman?"

"Yes," James said. "Just catching a little fresh air."

"Good idea," the agent said. "You might not have as much time to do that after tonight."

James nodded and smiled, then looked up. As the wet snowflakes dissolved on his cheeks, he closed his eyes and thought about Heath. The door opened, and Julie walked out to stand beside him at the railing.

"Pretty, isn't it?" she said. "The first snowfall of the season is always the most beautiful."

"I just wish I could enjoy it as much as we normally do. Everything just seems *black* with Heath gone."

Julie swung her arm through James's and pulled him close.

"He'll come back to us soon. I have a good feeling. The FBI is getting close."

"Not close enough," James sighed. "It's like finding a needle in a haystack. I'm sensing our time is running out. I'm afraid we may only have one option left—"

James heard a buzzing sound coming from overhead, about a hundred feet directly above him. He held his hand over his eyes and looked up, but the snow was coming down harder and he couldn't see anything through the streaks. Suddenly, he heard a plop sound on the deck and turned his head. Lying in the thin blanket of snow was a small gauzy bag, with a narrow ring of crimson seeping into the white pellets.

James lunged to pick up the bag.

"Congressman—*no!*" the Secret Service agent called, running toward the deck. "It could be a trap—don't touch it!"

James didn't care. All he could think about was Heath. He picked up the bag and quickly untied the string closure. Looking inside, he saw the unmistakable shape of a human ear. His eyes flew open and he clutched his stomach.

Then he leaned over the railing and vomited into his garden.

For the next hour, the Marshall household was a flurry of chaos. As Secret Service agents closed the circle to keep a close watch on James, Agent Marino and his FBI team studied the ear. Marino wanted to take it to the FBI lab to compare the DNA with the federal criminal database, but James insisted on keeping it in his refrigerator. If it belonged to Heath, he wanted to have every chance of successfully reattaching it. One of the agents took a blood sample from the specimen, and James supplied one of Heath's combs from the upstairs bathroom.

While he waited to hear if the DNA matched, he rejoined the others in the living room. As Maggie consoled Julie, Matías joined James at the bar, where he was pouring a large glass of whiskey.

"James," Matías said. "I don't know what to say. I just wish there was something I could do to help—"

"I appreciate that, Matías," James said. "But I think Maggie will need you more than I do in the days ahead. I'm going to need to take some time off…"

"Of course. We'll do whatever it takes to hold down the fort. Our thoughts and prayers are with Heath and your family—"

Agent Marino suddenly walked up to James and motioned to him. They walked to a quiet section of the hallway, where they spoke privately for a few moments. Marino nodded, and James closed his eyes and hung his head.

After a few minutes, he returned to the living room and sat down beside Julie, shaking his head.

"It's…Heath," he choked. "The DNA matched."

Julie fell into James's arm and sobbed uncontrollably. She'd tried to stay strong to support her husband through the whole ordeal, but now the reality of the situation struck home. First she'd lost her daughter, and now she was about to lose her son.

Maggie and Matías looked on awkwardly while the couple consoled one another. No one seemed to notice that the CNN election map was filling in in a sea of blue as it crossed the Mississippi. After a few minutes, Julie looked up with bloodshot eyes and said she had to look after Brooke, who'd been taken upstairs by a female FBI agent to separate her from the situation.

After she left the room, James turned to his running mate.

"Maggie, can I borrow you for a few moments?"

"Yes, of course. Anything you need—"

"I'm afraid I have a big favor to ask," James said, escorting her onto the deck.

"Meg," he said when they were alone outside. "I'm so sorry to ask this of you just as we're on the edge of achieving everything we've fought so hard for. But I can't do this any longer. My son needs me, and I'm being irresponsible. I want you to take over leadership of the party. I'm going to announce my resignation tonight."

Maggie looked at James for a long moment. She'd known he was having second thoughts about the Presidency for some time, but the timing nonetheless surprised her.

"I understand, James," she said. "And so will the American people. You've been an inspiration to me and millions of others since you started this campaign. You needn't worry about your legacy. I'll proudly carry your plans to the White House and get the bills passed as soon as possible—"

"I appreciate that, Maggie. But maybe you can hold off on that message—at least until we get Heath back. That's the only bargaining chip I have left. Once he's back safely, it's your prerogative to do as you please as the new President."

"What about *you*?" Maggie asked. "What will you do now? I mean, politically—"

"Fade into the woodwork, I suppose. I don't want to steal any of your limelight. I can't make any decisions right now."

Maggie nodded her head and put her arms around James,

holding him for a long moment. When they reentered the living room, Julie had returned from putting Brooke down for the night. She knew the moment she looked at James what he'd done.

On television, Wolf Blitzer announced that CNN was calling the presidential election for the Marshall-Castillo ticket. The landslide victory had also turned the balance of power in both the House and the Senate over to the Democrats. As the pundits began debating how the change in leadership would alter the political landscape, James's phone rang.

He already knew who it would be. He looked down at his screen and nodded, then turned to Maggie.

"I suppose we have a speech to make," he said, matter-of-factly.

58

Willard InterContinental Hotel, Downtown DC

November 8, 10:00 p.m.

The main ballroom of the Willard InterContinental hotel erupted in jubilation when James and Maggie entered the room. Their supporters had waited all evening for a glimpse of the conquering heroes, and the recent concession by President Templeton had raised the excitement to a breaking point. Like a dam opening its floodgates, thousands of people swarmed around the winning couple, cheering and chanting their names. Millions more watched on from their living rooms, as every major television network broadcast the scene live.

James waded through the throng with his family by his side, shaking hands and thanking his supporters for their contribution to his campaign. He felt strangely relaxed, as if the weight of the world had been lifted off his shoulders. Although he wasn't sure it would work, he felt at peace knowing he was about to do the only thing that could bring his son back alive. He forced a smile as he looked each supporter in the eye, while Julie followed behind, looking vacant and bleary-eyed. Unlike her husband, who had to put on a brave face for the cameras, her thoughts were still with Heath.

When they reached the stage and James and Maggie walked onto the platform, the crowd roared. James walked to the podium at the front of the stage as Maggie stood at his side, while Julie and Matías waited at the rear of the stage. The teleprompter panels had James's acceptance speech queued up, but he stared straight past them. He had a different speech to deliver this evening—one he hadn't prepared.

Normally, he and Maggie would bask in the adulation and share the excitement of the crowd before starting his speech. But tonight, he had no interest in delaying the inevitable.

Good news can be parsed and savored, but bad news is best delivered fast. Like a bandage from a wound.

"Thank you," he said, leaning into the mic.

The crowd had no intention of letting him talk right away. They wanted to give him a reception fit for a king.

Jim-Mee, Jim-Mee, they chanted, drowning him out.

James smiled weakly and nodded, then raised an open hand to signal he wanted to speak. It took more than two minutes for the din in the room to subside to a level where he could be heard over the loudspeakers.

"This has been one heck of a roller coaster ride," he said, as the room began to hush.

A gentle chuckle rose from the crowd.

"Honestly, I never knew when I signed up for this that we'd capture so many people's imaginations and get this far. I just hoped to raise the awareness of some important issues that were profoundly affecting me and many other Americans."

Many onlookers nodded tearfully, remembering Breanna's gang-land shooting.

"Reaching this point was something I could only imagine in my wildest dreams. But none of this would have been possible without all of your support. I'd like to thank each and every person who contributed his or her time to this campaign. Maggie and I will forever be in your debt."

As the crowd cheered, James turned and looked into Julie's eyes tearfully.

"As many of you know, this campaign grew out of a personal loss. As is so often the case in life, it takes a tragedy to make us stop and see the connection between our actions and consequences. Sometimes, we're so wrapped up in doing what we've always done that we fail to recognize the world around us has changed and that the status quo is holding us back instead of lifting us up. If I've opened your eyes and cleared some of the fog for you to see a better future for yourselves, then I've done the most important part of my job."

Many people in the audience looked at one another uncertainly, sensing an ominous announcement.

"Unfortunately, my own path has taken some unexpected turns recently, which has caused me to reexamine my situation and ask if maintaining the current course is in the best interests of myself and my family. In the last few days, we've had to deal with another personal crisis that has consumed my focus. It's become increasingly difficult to divert my attention from my first and highest priority, which will always be my family. For these reasons, I hope you'll forgive me in this moment of triumph for stepping down—"

"No!" someone cried from the audience.

James closed his eyes and bowed his head.

"We've come...a long way," he said, choking up. "We changed the conversation about what makes this country great and how we can improve the security and prosperity of *every* citizen. It's been my sincere honor and privilege leading the charge to a new vision for America. But it's time to turn the reins over to my running mate, who's already demonstrated her ability to lead our citizens with a progressive agenda. My fellow Americans, I give you the next President of the United States—*Maggie Castillo!*"

As the audience looked on in shock, James stepped away from the podium and hugged Maggie for a long moment. When they separated, they exchanged a few words, then James joined Julie and Brooke at the back of the stage.

As Maggie began to address the shocked group of supporters, James's mind wandered to thoughts of his son's kidnappers.

I've done my part, he thought. *Now it's your turn.*

59

Washington National Forest, West Virginia

November 8, 10:00 p.m.

*F*unny *how everything smells sweeter when you're about to die,* Heath thought. *Not funny ha-ha. Funny-ironic—like not what you'd expect.*

Even the smell of dirt.

After his captors cut off his ear and Heath stemmed the blood loss, he'd quickly set back to work. He was able to pry up the loose floorboard and dig a hole under the container almost two feet deep with his bare hands. The earth was pungent, filled with roots and insects. A whole living ecosystem, buried under a heavy steel box. Heath breathed in the redolent air.

The smell of freedom.

In the two days since his captors butchered him, Heath had a lot of time for self-reflection. He knew it was election night and that his time was likely running out. If his father won the election, they'd just keep cutting off body parts until he capitulated. But if his father lost, he'd be worthless to his captors, and they'd kill him quickly.

Either way, I'm not going to sit around waiting for these assholes to use me as a pawn.

The bleeding to his ear had stopped within a few hours after he wrapped the towel around his head and applied pressure over the open canal. It hurt like a son of a bitch, but there was a surprisingly small amount of blood.

I suppose it's mostly cartilage, he thought, as he continued digging. *I hope there's enough blood supply to reattach it. Did you save it, Dad? I'm sorry you had to deal with this—I bet it's been hard on Mom. What about Liv? Will she even want to kiss me again with this deformity? How long can a severed ear survive before all hope of reattachment is lost?*

I've got to get out of this place.

Heath clawed at the dirt with his fingernails, then poured another handful of loose soil into his shoe. He carried it over to his little window, stepped on his toilet bucket, and flung it out the window.

Hopefully, these bastards aren't watching the back side of the container, noticing the rising mound of dirt under my window.

Heath turned his good ear to the open hole to make sure nobody was nearby. He'd already received his night feeding, so there shouldn't be any reason for them to approach the container until morning, he thought. All he could hear was the distant sound of owls hooting their familiar song. It seemed strange to Heath how the cadence rarely changed. The pattern and timing of the hoots always was the same: one hoot followed by a pause, then three quick hoots followed by another pause, then two more.

Repeat.

Must be the same owl, he thought. *What's his deal? Is he looking for a mate at this time of the night? Is he coordinating an attack on some helpless rodent?*

Whatever it was, it never seemed to stop, like the owl was *taunting* him. Just to break the boredom, Heath would sometimes mimic the sound, mixing up the patterns to throw off the bird.

As Heath stood at the window listening to the sound of the owl, he heard another sound, slowly growing in volume. Holding his breath to listen more carefully, he realized it was the sound of a car's wheels on a dirt road. As the sound grew louder and louder, it became apparent it was coming in his direction.

Should he yell or signal if it comes here? he wondered. Could the cops have finally tracked his location down? Or could it be more bad guys, deciding to end this charade once and for all?

As the vehicle pulled up in front of the cabin, Heath pulled himself up with two hands and peered out the window. From the light of the porch lamp, he could see that it was a dark sedan. A lone figure emerged from the car and was greeted by his two captors, who were standing on the porch. The three men talked quietly in Spanish for a few seconds, then disappeared inside the cabin.

Great, more bad guys. What's the jig? Who's the new guy? Is it the one who drove off in the getaway van after they switched vehicles on the night of the abduction? It's not like they need another guard—I'm locked up in a steel box, for chrissakes. Are they on to my escape plan?

No, Heath thought. *If they knew what I was doing, they would have re-secured the floorboards and tied me up. It's got to have something to do with the election. Maybe they've come to move me.*

Or dispose of me.

Heath held himself up for a few more minutes as he watched the door carefully. He could hear the men talking and laughing inside the cabin and the occasional bark of a dog. He still had some time.

He scampered down off the bucket and returned to his shoveling task. It had taken him two days to dig a hole one foot deep and two feet long. He calculated the container was eight feet wide. Since he started digging from the middle of the floor, he figured he only had about two more feet to go underground before he reached the outside of the structure.

But he'd lost a lot of time on the first day tending to his severed ear. That meant two feet per day. If he sped up his pace, he might be able to free himself sometime tomorrow.

Do I even have twenty-four hours? he thought. *Whatever you do Dad, don't cave. Win this election and stay the course. The best way to beat these narco-terrorists is by replacing their business with good-old American free enterprise.*

I'm gonna get out of here. Then we'll see who ends up locked in a steel box.

60

Marshall Congressional Office, Longworth Building

November 9, 9:00 a.m.

James clenched his jaw as he read the front-page headline of the Washington Post.

MARSHALL RESIGNS, the main headline declared, filling the entire width of the page. *Castillo Appointed President-Elect*, read the sub-header. Almost the entire front page was devoted to the sensational story. Although the U.S. Constitution provided for the legal passing of the top executive position to the Vice President in such circumstances, many of the editorials suggested that James had stolen the election by abdicating so soon after being chosen the people's leader. Much further down the page, a smaller story headline read *Son's Abductors Still at Large*.

James shook his head and sighed.

No sympathy for the devil, he thought.

He put the paper down on his desk and turned on his computer.

Let's see what my congressional constituents have to say.

He clicked on his public email account and saw that he had over *one million* new messages. Scrolling through the subject headings from the top, most of the senders were asking him not to resign, with many others offering thoughts and prayers for his family. When he clicked to open one of the messages, he noticed some movement by his open door. He looked up and saw Ray standing at the entrance.

"I saw your open door," Ray said. "Thought you might like some company."

James turned away from his computer and nodded silently.

"Quite a maelstrom you kicked up," Ray said, seeing the newspaper headline on James's desk.

James sighed.

"God, country, family. Apparently, a lot of people think I got my priorities mixed up."

Ray took a seat in one of the armchairs and crossed his legs.

"At least you've got the 20th Amendment on your side. All this will pass. It won't take long for people to realize that Maggie's eminently qualified to take over and understand why you had to do this. Hang in there buddy—you've got more support than you know."

"Thanks, Ray," James said, tightening his mouth to stem back the tears welling in his eyes.

"Who's the new bodyguard?" Ray asked, referring to the unfamiliar agent stationed outside James's office. "I thought the Secret Service detail would disappear after your resignation."

"They *have*," James said. "He's with the FBI. They want a man with me at all times so they can intercept the next call from Heath's kidnappers."

"Have you heard anything?"

"Nothing for thirty-six hours. I'm beginning to get concerned that we'll never hear from them again. The FBI said if I resigned I'd lose all my leverage. The kidnappers may feel there's more risk returning Heath than—"

"You still have plenty of leverage, Jim," Ray said, cutting off any suggestion of a violent conclusion. "They know you can resubmit your nomination any time. State electors don't cast their official ballots for the President and Vice President for another three weeks. Plus, you still wield tremendous influence on policy matters. If they do anything to your son, they'll lose the only bargaining chip keeping you from driving through your agenda."

"That's what worries me. It could take four years or more before they think they're in the clear. In the meantime, there's nothing to stop Maggie from pushing the drug legalization bill through Congress now that we have a majority in both houses."

"Are you a hundred percent sure Heath's kidnappers are affiliated with the drug syndicate?" Ray asked.

"The FBI traced the accent of the last caller to a known haven in Colombia for one of the biggest drug cartels. It all adds up."

"Do they have any tips on the kidnappers' whereabouts?"

"They traced the last call to somewhere in the mountains of West Virginia. But they can't pinpoint it closer than a hundred square miles—or even be sure they haven't moved since then."

Ray nodded as he squinted his eyes.

"I was fishing out that way just a few days ago. If you need to take a few days off when this cools down, I know a good spot to catch trout and walleye. It's incredibly peaceful in that part of the Appalachians. All you can hear is the sound of the river and the owls in the forest."

James chuckled as he looked absent-mindedly out the window.

"What's so funny?"

"I was just thinking about Heath. He'd often imitate the sound of the owls when we went on camping trips. He talked about their distinctive call and never seemed to have difficulty engaging them in an extended conversation."

"I didn't think about that while I was there, but I guess you're right. They do seem to have a strangely consistent call pattern—almost robotic. This particular one had an alternating series of three short hoots followed by three long hoots, and he never let up. It was almost like he was trying to tell me something."

James laughed.

"Maybe he was trying to tell you to get the hell off his hunting grounds. You might have been stealing his next meal. Thanks for the offer, Ray, but I won't be able to take any time off until I get Heath back safely. Plus, my FBI minder wouldn't be too thrilled about the idea of traipsing off on a random fishing trip with me."

"No worries, Jim," Ray said, standing up to take his leave. "The offer is open whenever you want to get away. Good luck—and please let me know when anything breaks."

"Will do, Ray. Thanks."

As Ray exited his office, James leaned back in his chair and closed his eyes, thinking about his family camping trips with Heath. After a few seconds, his eyes suddenly flung open and he leaned forward, tapping furiously on his computer keyboard. He hit the return key and clicked his mouse to listen to an audio SOS signal. Then he turned to his open door and screamed Ray's name. His friend came running to the entrance and looked at James in surprise.

"What's the matter? Is everything—"

"Where *was* it exactly where you heard that owl?"

Ray shook his head in confusion.

"What?" He furrowed his forehead, trying to remember the location. "It was...in the lower section of the Cranberry River, a few miles off highway 39 in the Washington National For—"

James leaped out of his chair and motioned to the FBI agent sitting down the hall. Then he turned to Ray.

"Can you take us there? It's a longshot, but you may have just found my son."

61

Washington National Forest, West Virginia

November 9, 7:00 p.m.

Agent Marino crept toward the dimly lit cabin alongside twenty heavily armed SWAT agents, squinting through the darkness for any sign of activity. He'd instructed the team not to shoot unless fired upon and to take all suspects alive if possible. He didn't want to take any chance at losing valuable intel in the event Heath wasn't found on site. As the assault team closed in on the cottage, James and Ray watched from behind a truck parked hundreds of feet back.

Marino's team had scoped the property to search for any sign of Heath, but there was no indication of his whereabouts. Infra-red cameras showed three figures inside the cabin and none in the outbuildings—including a padlocked steel shipping container. Marino had instructed his men not to break the crate's lock for fear of alerting the kidnappers. If someone *was* inside, he'd at least be safe until they cleared the main building. The success of their mission depended on complete secrecy and surprise.

When the team reached the edge of the clearing surrounding the lodge, Marino kneeled and whispered over the intercom for the team to hold up. He pulled out his binoculars and scanned the exterior of the structure. A small porch light cast a dim ray about fifteen feet to the front and sides. The perimeter appeared to be clear of any spotters or obstacles. He panned across the windows, but they were covered in heavy drapes, obscuring the interior. He held up the hand-held infrared monitor connected to his helmet cam. The three figures were seated around a table, motioning with their hands, as if playing cards.

"Advance with caution," Marino whispered over the intercom. "Targets appear to be seated at a table near the southeast window. Location of captive is unknown."

The team emerged into the clearing and walked in a constricting circle formation, trying not to step on twigs or debris that might announce their position. Marino's plan was to get close enough to the window without being noticed to see if he could locate Heath's position before storming the interior. But when they were about twenty feet from the outside wall, the front door latch rattled and somebody stepped out onto the porch.

The man was too close for Marino to issue an audible warning. He held up his right hand in a fist and motioned with his left palm for his team to crouch as low as possible at the edge of the darkness. The man reached into his pocket and pulled out a cigarette and lighter. But when he flicked the lighter and raised it to his cigarette, Marino's infrared monitor lit up showing the flame, and the man paused, peering into the darkness.

"*Que mierda*," he muttered, then he screamed "*La Juda!*"

He reached into his coat for his pistol, but a rain of automatic fire riddled his chest and he crumpled to the ground. Within seconds, the panes of glass in the front windows shattered and machine gun fire sprayed the ground in front of Agent Marino. He rolled to his left and lunged toward the relative safety of the corner of the cabin.

"Fire the tear gas!" he shouted over the intercom. "Close in now!"

A poof sounded on both sides of the cabin, followed by the sound of more broken glass, then the interior of the cabin filled with smoke. Two separate teams using battering rams broke down the front and rear doors simultaneously, followed by SWAT officers holding ballistic shields. Marino heard ten seconds of automatic fire and shouting, followed by the sound of a dog barking, then someone shouted 'Clear!'

He held a handkerchief over his nose and mouth and stepped in through the front door. Two men lay prone and lifeless on the floor, oozing blood onto the pale hardwood.

Marino looked at the lead SWAT officer, who was holding a snarling bloodhound by the collar.

"Did you find the boy?" he said.

The SWAT officer shook his head.

"Just the three perps. We've searched the cabin. There's no one else here, other than the dog."

Marino kneeled down and placed his fingers on the neck of each of the assailants. They were all dead.

"Shit!" he cursed. "How the hell are we going to find the congressman's son now?"

"Agent Marino," someone called from outside the cabin. "I think you'll want to see this."

An agent waved a flashlight at Marino from the edge of the clearing. He was standing in front of the open steel container. Marino ran up and looked inside. In the middle of the unit was a hole in the floorboards and a tunnel dug into the dirt.

"Does this go all the way outside?" he asked the agent.

"Yes. It looks like whoever was in here got out before we arrived."

Marino shook his head in dismay.

It appears the congressman isn't the only enterprising member of the Marshall family, he thought.

"Take a team and search the woods. If he's nearby, he'll be injured and cold."

Marino searched the inside of the container with a flashlight. He walked up to a large white bucket in the corner of crate, under a small opening near the ceiling. Peering inside, he flinched and grimaced from the foul smell.

"Take a sample," he instructed one of his assistants. "If the congressman's son was here, this will confirm it."

James suddenly appeared at the front of the open container, breathing heavily, accompanied by another FBI agent. Peering inside, he shook his head in confusion at Marino.

"He was here," Marino said. "But it looks like he got tired of waiting."

62

Washington National Forest, West Virginia

November 9, 7:30 p.m.

"What now?" James asked Agent Marino.

"We'll search the area and put out an APB. He can't have gotten far in his condition. The good news is that we're not far from populated areas. The nearest access road is only a few miles away. He should be able to flag someone down and get help pretty quickly."

"That assumes he follows marked trails," James said. "It's the first place his captors would look once they found he escaped. He must have known their dog could track him down that way."

Marino furrowed his brow as he looked at James.

"You know your son best. Where do *you* think he'd go?"

James turned to the river running behind the cabin.

"How many cabins are on this river?"

"Our satellites located two others within a five mile radius. One's two miles upstream and the other's about three clicks in the other direction."

"Can you send a team to the one upstream? I'll check out the other cabin. In the meantime, if you can continue your search of the woods and local roads in the area, it's much appreciated."

"Of course. I'll give you a shout if we find anything."

James headed toward his car, then stopped and looked behind him.

"And Agent Marino..."

"Yes, Congressman?"

"Can we borrow your helicopter as soon as we find him? I've got a surgeon on call to repair his ear, but every second counts to have a chance at successful reattachment."

"I'll be happy to give *all* of you a ride. Without Congressman Bradley's help, we might not have gotten here in time."

"Thanks. I'll report when I get to the cabin."

F ifteen minutes later, James knocked on the front door of a log cabin, flanked by Ray and an FBI agent. An elderly woman opened the door and she looked at the three men inquisitively, then her eyes widened.

"President—" she said. "I mean...*Congressman* Marshall. What in heavens name—"

"I'm sorry to disturb you, madam," James said. "I'm looking for my son. We have reason to believe he may be injured and lost in this area. Have you seen a young man, about six feet tall with blond hair—"

"Oh my goodness," the woman said. "Harold and I have been following your story ever since you entered the presidential race. I'm so sorry to hear about your son. I haven't seen anyone matching his description, but my husband might have. He'll be back from a trip to the store any minute now. Would you like to come in for some hot chocolate? It's awfully cold out—"

"Thank you for your kindness, ma'am," James said. "But we need to continue our search." He scribbled a number on a card and handed it to the woman. "If you or your husband see anything, can you call me at this number?"

"Of course, and good luck." The woman paused. "For what it's worth, my husband and I are Republicans, but I don't think you should step down. You won that election fair and square. If you find your son, I hope you finish the job. I think you'll be a great President."

"Thank you, ma'am," James said, reaching out to hold the woman's hand between his. "But right now, there's only one thing on my mind."

James's phone suddenly rang. The screen read *Unknown Caller.*

"Hello?" he said, pulling the phone to his ear.

Dad, it's Heath—

"Heath! My God, where are you?"

"I'm in a car, traveling west on Route 39. This nice couple is driving me to the hospital—"

"No—wait there, son," James said. "I've made arrangements to fly you to Georgetown Hospital. They've got the best reconstructive surgeon in the area."

"So you saved my ear?"

James laughed as tears welled in his eye.

"Of course. It's well-preserved in our refrigerator."

"Don't let Brooke at it. You know she steals anything that looks like a snack—"

James swallowed as he choked up.

"Not to worry. It's got your name all over it. Now, give me the name of your nearest cross street, and I'll send a helicopter."

There was a brief pause on the line as Heath consulted the driver.

"We're just coming up on Summit Lake Road. We'll pull over and wait for you there."

"See you soon, son. I love you."

"Love you too, Dad"

The old woman was standing in the door listening to the conversation, and she smiled at James.

"Go get 'em, Congressman," she said. "I mean *President*."

63

Georgetown Hospital

November 10, 9:00 a.m.

The next morning, James sat with his wife and daughter at Heath's bedside as his son lifted his heavy eyelids after surgery.

"You guys are sure a sight for sore eyes," Heath muttered.

Julie leaned over and kissed her son's cheek.

"Oh baby, I'm so glad you're back safely..."

Heath reached up to feel the right side of his bandaged head and James quickly pulled his hand down.

"Don't *touch* it, for God's sake!" he said. "You have to leave that thing alone for a while to let it heal."

"Was the operation a success?"

"The doctors think they got it just in time. Another twenty-four hours, and it would have been a very different kind of operation."

Heath nodded, reflecting back on his escape.

"How did you find me anyway? Why were you were so close when I called—"

"It was a fluke, really. My friend Ray was fishing near your cabin when he heard your owl SOS signal. We didn't put it all together until I remembered the funny way you used to mimic them on our camping trips."

"That's pretty funny. Who knew that would come in handy some day. Talk about a lucky coincidence."

"Turns out we didn't need it. You seemed to have the situation under control the whole time."

Heath motioned to his bandaged ear.

"I'd hardly call *this* under control. Did you catch the bad guys?"

"Let's just say they won't be causing us any more trouble," James nodded.

"What was it all *about*, anyhow? Who was the ringleader?"

"Our contacts at the Colombia Justice Department traced the photos of the kidnappers to a prominent drug cartel operating in the region. They think a drug lord by the name of Carlos Rojas was behind it all."

"I figured it was something like that," Heath said. "Those guys had some pretty strong accents. Do you think they were the same ones behind your assassination attempts?"

"We may never know. There's no one still alive to connect the dots, other than the drug lord in Colombia. And we don't have enough evidence connecting him to the crimes to extradite him to the U.S."

Heath pinched his eyebrows as he shook his head.

"For someone operating from another country, these guys never seemed to have much difficulty knowing exactly where we'd be every time they carried out their operations. They must have had some local help, don't you think?"

"Maybe, but it's all moot, now. They no longer have any reason to target us."

Heath paused, remembering the conversation he and his father had on the helicopter ride to the hospital.

"You can't just step down after all this, Dad. You fought too hard to win the election. Now that everybody's safe and the bad guys are out of the way, what's stopping you from claiming what you've rightfully earned?"

"It's not as easy as it might appear. There's a new President-elect now—"

Heath saw some movement at his door and turned to see Maggie smiling at him.

"You mean the one who's standing outside my room right now? Why don't you two have a conversation while I get caught up with Mom and Brooke?"

James placed his hand on Heath's arm and smiled.

"Rest easily, son. You've experienced enough political drama for a while. Let me tie up the loose ends."

James excused himself and walked out into the hall, where Maggie hugged him warmly.

"Maggie," James said. "Thank you for coming."

"I came as soon as I heard," Maggie said. "How's your boy holding up?"

"Pretty good, under the circumstances. The doctors say he has a good chance at the reattached ear fully recovering. I'm just glad he's back in one piece."

"That makes two of us. Now that this little matter's been resolved, I wanted to talk with you about something else. There's no longer any reason for you to step down. I want you to take your place where you rightly belong, as President—"

"Maggie," James said, shaking his head. "I couldn't ask you to do that. And besides, there's no legal precedent…"

"I've already consulted the Attorney-General. The decision rests in the hands of the State Electors. As you know, they're obligated to follow the will of the voters. All you have to do is rejoin the ticket, as per the people's wishes."

"What about you?" James hesitated. "I'm uncomfortable taking away what I already promised you—"

"It's *you* the people want as their President. I was just along for the ride. You created the grand vision and carry the political capital to bring it to reality. It would be my greatest honor to serve at your side in the new administration."

James looked at Maggie, then peered through the door at his family by Heath's bedside.

"Can you give me a few days to think about it? Right now, I need a little quiet time with my family."

"Of course," Maggie said. "Just give me a call whenever you're ready, Mr. President."

EPILOGUE

Oval Office, The White House

January 21, 10:00 a.m.

James sat in the Oval Office, looking out his window at the South Lawn. In the distance, he could see the familiar obelisk of the Washington Monument rising from the National Mall. Glancing out his southeast window, he recognized the U.S. Capitol standing sentinel over the city. It all seemed so surreal. It wasn't so long ago when he viewed these monuments with awe as a first-term U.S. congressman.

He'd come a long way, he thought, after that fateful day when his daughter was taken from him by a drug gang. Now, finally, he could exact a measure of justice by turning the tables on the criminals and pass a bill that would make the streets safer for everybody. He wondered if his daughter could see him now and if she'd be proud of what he'd accomplished.

A soft tap on his door snapped him from this thoughts.

"Come in," he said.

The door opened, and Maggie and Nick walked into the room.

"Good morning, Mr. President," Nick said. "We have the briefing you requested."

"Thanks, Nick," James said, inviting his newly appointed White House Chief of Staff and Vice President to have a seat.

"So this is it," Maggie said, looking around the room. "The most famous office in the world. How does it feel, Mr. President?"

"It definitely feels strange. But not nearly as strange as everybody calling me Mr. President—especially my closest colleagues."

Maggie chuckled.

"It's our way of showing respect for the office, as much as the man."

"Thank you, Madam Vice President," James smiled. "Shall we get on with the briefing before we get hopelessly bogged down in decorum?"

Nick passed out three copies of a policy paper concerning the soon-to-be-introduced Recreational Drug Legalization Act. For the next forty-five minutes, James, Nick, and Maggie reviewed the provisions of the bill, deleting superfluous verbiage and adding a section stipulating the use of targeted tax revenue for drug rehabilitation programs.

"That should do it," James said, rising to signal the end of the meeting. "Nick, can you forward the revised outline to Ray Bradley? As the new Chairman of the House Judiciary Committee, he'll take the lead on introducing the bill for public hearings."

"Will do, Mr. President."

As James opened the door to his office to usher his colleagues out, he noticed Heath and Olivia entering the hall from the Rose Garden. He smiled as he approached them, then he called out to Nick.

"Nick, one more thing," he said. "Can you ask Ray to send me a summary of the public comments before the final reading?"

"On it, Mr. President," Nick nodded.

Heath suddenly snapped his head and looked at Nick with a puzzled expression.

"Is everything okay, Heath?" James said, noticing the sudden change in his son's demeanor.

"Yes..." Heath hesitated, looking confused. "I was just giving Olivia a tour of the White House. I didn't mean to interrupt you—"

"This is actually perfect timing. I've got fifteen minutes before my next meeting. Would you like to see the Oval Office, Olivia?"

"Um...wow," Olivia stammered. "I'd love to!"

James escorted Heath and Olivia into the office and pointed out some of the famous artifacts, including official portraits of previous Presidents.

"Why is President Kennedy looking *down* in his portrait?" Olivia asked. "All the other Presidents look so confident and commanding in their pictures."

"I often wondered the same thing," James said. "His was the only official portrait painted posthumously. It was commissioned by his wife Jacqueline, who asked the artist to create a different pose from the usual photos of him with his penetrating gaze."

After James finished explaining how the Resolute Desk was a gift from Queen Victoria to President Hayes, Heath looked increasingly distracted and asked Olivia if he could have a few minutes alone with his father.

"What is it, son?" James said, after Olivia left the office. "You seem out of sorts today. Has your ear been bothering you—"

"No, it's fine. It's something else. When I was abducted a few days before the election, I overheard a telephone call to one of my captors. They were speaking in Spanish, but the voice on the other end sounded familiar. I couldn't place it until now. Dad—I think your chief of staff was the inside man."

"*Nick?*" James said, looking at Heath incredulously. "Are you sure? I have a lot of staffers who speak Spanish—"

"It's *him*," Heath said. "The soft accent and that manner-of-speech he just used—I'm certain it's the same person."

James paused as he contemplated what to do next.

"I have to be sure before I accuse him of such a serious crime."

"Can't we just trace their *call records*?" Heath said. "If we find that he placed a call to one of my captors around that time, wouldn't that provide enough evidence?"

James looked at Heath blankly for a moment, then nodded.

"That could work."

He sat down at his desk and looked up Agent Marino's number. Then he picked up the phone and punched the keypad.

"Agent Marino?" he said into the phone. "This is President Marshall. Did you find the phone my son's abductors used to call me the night before the election? What about the number they called from—did you record it? Can we trace the call record from another phone to that number from three months' ago? It's just a hunch at this point. I'll get back to you soon."

James hung up and immediately dialed another number.

"Nick?" he spoke into the phone. "Can I borrow you for another couple of minutes? There was something else I wanted to talk with you about."

James walked to the door of his office and motioned for a Secret Service agent to come into his room.

"Gene," he said to the agent. "Can you accompany me and my son while my chief of staff is in the room? I may need your assistance detaining him."

When Nick came into the office, he looked at Heath and the Secret Service agent warily.

"Yes, Mr. President?"

"I need to see your cell phone for a minute," James said, as the Secret Service agent closed the door quietly behind Nick.

"Why?" Nick said, wrinkling his forehead. "I can't see how that—"

"Just give me your phone, Nick."

Nick handed over the device and James tapped the screen.

"Unlock code?"

Nick hesitated, as his eyes flitted between James, his son, and the Secret Service agent.

"Something tells me I need a lawyer."

"You're going to need a lot more than a *lawyer* by the time I'm done with you," James said.

OTHER BOOKS BY J. R. MCLEAY:

Crime Thriller:

Everyone has to come out in the open eventually.

Medical Thriller:

Remember when you said you never wanted to grow up?

AFTERWORD

Thank you for reading The Candidate. I hope you enjoyed the book. If you're interested in reading more books authored by me, you can find brief synopses and links on the following pages. If you'd like to be notified when I release new books or be a beta reader for one or more of these books, drop me a line at mcleayjr@gmail.com.

Please let me know how much you enjoyed this story with a brief review on my amazon book page. Even just one or two sentences with your impressions will help other readers find and enjoy the book. Your feedback is much appreciated and also helps me improve my craft. Click here to post your review.

1

UNLUCKY DAY

Times Square, New York City
July 4, 11:45 a.m.

W hose life will I extinguish today?

So many choices, so many worthy subjects. It's the Fourth of July in the epicenter of New York. The anthill is swarming with activity. Such easy pickings.

People are oblivious about their vulnerability as they travel about their everyday business. So lost in their little world with their self-important tasks, they can't imagine at this very moment someone could be drawing a bead on them. Mere seconds away from sudden death from the simple pull of a trigger.

There's a busy mix of tourists and native New Yorkers moving about Times Square today. It's easy to tell them apart. The natives so impatient to get from point A to B. Everybody trying to get ahead in the most competitive city on Earth. The tourists stroll about in lazy clumps, soaking up the flash and glitter of the Theater District. The locals try to wedge their way through the horde or walk onto the street to bypass the gawkers.

It's quite amusing, in an anthropological kind of way, to observe the different castes in action.

Every colony harbors insects worthy of extermination. Scanning the faces of these creatures, likely candidates abound. Like the well-to-do tourists, carrying their overstuffed Tiffany and Cartier shopping bags. What a waste of resources. One of those fancy diamond rings could feed a hungry child for a year.

Or the fat-cat investment banker, dressed in his bespoke suit and five hundred dollar shoes. How many mortgage-backed securities has he dumped on the market today? Building an ever-taller house of cards, poised to topple the economy and over-indebted homeowners at any moment.

How about the muscular guy wearing a wifebeater shirt? How many skinny kids did he torment in the playground growing up?

So many people who deserve to die.

Power is not just bestowed by genetics or social class. It can be wielded by anyone with sufficient motivation and will.

But I'm in no hurry to take my quarry today. I've still got a few minutes before the appointed hour. It's six minutes before noon.

My rifle scope shows a crowd milling about the entrance to the Hard Rock Cafe between 43rd and 44th Street. A young pregnant woman barely out of her teens is pausing to light a cigarette. She's not wearing a wedding ring. Yet another unplanned pregnancy by a promiscuous tramp. Will she too abandon her baby, only to have the child bounced from one abusive foster home to another?

So many thoughtless people in this world. My finger presses more firmly against the trigger.

I follow the tramp as she elbows her way through the throng northward along 7th Avenue toward Broadway. She's giving no apparent thought to the dependent child within her. Bouncing between one distracted pedestrian and another, she pinballs through the crowd, toxic smoke blowing from her lips.

Doesn't she know the prenatal months are the most critical in a developing child's life? My anger builds as my rifle traces her harried journey.

There are no longer any other persons of interest in my field of vision. I'm incensed. If I kill her now, at least the paramedics will arrive soon and have a chance at saving the baby. Child Services will put the baby up for adoption, and the circumstances of its delivery may find a sympathetic and caring family.

This tart isn't fit to be a mother. There is more than one way to separate an abusive parent from her offspring.

This is the child's lucky day.

The traffic light turns red at 45th Street, and the woman stops on the edge of the curb, directly facing me. I see her clearly in her red halter, a bullseye in the sea of vanilla pedestrians surrounding her.

She's waiting impatiently for the light to turn. This will be her last vision before the white light takes her somewhere else.

I glance at my phone propped on the window ledge beside my rifle. The time is just past noon. I squeeze the trigger and feel the recoil of the weapon against my shoulder.

Exactly two seconds later, pandemonium erupts at the corner of 45th and Broadway.

Read more...

Made in the USA
Lexington, KY
10 August 2018